CAST A COLD EYE

ALAN RYAN was born in The Bronx in 1943 and lived most of his life in New York City before moving to Brazil in 2001. He graduated from Regis High School in Manhattan and from Fordham University in The Bronx. Ryan taught English at Cardinal Spellman High School in The Bronx before turning to writing full time in the 1970s, first as a literary critic and book reviewer and later as an editor and author of fiction. In the early 1980s, Ryan was hailed as one of the bright new lights in the horror field, with several successful novels, including *The Kill*, *Dead White*, and *Cast a Cold Eye*. He also earned critical acclaim for his short fiction, which was collected in the volumes *Quadriphobia* and *The Bones Wizard*. Ryan also edited a number of important horror anthologies, including *Halloween Horrors* (1986) and *Vampires* (1987) (republished as *The Penguin Book of Vampire Stories*). After a long absence from the genre, Ryan returned with a new novel, *Amazonas*, and a new collection of short fiction, *The Back of Beyond*, both of which were published posthumously by Cemetery Dance. Ryan died in Rio de Janeiro in 2011.

BY ALAN RYAN

NOVELS
Panther! (1981)
The Kill (1982)
Dead White (1983)
Cast a Cold Eye (1984)
Amazonas (2012)

SHORT STORY COLLECTIONS
Quadriphobia (1986)
The Bones Wizard and Other Stories (1988)
The Back of Beyond (2012)

ANTHOLOGIES EDITED
Perpetual Light (1982)
Night Visions 1 (1984)
Halloween Horrors (1986)
Vampires (1987)
Haunting Women (1988)

CAST A COLD EYE

ALAN RYAN

VALANCOURT BOOKS

Dedication: To Doug Winter, for the hours spent together laughing at the dark

First published in hardcover by Dark Harvest in 1984
First paperback edition published by Tor in 1984
First Valancourt Books edition 2016

Excerpt from "At a Potato Digging" from *Poems 1965-1975* by Seamus
Heaney, copyright © 1966, 1969, 1972, 1975, 1980 by Seamus Heaney.
Reprinted by permission of Farrar, Straus and Giroux, Inc. Reprinted by
permission of Faber & Faber, Ltd. from *Death of a Naturalist* by Seamus
Heaney.

Excerpt from "The Hungry Grass" from *The Hungry Grass* by Donagh
MacDonagh, copyright © 1947 by Donagh MacDonagh. Reprinted by
permission of Faber & Faber, Ltd.

Excerpt from "Under Ben Bulben" from *Collected Poems* by William Butler
Yeats, copyright © 1940 by Bertha Georgie Yeats, Anne Yeats, and Michael
Butler Yeats. Reprinted by permission of Macmillan Publishing Co.

Published by Valancourt Books, Richmond, Virginia
http://www.valancourtbooks.com

ISBN 978-1-943910-41-0 (trade paperback)
Also available as an electronic book.

All Valancourt Books publications are printed on acid free paper that
meets all ANSI standards for archival quality paper.

Cover by Henry Petrides
Set in Dante MT

Centuries
Of fear and homage to the famine god
Toughen the muscles behind their humbled knees,
Make a seasonal altar of the sod.

—Seamus Heaney,
"At a Potato Digging"

Little the earth reclaimed from that poor body,
and yet remembering him the place has grown
Bewitched . . .

—Donagh MacDonagh,
"The Hungry Grass"

Cast a cold eye
on life, on death.

—W. B. Yeats,
"Under Ben Bulben"

PART ONE

These lonesome people in the wild places, it is
their nature to speak; they must cry out their
sorrows like the wild birds.

—Frank O'Connor,
"The Bridal Night"

CHAPTER 1

"Have you the blood, John?"

They sat there, four old men, as old as the dirt-floored cottage, a stone and thatch-roofed shebeen, and the rock-scattered hill it stood on, their shallow breath making thin white puffs before their lined and solemn faces. The one who spoke the needless question was Brian Flynn, the second eldest. He sat nearest to the closed wooden door, his back turned a little away from the chill dampness that entered through its cracks. His shoulders hunched forward beneath the shiny black cloth of his coat. The narrow frayed collar scraped against thin gray hair at the back of his neck. His hands were knotted together in his lap, great bony fingers and twisted swollen knuckles, all bloodless and gray with the cold and damp of the morning. He raised his eyes from a contemplation of the pitted dirt floor and squinted through the smoky interior at John MacMahon, the eldest.

MacMahon raised one slow hand, as gray as Brian Flynn's, and drew it across his mouth and chin, dry fingers scraping across the gritty stubble of a beard.

"I have," he said, in a voice as dry and gritty as his skin.

The other three men in the shebeen stirred, grunted, chafed hands together against the cold. At the end of the single-roomed cottage, the next-to-last sod of turf tumbled on its side and coughed out a puff of smoke that drifted toward the men, filling the room with its thick and acrid scent. Outside, the ceaseless drizzle pattered for a moment against the wood of the door, trying feeble strength against the smoky dryness inside, then subsided to its steady hissing on stone and gravel and thatch.

"Give us a look, John," said one of the two remaining men from his place on the end of the bench, in the corner. His name was James Brennan and he was the youngest of the four. The civil records of his birth and the church records of his baptism had long been lost to history, but he was understood, among the four of them, to be the youngest. He coughed around the half-burned cigarette in his mouth, squinted past the curl of smoke that touched the side of his face, and said again, "Give us a look."

"Do you trust nothing?" said John MacMahon, his voice as dry as thatch on a hot day. He turned his head a little toward Brennan. His watery eyes searched out the other faces in the hanging smoke from the peat: James Brennan, Brian Flynn, and the fourth, Martin Gilhooley. "All right, then," he muttered. "Here's a look."

He twisted a stiff arm and got the hand into the pocket of his coat. After a moment of rummaging there, stiff fingers grasping at a hard round object and wrestling it free from the cloth, he drew out a small stone bottle, stoppered with a smudged cork. The bottle might have held near a pint of something. He held it up for the others to see. They edged a little closer and Brian Flynn stood and moved across the cottage. His first steps were shaky until his legs limbered up.

"It's all right, is it?" asked Martin Gilhooley. He looked at the bottle in John MacMahon's hand as if he thought it might leap at him across the room.

"It is," MacMahon said, his voice edged with impatience. "What else would it be, and I after taking it myself?"

"Aye," Martin Gilhooley said. The others nodded.

MacMahon lowered the bottle and rested it on the thin bone of his leg.

"We'd best be going, I think," he said. "They'll be along in a minute now. See, would you, Brian."

Brian Flynn moved back to the door. His fingers fumbled for a moment at the ancient rusted latch, then pulled it free. The door, twisted by age and its own weight, swung back at a lopsided angle, creaking in protest. The rain immediately sought to enter the cottage, wetting the dirt floor and stirring the thick gray pall of smoke. Tiny wisps of smoke eluded it and slipped outside to dissipate in the rain. Outside, all was gray and silver, rain washing the world of color, leaving it only the cold dark shades of stone.

"They're coming along now," Flynn said over his shoulder, and turned back to watch outside. Behind him, the others pushed themselves to their feet, heavy shoes scraping on the hard rough floor, and came to stand beside him in the doorway.

The cottage was halfway up a hillside, at the end of a ragged path that led from a low stone wall at the edge of the road. The wall was tumbled down in places, and rambled on up across the slope and away on the far side out of sight. Once, in the distant past, the hill had been thick with growth, protecting the shebeen from wind and rain and the sight of strangers, but now it was empty of everything but stones and scrubby low vegetation pushed flat by the salty wind, and the view from the cottage door was unobstructed, except by the sheeting gray mist, across the other hills and the rain-soaked village below.

The mist drifted in shifting waves across the hillsides, touching everything with wet, cold fingers and occasionally spitting icy rain, like a handful of angry gravel, into slate-gray puddles on the hard earth, shattering the shiny surface that was the same blind color as the sky.

"Here," said James Brennan, and lifted one stiff finger to point.

The funeral procession moved slowly up the winding road, climbing the hill wearily beneath the weight of the cold, the rain, the grayness of the morning sky, and the dark wooden box carried on the shoulders of six of the mourners. The figures in the procession, black shapes gliding slowly, slowly, in the gray road, were blended into one form, robbed of sex or names or faces by the rain and mist that engulfed them. On they came, heads bowed, feet shuffling, climbing steadily up the hill toward the cemetery. Solitary at the head of the procession moved the priest from the village, his slow step setting the pace for the others, his long black raincoat clinging wetly to his legs. On they came, on and on, black shapes against the gray.

"They won't be long in this dirty weather," Martin Gilhooley said quietly.

"That they won't," John MacMahon agreed. He moved his right hand, brushed it against the damp wool of his jacket, feeling the heavy bulge and weight of the stone bottle in his pocket. "They won't, indeed."

The four of them moved back, without another word, into the smoky darkness of the cottage as the dark procession glided silently past the break in the wall and on up the hill to where the grave awaited. They watched until the black straggle of mourners was past and had flickered out of view around the side of the hill where the stone wall still stood high. They would be almost into the cemetery now.

"Best to close the door while we wait," John MacMahon said, and moved back to his place on the worn wooden bench, its boards shiny from the press of cloth during several centuries. Brian Flynn closed the door and came to sit beside MacMahon. Martin Gilhooley poked at the struggling fire with an old rod of twisted and blackened iron.

They sat in silence and waited, hands clasped between knees for evasive warmth or shoved deep in jacket pockets.

After a while, without reference to a watch but knowing it was time, MacMahon pushed himself to his feet. The others stood with him and, together, they moved to the door.

The rain was harder now and the wind a bit nastier still. They pulled their caps low on their foreheads, pulled collars higher about their necks, clasped lapels close over narrow chests, hunched shoulders against the damp, making a smaller target for the weather. Their shoes slopped on the wet earth as they walked down the path toward the road, then started up the hill.

The entrance to the cemetery was only a ragged break in the leaning stone wall and, inside it, a muddy path that climbed farther up the hill. The place was deserted now, the mourners having done their cold, wet duty and proceeded on to warm themselves and the priest at the home of the departed soul and his mournful relations. A little way up the path beyond the wall was a level stretch where the first of the graves lay soaking up the rain, and beyond that began a sparse stand of trees, climbing higher up the hill. The trees slouched tiredly beneath the rain, and added their dripping to the puddles on the ground.

Wordless, saving their breath for the walk, they made their way to the edge of the fresh grave, and stopped. It was only partly filled in, someone no doubt having said they'd finish it later when the rain was ended, and also no doubt unwilling to miss the warm wake at home. Rain ran down the muddy sides of the grave in rivulets and had washed one end of the coffin free of dirt. The ground at the edges of the grave was slippery, trampled by many feet, glittering with puddles.

The four old men paid no heed to the mud and came as close to the edge of the hole as solid footing permitted. They craned their necks, ignoring now the icy touch of the rain, and looked in, looked at the bare end of the coffin, the mud in which it rested, and the rain pooling at the sides.

John MacMahon was the first to raise his head. He looked around at the three others. Each of them met his gaze briefly, then looked back into the grave. MacMahon reached into his pocket and, after a moment's struggle, pulled free the stone bottle. With fingers stiffened by age and the cold and damp, he drew the cork from its neck and fisted his left hand around it. The others raised their eyes and watched him, watched the bottle. MacMahon looked to the muddy ground and inched a little closer to the edge of the grave. James Brennan moved then and came closer to Mac-Mahon, grasped his left elbow and steadied him.

MacMahon drew in a breath and looked around once more. The others continued to watch him and Brennan nodded. "Do it, John," he said.

John MacMahon stretched his right hand out above the muddy hole and the wet coffin. Then he hesitated. A wave of pain had suddenly washed through his stomach and twisted his intestines. It had been three days since he'd felt it last. And it had been five days before that time. It was coming always closer. He shut his eyes tight and held his breath and it quickly passed away, leaving only the memory and a lingering fright.

Rain spattered on his hand and darkened the cold stone of the bottle. He tilted the neck of the bottle and a thin, slow stream of dark red blood dribbled from it into the grave. He moved his hand to the right and then swept it slowly to the left, to the other end of the grave, regulating the red stream to spread it evenly. The blood, mixing with the rain, dripped into the dirt and mud at the bottom, stained the wood of the coffin with fat drops, and blended in, becoming one with the ancient earth. After a few moments, the blood stopped dripping from the bottle but John MacMahon, breathing deeply, continued to move his arm back and forth. One final drop of red clung to the lip of the bottle, clung and shivered as he moved it, and then at last that drop too fell off and mixed with the mud of the grave.

That done, the four of them stepped back from the edge, minding now where they put their mud-caked shoes on the slippery ground. They huddled together silently, cold breath pluming from their mouths, while MacMahon pressed the stained cork back into the bottle and replaced the bottle in his pocket.

"That's done, then," he said, and the others nodded. Then, without looking again into the muddy grave, they started down the path toward the wall and the road and the cottage.

When they reached the cottage, its dark interior was still thick with warmly scented smoke but the fire was dying out. Martin Gilhooley bent into the corner and added three crumbly dark bricks of peat to the fire and rubbed his hands in front of it, waiting for the warmth. John MacMahon pulled the stone bottle once again from his pocket and, without speaking a word, replaced it in the niche between two stones in the wall beside the fireplace. Then he too rubbed his hands before the fire and James Brennan and Brian Flynn came and stood beside them and did the same.

After a few minutes they began to feel the new warmth from the burning turf and their tight shoulders eased and began to slump and relax. The smell of the peat, ancient, bitter, and warm, filled the cottage, mixing with the raw smell of earth and the thick aroma of rain-soaked wool.

"So it's done another time," James Brennan said, his eyes fixed steadily on the fire, hands still moving.

"It is," John MacMahon said quietly, and then added, "until the next death."

Brian Flynn's head bobbed once in agreement but he said nothing.

Suddenly John MacMahon gasped, pressed a tight-clenched fist against his stomach, and squeezed his eyes shut for several moments until the twisting pain receded. James Brennan's hand came to rest lightly on his shoulder.

"Will you last it out, do you think, John?" Brennan said, his voice barely louder than a breath. "Until the time, I mean."

MacMahon took two deep breaths to be certain of his voice, and then answered softly, "With the help of God, I will."

No one said anything to that and they continued standing

there, rubbing their hands before the fire as if the cold would never leave them.

CHAPTER 2

The sun was shining brightly on Dublin when Jack Quinlan first saw the city. The yellow double-decker buses were freshly washed by the morning's rain, the taxis sparkled, the stone of the O'Connell Street bridge was newly cleaned and dried white by the fresh cool air, and even the River Liffey itself, normally brown and thick and sluggish, seemed to flow more easily and even sparkled once or twice, as if the unexpected sun insisted that it smile too. The green of Trinity College was bright as emeralds, the store windows of Brown Thomas and Switzer's in Grafton Street tried vainly to lure unwilling shoppers from the sunshine, and the columns of the G.P.O. stood tall and white and proud. There were beggars in the streets, in O'Connell Street itself and in the busy, narrow lanes around the post office, but the sun shone on them too and on the peaches and oranges they sold from rusty carts and wobbly prams and strollers, and the crowds waiting for buses in front of Clery's Department Store stood out full in the sun, sporting bright colors, white Aran Island sweaters, and pink-cheeked smiles.

This is like coming home, Jack thought. After all this long while, a whole lifetime, of hearing about Dublin from my grandmother, from friends and relatives and neighbors, all the stories, all the memories, all the songs, it's just like coming home. I know this place. It's mine.

He had just come out the front door of Clery's into the bright colors and bustle of O'Connell Street. Under his arm was a bulky parcel containing an oatmeal-colored Irish knit sweater he'd just bought. Shop at Clery's for the bargains, they'd told him at home in New York, you'll only do better out in the country. And they'd been right. The sweater would have cost at least twice the price in the States—he was already beginning to think of it that way, as a far-off land: the States—if you could find such a thing at all. He'd get another when he reached the country itself; he'd be there by tomorrow evening. Now he stood beside the busy doorway of Clery's, lit a cigarette, and gazed happily about at the scene.

He had arrived in Dublin by Aer Lingus only that morning and taken a taxi directly to the bed-and-breakfast house in Clontarf, out along Dublin Bay, where he'd reserved—no, where he'd *booked*—a room from the States. Luckily, the movie projector on the plane had suffered blessed mechanical trouble and he'd been spared the bother of a movie. Even with his long legs feeling cramped in the narrow space, he'd managed to sleep through most of the flight, including the twenty-minute stopover at Shannon. Though he was still tired from the trip and the last-minute packing and the excitement of seeing Ireland for the first time, he'd let the landlady show him where breakfast was served, then settled quickly into his room, and hurried off to catch a bus to O'Connell Street.

Things were falling nicely into place. He would have liked, given all the time in the world, to spend more time seeing Dublin—his grandmother had grown up here, walked these very streets, shopped in many of the same stores—but he was even more eager to get done what had to be done here and get out into the country where his house was waiting.

He checked the list in his mind. He'd already called the auto rental agency and they'd promised to deliver the car—a Ford Escort automatic, and didn't they sound impressed that he was renting it for three entire months!—by ten o'clock in the morning. "You'll have it by the time you're done with your breakfast," the pleasant lady on the phone had told him, and he'd smiled at the typically Irish conception of time. There's real time and there's Irish time, they'd told him back in the States. He hoped to see the car by eleven.

He'd intended to buy a good sweater and that was done now. He'd been warned at home about the cool Irish weather, especially in September, and he could vouch for it now himself. As bright as the sun was at the moment, he was already thinking about putting the sweater on beneath his brown corduroy jacket. If he went out this evening, he'd surely need it against the night's damp chill.

That left two items of business to attend to, the computer and a supply of books.

He'd bought a green Geographia map of Dublin at the airport and studied it later on the bus. If he remembered right, the Radio Shack store was on Bachelor's Walk, facing the River Liffey just off O'Connell Street near the bridge. He turned to his left and began strolling toward the river, crossed O'Connell Street, then went around the corner and found the little Radio Shack store right there where it was supposed to be. He caught himself grinning at the familiar red sign, seeming so out of place in this foreign city, yet a comfortable touch of home.

The shop was tiny, not at all like the Radio Shack Computer Center on Fifth Avenue where he did most of his business and where the manager took good care of him. But, once he was inside the doors, looking at the familiar displays, he felt he was back in his own territory. Only the soft Irish accents were different.

"May I help you, sir?"

"Yes. My name is Jack Quinlan. You should have—"

"Oh, of course." The neatly-groomed young man smiled happily. "We've been expecting you. I think you'll find everything is in order. Would you like to step over here?"

"Terrific," Jack said, and took a seat beside the young man's desk.

Everything, it turned out, was indeed in order. Jack's literary agent in London had taken care of the arrangements long in advance, as soon as Jack had planned this trip. The clerk even had the papers filled out for the three-month lease on the word processor, and a carton on the floor by his desk was already filled with an adequate supply of disks, paper, and ribbon cartridges for the printer. It was all infinitely easier than Jack had hoped or expected, especially in light of everything he'd heard at home about Irish efficiency.

"Well, thanks very much," Jack said when the papers were signed and the contents of the carton checked against the clerk's list. "You've gotten me off to a good start."

"That's no trouble at all, Mr. Quinlan," the clerk said. Then he seemed to hesitate for a second. "I wonder," he said, "would you mind terribly . . ."

"Yes?"

The clerk pulled open a drawer by his knee and took out paper-back copies of four of Jack's novels. Two of them were British editions, but the other two were American books; those novels had been his first and hadn't sold in England. "Would you mind very much taking the time to sign them?" the clerk asked.

Jack grinned happily and pulled the books over in front of him. "Not at all. I'd be delighted. But where did you get these?" he said, tapping the two American books.

Now it was the clerk's turn to grin. "I have a cousin in the Bronx," he said. "She sent them to me."

Jack signed the four books with elaborate inscriptions and he and the clerk smiled happily at each other all the way to the door.

"Are you writing a book while you're over here?" the clerk asked when they reached the doorway.

"I am," Jack said. He almost burst out laughing, hearing the sudden Irish phrasing and rhythm in his own voice. "I'm doing some research for it in the west, in County Clare. I hope to get a first draft done while I'm here."

"Would you mind if I asked what it's about?"

"Not at all," Jack said, happy to find a fan this far away from home. God bless the printed word, he thought. "It's about the Famine. It's an historical, bit of a change of pace for me."

The clerk's face had clouded over a little. "About the Famine, is it?" he said.

"Yes."

"A sad time for Ireland," the clerk said, the smile gone now completely from his face.

"Yes," Jack said again. "I've been doing the basic research, of course, but now I want to see some of the settings." He was choosing his words with care now, suddenly, sharply, reminded by the tone of the young man's voice—how old could he be? twenty-two? twenty-three?—that the pain of the Famine and events that took place almost a hundred and fifty years ago were still fresh and tender in the thoughts of the Irish. Here, in a land as ancient as Ireland, history was only yesterday and the distant past breathed fresh and sharp and painful in living memory. "I want to get it right," he added.

"Oh, yes, of course," the clerk said. Then his smile—or some of it, at least, Jack thought—returned and he said, "I'll look forward to reading it. Has it a title?"

"No, I'm afraid not," Jack said, glad to be back on more solid ground. "Still working on coming up with the right one." The clerk was nodding. "Well, then, I'll see you tomorrow when I have my car to pick up all that stuff."

"Right, then," the clerk said.

"Right," Jack said, and stepped down to the sidewalk.

Still wondering if the young man's reaction was really a universal Irish response to mention of the Famine, Jack crossed the busy street toward the river and leaned on the stone wall, peering over it down to the brown depths of the Liffey.

His grandmother used to talk about the River Liffey, mostly about the terrible way it smelled in the nineteenth century because the breweries used to empty their waste into it. Lucky thing I've come along, he thought, his smile returning. He'd never quite gotten the hang of drinking Guinness, not even in the Irish bars of New York, but he expected to do some serious damage to the local supply of Harp. God willing, there'd be a decent cozy pub in the village, preferably within walking distance of the house. God willing. I'm doing it again, he thought. I am naturally mimetic, a lucky thing for a novelist. And the top of the morning to you too, Johannes Gutenberg.

He turned away from the river and placed his elbows behind him on the wall, leaning back comfortably, gazing happily around, drinking in the foreign details, the different shapes of cars and street signs and lamps and windows, the different complexions and angles of faces.

I've come home, he thought. This will be fine. Just fine.

He was back at the bed-and-breakfast house in Clontarf before he remembered about the books.

The strain of travel was beginning to take its toll and he sat on the edge of his bed, thinking through the rest of the day. There was still time to make it to a bookstore. If he got that out of the way this afternoon, he wouldn't have to do it in the morning. Then all he'd have to do would be to make the brief stop to pick up the computer and he'd be on his way. Much more civilized like that, he thought, and bent to pull his shoes on again.

Mrs. O'Keefe, the landlady, told him there was a fine and well-stocked bookshop just down the road, go under the railroad tracks, turn right, walk for a minute or two, and it'll be right there. The Clontarf Bookshop, it was called, and be sure to mention her name, she sent many of her guests there as she had so many professors and other professional gentlemen from all over the world. He thanked her and was on his way.

Clontarf, he had read in the guidebooks, was a wealthy and upwardly mobile suburb, and his walk to the bookstore—the "minute or two" was closer to fifteen—bore that out: neat streets lined with well-kept homes, bright-faced young wives returning from shopping trips, well-mannered children playing on the lawns. No poverty here, he thought.

The bookstore, when he reached it at last, suited its location: bright, large, well-stocked, just what he was looking for. He wanted to load up on books now, at the beginning of his stay. He didn't know when he'd get back to Dublin and he had little hope of finding a bookstore anywhere near where he'd be living, no more than he had hopes of seeing neat streets and manicured lawns.

He received a smile from the pretty girl at the counter near the door as he entered, a tiny bell tinkling overhead, and looked around for a moment to orient himself.

"Can I help you find something?" she asked. Her voice was soft and shy, in contrast to her frank smile and dark eyes that met his own.

"Well, I will need help, I think, but I'd like to look around for a bit myself."

"All right," she said, "take your time," and lowered her head again to the book she was reading.

Jack's eyes lingered on her briefly. She was rather the classic Irish beauty of the dark variety: milk-white skin and thick and silky jet-black hair, heritage of lusty Spanish seamen in centuries gone by. Very pretty. Extremely pretty.

He spent forty-five minutes wandering through the store, enjoying the different look and feel of the Irish and British books, the different covers on familiar books, and was delighted to find three of his own novels in the fiction section, in their British editions. When he had made some selections—a few American bestsellers he hadn't read, the latest British bestsellers, several Irish authors (he'd always meant to read James Plunkett and this was a perfect time to get to him), and several books on Irish history, he carried a dozen of them up to the counter. The girl looked at him curiously as he set the pile down and went back for more. There were about three dozen in all when he was done, probably more than he'd read in the three months, but better to have too much than too little.

"Are you off to live in a cave?" the girl asked, smiling. The smile made her extraordinarily pretty, with those dark eyes that seemed almost to glitter, the milky complexion, and the black hair that fell softly across her shoulders. She was sitting on a high stool with apparent ease and wearing jeans that revealed long legs and slim hips. A bulky white sweater, however, suggested a full figure. Coltish, Jack thought, and for an instant, wished he had more time in Dublin. He had, from the day he planned the trip, resigned himself to looking at nothing but hefty farmgirls during his stay.

"Something like that," he said, and returned her smile.

"Are you from the States?"

"I am," he said, thinking as he said it, I'm doing it again. By the time I leave, I'll be able to pass for a native.

"Your people mustn't be very good company if you have to bring so many books," she said.

"Oh, no," he laughed. "I have no people over here. Or if I do, I don't know them. I'm on my own, actually." Jack, you sly devil, he told himself.

"Are you?" she said without a flicker of the friendly smile. "You must be a great reader. I am too." She held up as evidence the paperback in her hand and, Jack noted with pleasure, slipped a bookmark into it and put it down on the counter. She was prepared to talk. Jack caught himself wishing that the book had just happened to be one of his own.

Just then the telephone beside the cash register rang and the girl smiled apologetically at him as she reached for it. Jack wandered again through the aisles but didn't see anything else that caught his fancy. He kept one ear on the girl's quiet conversation. As soon as she was off the phone, however, another customer had several questions for her and she disappeared into the back of the store to look for something. Jack continued strolling through the aisles, then remembered two other things he'd meant to pick up here. One was a copy of Liam O'Flaherty's *Famine*—jet-lag must be killing my memory, he thought—which he'd looked for in the States but hadn't found. And he'd also meant to pick up copies of his own books, if they were available. A gift of an author's book could go a long distance toward smoothing the way sometimes. He took four copies of each of his books and carried them back to the counter as the girl was saying goodbye to the other customer.

She looked even more curiously at these books than she had at the other piles he'd made. "He must be your favorite author," she said.

"He is," Jack said, smiling. "I've read every word he's written."

"Have you?"

"I have."

"You're him."

"I am."

They laughed together.

She started to say she knew his books, but then blushed pink and confessed she didn't. Jack told her it was quite all right; after all, most of the human race hadn't read his books.

They chatted for a minute.

"It's not fair that you should know my name but I don't know yours," Jack said when the conversation lagged briefly.

"Grainne," she told him.

"Say it again."

"Graw-nyuh," she pronounced carefully.

"Grainne."

"That's right. It's Grace in English, like the great warrior queen, Grace O'Malley, but I like it best in Irish."

She asked what he was doing in Ireland and he told her he was staying for at least three months to research and write a book.

"Which reminds me," he said. "I was looking for a copy of *Famine* by Liam O'Flaherty."

"Are there none on the shelf? Wait, I think there's some in the back."

She hopped off the stool and Jack watched her walk to the rear of the store. She moved with an easy feminine grace, long-legged and liquid, black hair swaying softly at her back. He guessed her to be about twenty-two. Again, for an instant, Jack wished he could stay longer in Dublin . . . although, from what he'd heard of Irish girls, it wouldn't make much difference; apparently, you had to meet them in church, preferably in the line waiting to take Holy Communion, or it didn't count for anything. When she reappeared, she had a copy of the book in her hand.

"Great," he said, "I've been hoping to find this."

"Has it something to do with the book you're writing?" she asked.

He told her briefly that it was an historical novel, set in the west of Ireland, about a family and its struggles to survive through the Famine of 1846 and 1847, and about the horrible thing—Jack shuddered internally, just thinking about it; that was going to be a hard part to write—that happened to three members of the family in particular.

She listened to him gravely. "It'll be a sad story, then," she said.

Jack waved a hand non-committally. "We'll see. I won't really know until I do it. Stories have a way of writing themselves sometimes."

She was smiling again, interested now and not interrupting, so Jack continued chatting about writing in general. Whenever he slowed down, she asked a question, intelligent, thoughtful, informed, and the conversation fell into a comfortable two-way rhythm. Jack was glad that no other customers had entered the store. After a few minutes, Grainne told him that she had just finished her degree at Trinity and had read history there, concentrating on Irish history.

Her words suddenly raised possibilities, unformed but almost tangible in the quiet air between them. Each seemed waiting for the other to speak.

"Well," Jack said, "if I need any historical guidance, I'll know where to come."

Grainne glanced away for a moment, and Jack flattered

himself that a slight blush colored her fair skin. Then she raised her eyes and met his gaze. "That would be nice," she said shyly. "It would be interesting."

As my sainted grandmother used to say, Jack thought, in for a penny, in for a pound. "It *would* be interesting," he said. "For both of us. If there's a nice pub nearby, perhaps we could talk about it some more."

This time she definitely did blush. "I'd have to close up the shop first," she said. "It's closing time anyway." She spoke so softly that he could barely hear her.

"I'll wait," Jack said. He kept his smile within what he hoped were decent limits.

The pub, on Clontarf Road about half a mile beyond his bed-and-breakfast house, faced the choppy waters of Dublin Bay and was called The Ship. It was filled with what Jack would have called, in American terms, upper-middle class or possibly lower-upper class businessmen, most still in their three-piece suits, stopping off for a pint or two with their cronies on the way home for the evening. Most were in their twenties and thirties, with a sprinkling of bright young women among them in pairs and groups. It was definitely not a pick-up or dating bar, as it would have been in the States: these young men had old-fashioned wives at home, rocking the young ones and fixing dinner at this very moment, waiting for their men; the bright young women would find no husbands here; they'd have to go to London or Dublin or back to the corridors of the University for that. Everyone seemed to have at least a nodding acquaintance with everyone else.

Jack and Grainne found a place in a corner, near the bar, and after they'd finished the first pint—foaming Guinness for her, lager for him—she persuaded the barkeep's wife to fix them a couple of sandwiches. They ate quickly and Jack went back to the crowded bar for refills on the pints.

The conversation, smoothed by the beer, the food, the warmth of the pub, and by the tiredness now creeping all through Jack's body, was easy and natural. They liked each other, and each of them knew it. Chemistry, Jack told himself as he listened to the musical cadences of her voice.

She told him her name was Grainne Clarkin, she would be twenty-three in December, her parents owned the bookstore and she was helping them run it for a few months while they took some time off and made visits to relatives, and while she decided what she wanted to do . . . or until she was able to find a real job, there not being many jobs of any sort to be had in Ireland, even for a Trinity graduate, she spoke and read Irish—Jack confessed that he only knew half a dozen words—and she promised to read all of his books right away, now that she'd met him and knew him.

Jack told her he was thirty-two years old, he'd written seven novels—serious suspense novels, he called them—had lived most of his life in New York except for periods of travel that included most of western Europe with the notable exception of Ireland; this new book had earned a sizable advance on his proposal for it and he was using part of the money to finance the research trip, partly because the subject truly interested him and gave him a chance to see the land of his ancestors and, besides, it was tax-deductible; and he'd certainly be back in Dublin again as soon as he was settled in the house and the book was actually started, and he'd very much like to see her again and he hoped she felt the same.

Midway through the third pint, his hand was resting lightly on hers on the worn leather cushion between them. By the end of the third pint, her fingers were gently gripping his.

But, in spite of his best efforts, Jack's eyes were closing from fatigue. It suddenly struck him that three pints of beer was a quart and a half. God, talk about getting acclimated quickly. They voted against another pint, and she drove him down Clontarf Road in her rattly Toyota. When she stopped in front of the house he pointed out, the only thing awkward about parting was the box of books he clutched on his lap.

"I'm awfully glad we met," he said.

"Irish girls are not supposed to be so forward," Grainne said quietly.

"I suppose that's what a university education will do."

"It is," she said. "I'm terribly corrupted." With only a little encouragement, Jack thought, her smile might have turned into a grin.

"Will you be in the shop in the morning?"

"Yes."

"I'll stop by."

"All right."

At home, he would have kissed her. Here, he knew he shouldn't.

He stood on the pavement, with the box of books held up against his chest, watching until the Toyota's taillights blended into the traffic.

In the morning, he ate breakfast ravenously and finished all the brown bread in the basket. The car, a blue Escort, was delivered as promised, and by ten-thirty—he was comfortably falling into the slower Irish ways—he was driving away toward the Clontarf Bookshop.

She was there. When he walked in, he saw that she was reading one of his books.

He wrote down the address and telephone number of the house he was renting. She gave him one of the bookshop's cards and added that she lived upstairs.

She walked him to the door and, when he'd opened it, spontaneously leaned forward—she was almost his height—and kissed him lightly on the mouth. She seemed quite as surprised as he was. For the moment they touched, her lips felt full and soft on his own.

"I'll see you again," he said, and she nodded. He thought her eyes still looked startled at her own boldness.

He saw when he glanced back that she stayed in the doorway until he'd driven out of sight.

The clerk at Radio Shack had everything ready as promised, and helped him carry it all outside and wedge the cartons securely into the trunk and back seat of the car.

The sun was shining again as he threaded his way through traffic alongside the Liffey, searching for unfamiliar road signs, and then onto the N7, heading west toward the rocky hills of County Clare and his waiting house near the village of Doolin on the coast, just at the edge of the Burren.

CHAPTER 3

In the village of Doolin, where the breezes carried the salt and scent of the ocean onto the stone-strewn hills, a man named Padraic Mullen was nearing death.

He was seventy-three years of age, hearty and in good health, still working his patch of hillside right up until spring planting time earlier that year. One morning, just as the planting was nearly done, he had urinated blood. He'd stood there for a long time, breathing deeply, his lips moving in sudden devout prayer, asking God Almighty that when he opened his eyes it would all be changed and he might be permitted a longer time on this earth with his children and his wife, God willing. But God was not willing and when old Paddy opened his eyes, the urine was still bright red. Oddly, there was no pain, no burning, and for another week everything was normal. Eleven days later, he stood before the toilet in the morning, forgetful, for the first time, of that big fright. And the urine was bright red again, accompanied this time by a horrible burning that made him cry out and double over in a vain attempt to stop the flow.

The next day, a Friday, his two sons, Michael and Patrick, had driven him in the truck to the hospital in Galway—Father Henning had said that would be the best place for this sort of thing—and, with many reassuring pats on the shoulder, had left him in the care of the sisters who managed to smile and yet look stern at the same time. The brothers had then driven on to Salthill, the beach resort just a few miles farther out on the coastal road along Galway Bay, taken a room at the Monte Cristo Hotel, and proceeded to the serious business of getting roaring drunk in one of the local dancehalls. When they were ejected from that place, they found another, more congenial establishment where their noisy custom was welcomed until closing time. They made a terrible racket getting up the stairs to their room at the Monte Cristo, and they were embarrassed and penitent when they faced the frowning landlady the next morning over breakfast. They were still red-eyed an hour later when they reached the hospital and enquired for the doctor whose name Michael had written down carefully on a grubby bit of paper. The doctor, a hard-eyed young man whose accent was more British than Irish, told them in a straightforward manner that their father had cancer of the pancreas and would be dead within six months. They took the old fellow home that afternoon, put him to bed, told the tale to their weeping mother, and repaired to the local pub, it being Saturday night anyway, where they repeated the previous evening's performance on a quieter scale to ease their sorrow.

Now, in mid-September, Padraic Mullen, his flesh gnawed away by the cancer, his eyes glazed, cheekbones threatening to tear through the jaundiced skin of his face, hands reduced to claws, was coming to the end at last.

Michael Mullen came out of the bedroom, secretly glad to escape the heavy smell of sickness and death, and closed the door behind him.

"It can't go on much longer," he said to Patrick and his mother, who kept one hand pressed tight over her mouth. "Please God, it'll be easy and he'll just go quiet-like."

Peggy Mullen's eyes narrowed as she forced back the sobs. Her voice, schooled by countless generations of getting by in the face of the worst, hardly wavered when she said, "I'll sit with him. You come in, the two of you, in a few minutes." Hand still pressed firmly to the side of her face, she opened the bedroom door and went in to sit with her husband. She and Padraic had been married for almost forty-one years.

When the door was closed, Michael turned to his younger brother. "You'd best go for Father Henning," he said. Michael was thirty-seven, four years older than Patrick, and now the head of the family. "It won't be long, I'm thinking. It's as good as over. Get on with you."

Patrick pulled on a coat and, head bowed, hurried from the house and down the road toward the church.

Michael sat in the front parlor for ten minutes, smoked two cigarettes, then got up and went to join his mother in the bedroom. He avoided looking at his father's ghastly face, which was mercifully lost in shadow. The room was lighted dimly by a single lamp.

There was a cane-bottomed straight chair in the corner of the room and he sat there, thick hands between his knees, listening to his father's body in its weary struggle for breath. His mother sighed and occasionally shook her head from side to side.

After a while, Patrick returned with a sad-faced Father Henning. They came into the bedroom quietly and the priest—who had been born in the same year as Padraic Mullen, who had married the couple four decades earlier, who had been three times offered retirement in a home for aged priests in County Limerick and who had three times refused—put a comforting hand on the shoulder of Peggy Mullen and moved his dry lips in silent prayer.

Then he sat carefully on the edge of the bed and performed for his boyhood friend the rite of Extreme Unction, murmuring the words of the prayer in a hoarse voice and tenderly anointing the dying man's body with holy oil. The moment after he straightened up from this office and was turning to speak some comforting words to Peggy Mullen about the irresistible will of God, the old fellow in the bed sighed loudly, made a soft rattling sound in his throat, and conceded victory to a greater force.

His wife, now his widow, cried out at last. The men let her stay for a few minutes, stroking her dead husband's face, then firmly led her from the bedroom and made her sit on the sofa in the front room, where she huddled, sobbing, in the corner, twisting a damp handkerchief in her hands. The two brothers and the priest retreated to the kitchen.

"Father, will you have something against the chill?" Michael asked after a moment.

"I will," Father Henning said, "but just a drop, and I'll take it in honor of him inside."

Michael crouched and pulled a bottle from a cupboard beneath the sink. The dusty bottle bore no label and had come from no shop that paid taxes to the government. Michael pulled the cork from it, rubbed his hand on the mouth of the bottle, and handed it to the priest. Father Henning raised it to his lips, sipped quickly at the colorless poteen, ancient and illicit product of the hills and the only proper libation at a time like this, and passed the bottle to Patrick. He drank and passed it to Michael, who took a mouthful, then stoppered the bottle again, and replaced it in the cupboard.

"Well, then," Father Henning said, "I'll be off now, but I'll come by tomorrow to say a prayer with you. It's best this way, lads, you know that. He's out of his pain now, God rest him."

The brothers lowered their eyes and nodded.

"I'll send the woman to help with the body," the priest added quietly. "And I'll telephone for you to Will McKeon." Will McKeon was the undertaker who served the needs of all the remote villages in this part of County Clare; he'd made a fortune, so it was said, on the grief and loss of others, and was simultaneously resented and admired for it. "You'll be waking him here, of course."

"Yes," Michael told him.

"That's best," the priest agreed. "There's no point in putting yourselves to needless expense. Will McKeon already has more put by than all the rest of us together." He looked at the brothers. They each managed a thin smile in reply, and the touch of normalcy marked an end to the little ceremony in the kitchen.

Father Henning stopped for a minute to speak a few soft words to the widow. Patrick sat down beside his mother and put a clumsy arm around her shoulders. Michael saw the priest to the door. It was dark out now.

"Mind your step in the road, Father."

"I will."

Back in the front room, Michael said, "I'll bring you a cup of tea, mother." She nodded but said nothing. Michael gestured his brother to follow him into the kitchen.

Looking directly into his brother's eyes, Michael placed a hand on Patrick's arm and said, "Pat, I want you to go for John MacMahon. It's best to do it and be done, before the women are here."

Patrick drew back a little but Michael held his arm. "Must we?" the younger brother said. "Is it necessary?"

"It is," Michael said.

"But—"

"Don't be arguing with me, Pat. It must be done and that's all there is to it. It's been done and done, you know that, and I'll not be the one to let it go. That's all there is to it. Now be off while there's still time. Go on. Go on, I said."

Patrick took his coat from the back of the chair where he'd left it and went out through the kitchen door into the night.

Michael fixed the tea for his mother, sat with her a few minutes holding her hand, fixed her a second cup, went to the bedroom and bade a brief farewell to his father, then returned to the kitchen door and waited there until Patrick came back with John MacMahon.

Without a word spoken, he led the old man into the bedroom and closed the door on him; he had no desire to watch or be present while the blood, even a small amount, was drawn from his father's body. He waited in the kitchen and Pat sat in the front room to make certain their mother didn't stir. If she heard strange movement in the house, she gave no sign. Besides, she no doubt knew just what they were doing. Hadn't her own husband been fetched from the house many a night to do the same for others that was now being done for him?

Then John MacMahon was back in the kitchen. Still without speaking—Pat was still in the front room with the mother—Michael drew out the bottle of poteen once again. Silently, he and John MacMahon drank from it. Then the old man nodded, silent and solemn still, and went out, as the priest had, into the darkness of the night. Michael followed him with his eyes until he was out of sight and tried not to look at the heavy bulge in the pocket of the old man's coat.

The house, Jack Quinlan thought when he finally reached it that evening, was everything he'd hoped for and infinitely more than he'd expected.

He got there at about seven-thirty, squinting in the fading light at the baroquely complicated driving directions the house agents had provided. It was amazing how misleading the directions could be in a country with so few roads. Fortunately, he'd driven on the left-hand side of the road several times in England before this, so that part of the journey, at least, was no problem. By the time he was out of Dublin traffic, he felt comfortable in the car. He'd been warned that Irish roads were like no others in the world: narrow, twisting, treacherous, confusingly marked, when they were marked at all, and haunted by fire-eyed demon drivers with not a whit of safety-consciousness and seemingly even less sense of self-preservation. All of it, everything Jack had ever heard, turned out to be the truth. What passed for a national highway route in Ireland wouldn't have passed muster as the lowliest county road at home. After an hour of driving, including twenty minutes rolling slowly along a single-lane road behind a lumbering wagon filled with shuddering bales of dusty hay, he was making daredevil passes with the wildest of the native drivers. In the end, the trip that he'd estimated would take three hours took, in fact, closer to seven. When he was still only halfway there, as best he could reckon the distance on his Geographia map, he settled back and resigned himself to living on "Irish time."

But his first view of the house made it all worthwhile.

It was at the top of a boulder-strewn hill that sloped so regularly toward the ocean's edge that he was sure the hillside simply continued, uninterrupted, beneath the water's white-capped surface. A blazing red-gold sun was just flashing its final light beyond the Atlantic horizon, staining a rippled streak of water with its own brilliant color, and outlining in shadow the dark, sea-girt, rocky hummocks of the Aran Islands. Jack had stopped his car near the ocean, at the bottom of the hill. When he turned his head away from the sun and looked up to his right, toward the house, the broad expanse of windows flashed back the sunset in dazzling flames of orange, gold, and red. The sky beyond was indigo velvet. The air was fresh, cool, salty with evening seaspray.

"I may never see Times Square again," Jack breathed. "Or miss it." He put the car in gear and continued up the hill.

Whether the house had ever actually been the home of an architect—every attractive house offered for long-term leases back in the States was advertised as being the former home of an architect—it was certainly everything the agents had promised: traditionally styled but with that very modern row of windows facing the ocean, comfortably furnished, with all amenities, including two bedrooms, a study (that would be his office, where

he'd write), a dining room, and a modern kitchen big enough to
eat in. It made no difference to Jack that it wasn't exactly "within
walking distance" of a church, as the listing had promised—
although maybe it was, by Irish standards—but he had no doubt
there was a church in the town itself. Beyond his own hillside, to
the north—he was just in time to see it as the light of sunset died
away into darkness—was the clearly defined edge of the limestone plains of the Burren.

For the next hour, in an excess of enthusiasm that he regretted only when he was finished and sat down to catch his breath,
he unloaded from the car his three suitcases, the computer and
printer, the carton of supplies and two heavy cartons of paper,
the box of books, and—he blessed himself for his own foresight,
even if he'd only thought of it late in the afternoon—the sack
containing tea, bread, cheese, and jam that he'd bought in some
nameless little town along the road.

He sat on the couch, looking about wearily but with great and
warm satisfaction, at his new domain.

After a few minutes, he became aware of the strain his back
and shoulders had suffered from sitting in the car all day, negotiat-
ing unfamiliar and difficult roads, followed by a spell of hauling
heavy cartons around. And he was famished. Before he could
fall asleep on the couch, he got up quickly and went out to the
kitchen, found a kettle, and put water on to boil. While he waited
for it, he made a cheese sandwich and had finished it before the
kettle began to whistle. He ate another while the tea was steep-
ing. When it was ready, he carried the steaming mug out to the
living room and stood at the windows, looking out to the west,
down the long slope toward the ocean. He could just make out
the sound of waves rolling in and breaking on the shore.

"Home, indeed," he said out loud.

When he turned to go back to the couch, he spotted the fireplace for the first time. Somehow, in the excitement of arriving
and unpacking and settling in, he'd completely missed it. He
walked over to it now, admiring the fine stonework and broad
white mantel, which was at the level of his shoulder. He'd have
to find things to put up there, things that would personalize the

living room, make the house his own. He looked around for fire-wood but there was none. Then he stopped suddenly, grinning at himself. Of course there was no firewood. This is Ireland, not Vermont. The English destroyed the Irish forests centuries ago. Here we burn peat. Snapping his fingers, he headed for the door.

The turf was stacked high, thick brown earthy bricks of it, against the end of the house. Jack had no idea how much of it to use or how long it would last—and the learning of such things was the very kind of mundane knowledge he'd come this dis-tance to find—so he gathered as much in his arms as he could hold onto and carried it into the house.

He dumped it on the stone flags before the fireplace, then piled it neatly against the wall. Then he stood back, put his hands on his hips, and realized that he'd never built a fire before in his life, even out of wood, much less peat.

He lit a cigarette and wondered if the lighter would do the trick or if he'd have to wait until he could get to a shop and buy wooden matches. But he wanted the fire now; it would be the perfect thing for this first night in his new home.

Then he thought of Grainne.

He realized instantly that his thoughts were running away with him. He hardly knew the girl, had spent no more than a few hours with her, might never see her again, and here he was pictur-ing her sitting beside him on the floor in front of a cozy turf fire. The image was vivid and warm in his mind: her glistening black hair, dark eyes, milky white skin, the touch of her lips on his, her slender legs and hips and full breasts. He'd been aware, certainly, of all of that the evening before and again this morning, when he'd stopped briefly at the bookshop, but the wave of new scenes, things to do, things to think about, had blurred and softened the impression of her face, voice, words, touch. He told himself quickly that, of course, he'd felt, and felt now, an immediate closeness to her; after all, she was the only person he knew—and even that was stretching a point pretty far—in the whole country. And at the same time, he wanted to tell her how much he loved the house. Besides, he had to find out how to build a peat fire, right? Right.

Humming a tune he knew from a Clancy Brothers album but

the title of which he couldn't recall, he got the bookshop card from the pocket of his jacket and went to the telephone in the kitchen. He was relieved that it worked. He dialed the number in Dublin—it suddenly seemed awfully far away—and listened happily to the foreign-sounding burr of the phone at the other end.

"Hello?"

He knew her voice instantly.

"Grainne, it's Jack Quinlan."

There was a moment's silence, then she said, "Oh!"

He sat back in the kitchen chair and put his feet up on a counter.

"What's happened?" she asked quickly. "Did you find it? Are you all right?"

"Yes," he laughed, "I'm fine. Everything is fine. The drive took about three times longer than I expected, but I'm here and the house is terrific. It's big, it faces the ocean, it has a great view, and I love it."

"I'm glad," she said, sounding pleased but still a little puzzled.

"I wanted to tell someone."

"Oh?"

"And, right now, you're the only friend I have in the world."

She said nothing and the telephone crackled a little in the momentary silence.

"That didn't come out right, did it?" Jack said. "What I mean is, you were the first person I thought of."

He thought she was smiling when she replied, "Well, that does sound a little better."

"It really is beautiful here, Grainne. I wish you could see it."

She said nothing to that.

"Actually," Jack went on quickly, "the *real* reason I called is purely a business matter."

"It is?"

"Oh, yes. You see, I've read all the books I bought—I read them while I was driving—and now I need a new supply."

"Do you?" she said, and now he could definitely hear the smile, almost see the curve of her lips. "You must be an awfully fast reader."

"Oh, I am. In fact—"

"I read your book," she said quietly. "The shop wasn't at all busy today and I finished it."

Now it was his turn to say, "Oh."

"I liked it."

"Good."

"Do you not want to talk about it?"

"No, nothing of the sort. It's just that . . . Well, as soon as you said you'd read it, it suddenly mattered a great deal whether you liked it or not."

"Oh," she said again, then added quickly, "I keep saying that, don't I?"

"So do I."

"I did something else, too. I was thinking about your book, the one you're writing, and I made a list of books on the Famine. You may have read some of them but I could get them for you if you wanted. I did it, you know, just on the chance you might phone." Her voice trailed off uncertainly.

Jack slid lower on the chair and crossed his ankles up on the counter.

"Well, I've phoned," he said.

"Yes."

"Yes."

They both laughed easily.

"I meant it, Grainne, when I said I wished you could see this place. Maybe you'll come here and see it. You could come here for a weekend."

"The university didn't corrupt me *that* much, Jack Quinlan," she said at once.

He was about to reply when she added, "You'll have to steal me away."

"I might just do that," Jack said. "I'd just toss you in the box with the books."

After that, she steered the conversation toward more neutral topics and they chatted easily for another ten minutes. He promised to call again in a couple of days.

He'd hung up the telephone and strolled out to the living room before he remembered he'd meant to ask about the peat fire. Too late, he thought. And he was too tired, anyway, especially with all he'd done and two days' worth of jet fatigue to get over. Yawning, he walked into the bedroom, opened a window to let in some fresh air, tested the mattress and found it as hard as he liked, peeled off his clothes, and climbed in.

As he dozed off, he thought he heard a distant high-pitched keening sound, borne on the dark night breezes, but then it blended with the rhythm of his own breathing and he was lost in sleep.

At some time during the night, a thick, damp fog drifted up the hill from the ocean and came curling in the open bedroom window. Jack stirred in his sleep and rose naked from the bed, shivering and grumbling at the cold touch of the air. He closed the window and got back under the covers and, not remembering, slept peacefully the rest of the night.

CHAPTER 4

He slept until almost eleven in the morning and awoke clearheaded, filled with energy, and ravenous. He blessed himself again for thinking of the bread and cheese and tea, and thought the whistling of the kettle on the stove was nearly the sweetest, homiest sound in the world.

Outside, it was raining and the world was gray and still and wet.

He stood at the living room window, drinking a cup of tea and eating a slab of bread liberally covered with strawberry jam. His view stretched down the hillside toward the ocean—he could just see the foamy surf rolling in and breaking on the rocks and, if he pressed his forehead against the cold glass, he could catch a glimpse, off to his right, to the north, of the gray-white blur of the Burren—and he thought the scene was grandly picturesque.

The only sounds to be heard were the patter and drip of the rain. The only human sounds were his own.

"King of the mountain," he said out loud.

He finished the bread and tea and, before returning to the

kitchen to fix more, he made the rounds of the living room and turned on all the lights. Instantly, the room seemed warmer, and the gray, wet world outside retreated and, thus challenged, grew darker still.

Jack spent another hour or so doing odds and ends in the house. He sat at the kitchen table and made a shopping list of foods he needed and another list of shops and services he'd have to locate. He wondered how far he'd have to travel—possibly all the way to Galway city?—to find, say, a dry cleaner's. Or a Xerox machine. He smiled at himself; this, after all, was what he'd come here for. He turned his head and looked out the kitchen window, and saw the top of the pile of peat stacked beside the house, ready for the cold, wet weather ahead. He sighed with satisfaction. Good move, he told himself.

When he was done with the lists, he delayed going out a little longer while he arranged his books in the empty bookcase he found waiting in the study. Looking at them and handling them made him think of Grainne. He supposed it had been pretty bold of him, from the Irish point of view, even to mention the idea of her coming here. But she hadn't instantly ruled out the possibility of coming to visit. If she thought it was out of the question, she would have said so, right? And she hadn't, so the possibility remained . . . a possibility. He wasn't surprised at all to find that he was still thinking of her as warmly as he had the night before. He only even became conscious of how he was lost in thought when his knee became cramped from kneeling in front of the bookcase. He changed his position and finished putting the rest of the books on the shelves, grouping them into several sets. When he came to the multiple copies of his own books, he wondered what Grainne really thought of them . . . and what she thought of him after reading them. And if she really would . . .

Daydreaming. Wasting time.

He stood up and stretched the stiff knee.

Take it easy, he warned himself. Grainne Clarkin was indeed very easy to look at, very pleasant to be with, very interesting to talk to, and, from what he knew, seemed to care about all the same things he cared about. She was also the only person he knew in this entire country, and here he was facing three celibate months—like some medieval monk—on the cold, wet rocks of western Ireland with winter coming on apace, and with nothing for company but his own imagination and the winds from the North Atlantic. What he felt was all the product of circumstance and wishful thinking, nothing more. Besides, she was Irish, wasn't she, born and bred to it, and that meant Virgin City, university education or no university education. Forget it, he told himself. You probably scared the hell out of her on the phone by even suggesting such a thing.

He decided he'd call her again the next evening, and went off, whistling, to get the yellow rain slicker he'd brought and the car keys.

He spent most of Wednesday doing shopping in the tiny village, wandering around, taking in the sights, such as they were—part of his mind told him they were really pretty dismal, while another part rejoiced in the sheer and primitive *foreignness* of the place: stone walls, ancient wooden signs, sidewalks only a foot wide in places, where there were sidewalks at all, and, visible through the narrow lanes between buildings, the green-gray fields and slopes of the hills, all of them dotted white with wandering woolly sheep. There were three pubs and he stopped in to sample two of them, eating his lunch in the first he came to, the Seafoam, and passing on afterwards to McGlynn's. Both were clean and plain, surprisingly bright, and sported identical arrays of colorful posters on the walls, advertising popular Irish groups, singers, and musicians, De Danann, Clannad, Mary Bergin, Liam O'Flynn, and others. Each also had, among the posters, hand-lettered signs promising traditional music on Friday and Saturday nights. It was all in keeping, Jack thought, just as advertised; he knew from several guidebooks that Doolin, unlikely as it seemed for this remote coastal village, was something of an international center for traditional Irish music. He was looking forward to it; the music of the fiddle and bodhran and uilleann pipes, passed down from teacher to student before a peat fire and unspoiled by commercial influences, was something he sought out at home when groups appeared at Town Hall and Folk City. Here he could have it at the source. And, thank God, something to do on the weekends. He'd toyed with the idea of buying a bodhran, the Irish goatskin drum that was played with a two-headed beater and whose ancient, hollow sound evoked visions of naked, blue-painted Celtic warriors running in shrieking hordes down the hills. Maybe he'd buy one now. Surely in Doolin he could find someone to teach him how to play it.

He enjoyed the afternoon. He filled the back seat of the car with his purchases and worried not at all, as he would have at home, about the milk and cheese and eggs and fish he'd bought. They'd be fine; the Irish didn't worry overmuch about refrigeration and, besides, the weather was cold enough to keep them. He ended up in McGlynn's with a pint of lager in front of him, his head whirling with scenes he wanted to use and describe in his book.

When he reached home at last, it was already getting dark. He wasn't much of a cook—he was going to have to find somebody to come in and take care of that for him—but he made a valiant effort at frying the piece of fish he'd bought. The result was less than spectacular, but edible. As he washed the one plate he'd used, the pan, and the pot he'd used to boil two potatoes, he found himself lost in thought about the book. There were notes he wanted to make, reminders he wanted to jot down. In the study, he worked for an hour, then pulled out his files of notes and added the new pages. He spent almost another two hours connecting the computer and the printer, setting up a disk for the new book, and testing the system. Tomorrow, he thought. Tomorrow he'd start. That was always the hardest part, the first few pages, but he'd do it tomorrow.

By the time he pushed his chair back from the desk, it was too late to call Grainne.

It was Thursday, his second morning in Doolin, that he saw the funeral.

With a couple of good nights' rest behind him, he was up early and at his desk, feeling extraordinarily virtuous and filled with ideas, by the time the gray light of dawn had firmly established itself over the land. Sitting before the keyboard of the computer, the words came easily. The first sentence of the book had been in his mind for a month. He typed it in and looked at it on the word-processor screen. It was good. The next sentence came and he typed that. And a paragraph. And a page, and another page. When he finally sat back, longing for another cup of breakfast tea, he was already a third of the way into the prologue, with the rest of the scene taking shape clearly in his mind. He was safe now. The book was started.

He had only explored the village itself the day before. Now he thought he'd take the car and spend an hour or two driving the narrow, rutted roads of the area, along the rocky coast and up among the hills and the farms.

It wasn't raining as he started out, but the sky looked as if it might open at any moment. He drove back the way he'd come on Tuesday and, moving slowly, letting his gaze drift easily over the rocky landscape where muddy sheep were the only things that moved, he circled to his left, making a wide swing around the neighboring hills and the village of Doolin itself. After about three quarters of an hour, as the car topped a rise on a tight bend, then straightened out, heading downhill, he saw the line of black-clad mourners gathered just ahead.

He brought the car to a stop, taking care not to go into the deep, weed-filled ditch at the side of the road. As he shut off the motor, a few fat, clear raindrops spattered heavily on the windshield.

The shuffling, dark line of people was turning in through a break in the tumbled-down wall that lined the road on his right. He could see six elderly men, all dressed in rumpled dark suits and wearing dark tweed caps and scarves, sliding their feet slowly over the gravel of the roadway, while a plain wooden casket trembled on their shoulders and grew slightly darker as the raindrops fell harder and the water stained the raw wood. At the head of the procession walked a tall, elderly priest, one hand clutching a raincoat closed over his chest. His black scarf flapped like an angry bird at his throat.

They were obviously people from Doolin and Jack wondered for a moment if he should join the procession and say a prayer (or at least pretend to) at the grave. After all, he was a member of the community now, even though, so far, he'd only met a couple of the shopkeepers. Then he thought that might be regarded as intruding, and he decided against it.

The funeral procession had moved on into the field and turned uphill toward the straggly line of trees. The mourners were out of sight now. Jack sat in the car, smoking a cigarette.

He needed to see a funeral, for a scene in the book, and this one would be perfect. He wouldn't even need to adapt it to his purposes; all he'd have to do is describe it. Writers can be ghoulish when they need to be, he thought. He sighed, stubbed out the cigarette in the ashtray, and got out of the car. He hesitated for a second, then, from force of habit, reached in and took the keys from the ignition.

It was easy to climb over the wall, but the hillside beyond it was rough, uneven, thick with nettles and tangled, ropy vegetation that concealed treacherous rocks. He moved with care, trying to watch where he placed his feet and, at the same time, angle across the slope in the direction the funeral procession had taken.

He had just reached a few dark, slouching fir trees when he saw the party gathered at the grave.

They stood with heads bowed beneath the rain and their grief, and Jack could just hear on the chill, salty wind, the murmurings of the priest's blessing on the deceased and the mourners' mumbled responses. The sounds reached him, faded, touched him again, as the wind danced over the hill. He shivered, pulled his collar up close against his chin and held it tight across his throat. Cold rain struck his face and he felt his hair getting wet. He could see the open grave, a dark patch at the mourners' feet. A pile of raw dirt, dotted with stones, stood beside it. As he watched, the priest made the sign of the cross over the coffin and the six pallbearers lowered it on ropes into the hole. They tossed the ropes in after it, then immediately picked up waiting shovels and began pushing in the pile of dirt. The other mourners were already beginning to move away. Jack thought he could pick out the principals among them, a woman and, apparently, two grown sons.

Now, with the coffin buried and the prayers said over it—and with the chilling rain coming harder and faster—the party moved more quickly away from the cemetery. In less than five minutes

—while Jack tried to memorize the details for the scene he was going to write—they were gone and the hillside was quiet except for the patter of rain.

Jack was soaked already—buy a tweed cap, he added to his mental list—but, as long as he'd seen this much, he thought he'd take in the whole sight and be done with it. Funerals and grave-yards hadn't changed much in a century and a half, especially in rural Ireland, and this whole event he'd witnessed was like a scene from the book. He knew just where it took place in the story. He shivered, pressed his teeth tightly together to keep them from chattering—get another Irish wool sweater, he added to the list—and took a step out from the trees. And drew back instantly out of sight.

Four elderly men had appeared from the trees and rocks on the uphill side of the grave.

They stood in a tight cluster, as if conferring, heads bent and looking down at the freshly turned earth of the grave, even now turning to mud as the rain struck it. One of them, the tallest, appeared to be the leader—the others seemed to be clustered about him—and Jack saw him turn his head and speak to his com-panions. His heart beating fast with surprise and curiosity, Jack strained to hear what the old fellow was saying, but the wind was at his back now and the only voices he heard were those of wind and rain.

He stepped back, hoping the scrawny wind-blown trees would conceal him, and watched.

The tall old man, the one who seemed to be in charge, strug-gled for a moment to pull some thick, heavy object from the pocket of his jacket. When he finally got it free, Jack thought it looked like a bottle. My God, he thought, don't tell me they've come here to a gravesite to drink in the rain. The old man pulled a stopper from the bottle—the three others watched him closely —and then leaned forward over the mounded dirt of the grave. Stretching out a hand, he slowly poured the contents of the bottle into the dirt, moving the bottle back and forth over the length of the grave so the liquid touched it all. Then the old fellow stop-pered the bottle again—Jack couldn't be sure but he thought the whitish bottle might have been stone—and pressed it back into his pocket. Then the four old men, three of them helping the eldest, came around the grave and, without once looking back at it, made their way down the rough path, toward the break in the wall, and continued till they were out of sight.

"I am a stranger in a strange land," Jack whispered out loud as the old men disappeared from view. "There are stranger things in heaven and earth, Horatio, than are dreamt of in your philosophy. And so on and so forth."

His jacket and sweater were completely soaked through now —he hadn't brought the slicker because he hadn't expected to be getting out of the car—and he hurried, as best he could, back to the road.

It occurred to him as he started the engine that the mourners as well as the four old men might have seen the car and wondered who it belonged to—or knew; this, after all, was a small town and news always traveled fast. But there was nothing he could do about it now.

He sat in the car for a minute, waiting for the heater to take effect, enjoying the spurious comfort of a cigarette, and wiping the rain from his face. By the time he reached the bottom of the hill and the rain-gray town of Doolin, the mourners, and the four strange old men, had disappeared, as if they had blended with the rain and the mist.

"Henning," the priest said. "Father Malcolm Henning. Come in out of the wet."

Jack stepped inside and the priest closed the door solidly behind him. "Jack Quinlan."

"This way," the priest said, leading Jack into a small sitting room at the front of the house. "We'll have you dry in a jiffy. Can I get you a hot cup of tea or something?"

"No, thanks, Father," Jack said. He pulled off the coat and the new cap he'd just bought on his way here to the priest's house. While the older man was putting the coat away, Jack's curious eye took in the details of the room: heavy overstuffed furniture that looked as if it might have been there since the turn of the century, used by eight or nine decades' worth of village priests, a sofa that was clearly intended for callers to the house, and, facing it, a large old wing-back armchair that was just as clearly reserved to the exclusive use of the priest himself. Both sofa and chair were done up with fine lace antimacassars on the back and arms.

"Are you sure you'll have nothing?" the priest said as he returned to the room.

"Really," Jack said. "Thanks, Father, but no. I just came by to say hello."

"And to ask a favor, no doubt," the priest said as he settled back into his chair.

Jack couldn't help smiling. "Well, yes, I did want to ask a favor."

"I'm not surprised," Father Henning said, his tone light and pleasant, easing the directness of his words. Jack studied the priest's face and thought he must have been a hearty and handsome fellow in his youth. Even the crisscrossed wrinkles that marked it now could not disguise the strong line of the jaw and the bright, intelligent eyes. "Indeed," the priest went on, "you'll no doubt be wanting more favors than one. I'll be glad to do what I can for you. I'm not what you might call a travel agent, but I know a thing or two about Doolin."

Jack decided he was going to like this man. It had been a wise move coming to him first. He sat back in the sofa and crossed his legs comfortably. "You seem to know all about me," he said.

"Well, let me see," Father Henning said, and joined his large-jointed fingers lightly together. If this was a friendly game they were playing, the priest was obviously enjoying it. "I know that you arrived on Tuesday. I know the house you've hired. People come and go in it, you know, but it's been empty this long while now. Painter, last time. Pretty good, too. He used to be showing me all his pictures, and they were lovely, lovely, I can tell you that. Rocks and hills and the sea, oh, and the waves coming in at Doolin Point. And the Burren, of course, they all want to be painting the Burren." He waved one long-fingered hand. "The Burren, that's the hard one to catch. You're not a painter, now, are you?"

"I'm a writer. A novelist."

"A writer, is it? Well, that's good. We're honored to have you among us. Writers and such are held in high esteem, you know, in Ireland."

Jack grinned. "They don't pay any taxes."

"They don't, that's true. It's not so different, you know, from the old times, the ancient times of the kings and the bards, when a poet would travel about the land, singing his songs and telling his tales, and find a warm welcome at every castle he came to, and a roof over his head at every inn along the road and a meal on his plate. Things don't be changing too terrible much in Ireland." He looked over the tops of his glasses at Jack. "You may have noticed that."

"I have. It makes it very attractive."

"Have you people here? In Ireland, I mean?"

"No, I'm afraid not. My family was small and just sort of lost track of relatives over here through the years. There probably are some—cousins, I guess—but I haven't a notion who or where they are."

"Ah, that's a shame. But then, it's so hard to be keeping up at such a great distance as the years go by. Is that why you're come here? To find them?"

"Well, no. I'm here to do research for a book. On-the-spot research, you might say. Atmosphere, daily life, local color, that sort of thing."

"Well. I should think you'd find us very quaint and backward here in the west of Ireland. Or is that what you're after?"

Jack saw that Father Henning was watching him closely now, despite the friendly look on his face. "Well, Father, if you mean, have I come here the way a person might go to a museum, to gawk at the strange people and ways, I'd have to tell you that's not really it. I *have* come, though, to learn as much as I can about . . . well, to learn what it's like to live here. I want to know the details, yes—and I *need* to know them—but it's because I want them to be right in the book. I want the whole thing to look and feel and sound right. I can't do that sitting in an apartment in New York."

"That's a good answer," the priest said, "a very good answer. So it's New York you're from, is it?"

"Yes."

"I've been there."

"Have you?"

"I have. I was there three times. I was there in nineteen

hundred and forty-nine, nineteen hundred and fifty-eight, and in nineteen hundred and *seventy*-eight."

"Well," Jack said. "Did you like it?"

"I hated it!"

They laughed together, as if, Jack thought, they had just been testing each other with lines from an old Abbott-and-Costello routine and found that each of them knew it by heart.

"I had two cousins there but they're both dead now, may God have mercy on them. It was only for them that I went at all. I wonder did you know one of them, John Mulcahy, he was pastor of St. Mary's, in Riverdale, until he passed away."

"No, I'm afraid not."

"No, well, of course, you wouldn't, I guess. Are you Catholic?"

"Mostly."

"Ah."

Jack saw that the priest had clearly *decided* not to pursue that, and he admired him for it.

"Father," he said, "I don't want to be taking too much of your time. I—"

"You wanted a favor."

"Just information, and I thought you'd be the one to ask. I'd like to hire a housekeeper, if there's someone available. House-keeper and cook, actually."

"Ah hah," the priest said. "Housekeeper and cook. Well, now, let me think."

"I'll be glad to pay whatever the going rate is, and be generous besides."

"Ah hah. Yes, I know the very person. A good woman who just lost her husband, we just buried him this morning. I'm certain she'd welcome a little extra coming in. How long did you say you're taking the house for?"

"I'll be here for three months," Jack said, then added quickly, "at least."

"Three months," Father Henning said, then, looking over the tops of his glasses again, added, "at least. Ah hah. Well, I think it will all work out for the best. I'll say a word to her, if you'd like."

"I'd appreciate it, Father."

"Of course. But you'll have to potter through as best you can for a few days or a week, you know, until she grows accustomed to the loss of her husband. Peggy Mullen's her name."

"Peggy Mullen. Yes, of course."

"Well, then," the priest said.

"Well, thanks very much, Father. I appreciate your help."

Father Henning was already unfolding himself from the chair. Jack stood with him, and they walked together to the door. The priest insisted on holding his damp jacket for him.

Jack couldn't resist one more question. "How long are you here, Father? I mean, in Doolin."

The priest laughed and the lines crinkled deeply around his eyes. "Oh," he said, "on a cold, wet, nasty day like this, I feel it's been all the ages. The damp gets into old bones something terrible. On a day as wet as this one, I feel as old as the Burren itself."

I'll get nothing from him, Jack thought as he drove away. The old priest had learned a great deal about him but told almost nothing himself, not even the length of time he'd served the village. It would take a long time to warm up *that* old fellow. And it would be an even longer time than that before Jack could ask questions about anything as odd as what he'd witnessed that morning at the grave.

Doolin, apparently, had its little secrets, and, just as apparently, meant to keep them.

Jack called Grainne that night, as he'd promised himself he would. She was out. It was, he assumed, her mother who answered the telephone. He wasn't certain if Grainne had mentioned his name to her parents—and why in hell did he feel like he was sixteen again as soon as he heard the woman's voice?—so he told her his whole name, resisting the automatic impulse to spell it—you didn't have to spell Quinlan here, the way you often did in New York—and said he'd appreciate her telling Grainne he'd called and that he'd call again.

When he was off the phone, he sat for several minutes at the kitchen table, telling himself firmly that it was absolutely ridiculous for him to be wondering where she was or what she was doing or who she was with.

He spent the rest of the evening reading. Trying to read.

After a while, he went out to the kitchen and added "radio" to his growing list of things he needed to buy.

At about one o'clock that night, as he was reading in bed and just beginning to think he'd turn the light off and try to get to sleep, he heard a man's voice groaning somewhere outside the house.

Jack froze, the book still clutched tightly in his hand, and listened. He heard it again: a long, deep moan, hinting at shapeless words and agonizing pain.

Shivering, Jack tossed the book aside on the bed, pushed the covers back, and grabbed for his clothes from the back of a chair. Still pulling a jacket on over his half-buttoned flannel shirt, he hurried through the living room to the front door of the house. He pulled the door open and stood there, breathing heavily, listening.

There was no sound, only the wind from the ocean beating against nettle and thistle and burdock and weeds and striking hard upon the rocks of the hill. It pushed his jeans tight against his legs, flapped his jacket out behind him, whistled in his ears and tossed his hair against his forehead. Nothing human.

He must have imagined it. He waited a little longer, still listening, trying to hear past the rush of the wind.

It came again, from the direction of the road that wound up the hillside and past the house: a voice, a man's voice, groaning in pain and fear.

He must have been hit by a car, Jack thought. He dashed back toward the kitchen to get the flashlight he'd bought the day before. Behind him, through the door he'd left open, the loud wind rushed into the house.

The flashlight wasn't where he thought he'd left it and he had to rummage around, pulling doors open, in order to find it.

He couldn't have been hit by a car. There *are* no cars here. And when one does go by, you can hear it coming for ten minutes before it passes. Maybe he had a heart attack or something.

Flashlight in hand, its beam dancing before him, he ran out of the house. He had only put on his slippers, not bothering with shoes in his rush to get dressed, and now he felt every stone of the weedy gravel between the house and the road.

The night was clear, the wind from the ocean having blown away the mist, and the hill was bathed in moonlight. The sky was black and a three-quarter moon shone white and cold. The green-black vegetation of the hill whipped in a frenzy before the salty wind.

Jack stood panting at the edge of the road, looking uphill and down, but seeing nothing, no body, no person. There was no way to tell from which direction the voice had—

—from which direction the voice had come. But how had he heard it in the first place? He couldn't possibly have heard a voice from outside the house, not with the wind howling like this and all the windows closed tight, and a voice that was only a moan to begin with. He must have imagined it. Had to.

"Shit," he said at the night, breath panting in his chest. He snapped his head to the right, looked down the hill, to the left, looking up.

The voice came again from his right, downhill, on—he thought—the far side of the road.

Goosebumps prickled at the back of his neck, the result of fright and darkness and chilly wind conspiring against him, and he sprinted toward the sound.

The man lay on his stomach at the side of the road, the upper half of his body hanging down into the weed-filled ditch at the edge. His face was turned to the left, away from Jack. His head was bare, he was almost bald, and he seemed to be wearing a long black coat that Jack saw at once was in tatters. Jack crouched beside him, scanning the man quickly for obvious injuries, and saw that his feet were bare. They were so black that he'd missed that point at first.

He put a hand on the man's shoulder and instantly felt the knobby bone beneath the cloth.

"Can you hear me? Can you hear me?"

The man moaned a little but did not move.

Jack knelt quickly beside him and reached over the man's back to grasp his left arm. At first he thought the sleeve was empty, the arm itself missing, so slack was the cloth. Then he felt the bone inside and, shivering, grasped it, and tugged the man over onto his back.

"Okay! Okay!" Jack said, as much to himself as to the sick or injured—dying?—man before him. "It'll be okay!"

He took him by the shoulders, feeling the fleshless bones again, and slid him up out of the ditch until he lay flat on his back in the road. The movement unleashed a cloud of stinking stale sweat and the sour stench of putrescent disease. When the man's left hand struck the road, Jack saw that he was clutching something . . . a tangled bunch of weeds?

"Can you hear me?"

The man's head moved a little from side to side, his lips opened, but no sounds came out.

He was as pale as a corpse in the windy moonlight, his head and face little more than a skull: eyes now hollow sockets, bony ridge of forehead protruding, parchment cheeks empty of flesh, white teeth exposed by withered lips. The lips and chin were stained and a dark saliva dribbled from one corner of his mouth and ran down onto his neck. Green, Jack thought, and leaned closer over the man's face to see better. The stains on the man's mouth and chin were green and the bubbling saliva on his lips was green. He'd been eating what? The weeds? He'd been eating the weeds?

"I'll get help!" he said loudly to the man. The man did not respond. "I'll get help! You'll be okay!"

He stood, turned, ran three long steps toward the house, stopped, thought: cover him up first. Already pulling off his jacket to throw over him for warmth, he turned back to the man, took a step, stopped again.

The man was not there. He was neither in the ditch nor in the road, neither up the hill nor down. He was nowhere, gone, not there, never had been.

"Oh, God," Jack whispered, and stood frozen, trembling, staring at the spot.

Where the man had lain, cold moonlight the color of ice shone on the undisturbed gravel of the road, and on a knotted clump of weeds, stringy dirt still clinging to the roots, that was crushed as if a dying hand had held it.

CHAPTER 5

Despite his troubled sleep after the strange occurrence that night in the road, Jack's weekend passed without event.

He spent the next several days working in the study on the book, alternately writing a couple of pages on the word processor, revising them, thinking about them, sometimes keeping them. Often, he found, he had to force himself to stick with it, more so than he usually had to do while he actively worked on a book, but gradually, day by day, the story and characters came clear and alive in his mind, they moved and spoke and took on a life of their own, and after his first four or five days of working at it, immersing himself in it, he knew the book was truly started and safe.

He had done some of the basic research already, back in New York, but had limited his reading on the period of the Famine, 1846 and 1847, to a fairly small number of readily available books. He had only a moderate belief in the value of research for a novel. So long as the basic facts and issues remained true-to-life, he had no hesitation in taking liberties with accuracy or inventing whatever he needed for dramatic purposes. Too much research tended to turn a novel idea into an historical study; he'd made that mistake on one earlier book—the reviewers, bless their critical hearts, had seen at once where he'd gone wrong—and he'd sworn he'd never do it again. No, what mattered were the characters, the people of the story, and what happened to them.

As for this trip to Ireland, he was already getting plenty of what he needed: a sense of the land, the air, the weather, the look of the people, the shapes of the houses, the sky and the shadows at dawn and dusk. None of that had changed from the time of the Famine and he was determined to make his book, in those regards, as true as possible. He felt already that he knew well the family at the center of his story. Being here himself, he could only know them better.

And it was his research into the history of the Irish Famine that, later in the night, when the shock had dissipated a little, made him realize what it was he'd seen—*thought* he'd seen—in the road.

In early June of 1846, the blight had first been seen on the potato crops of several farms in County Cork. By the end of the month, it had spread throughout all of Ireland. The potato crop, the only food of the Irish people—most lived their lives from birth to death without ever tasting meat—was destroyed, reduced to a stinking pulp, and there was, with stark suddenness, almost overnight, nothing to eat. The English landlords, whether absentee or resident, had plenty, of course, but for the peasant Irish who worked the land nothing at all remained. They starved, begged, walked the roads of Ireland, and starved still. And in the wake of starvation came dysentery and typhus and despair. And after the summer of deaths and disease and the burial of hollow-eyed children, came the cold and wet of the winter. Often, while caught up in even the limited amount of research he'd done, Jack had found himself staring at the pages of the books, unseeing, with the visions of men and women starving to death filling his mind.

And that was what he'd seen in the road that night.

It must have been that; the vision matched the very things he'd read. It was not at all unusual, in those two terrible years of the last century, for a man to be found dead at the side of the road, his wife and starving babies left in a hovel or a ditch while he went out to beg for them what he could. Disease and despair tumbled him at last where he stood, even while he pushed himself forward in the endless effort to feed the ones he loved. Many such men, reason having left them and their bodies reduced to little more than skeletons, were found with their mouths stained green from trying to fill their aching stomachs by eating the grass and weeds along the road.

That was what he'd seen. It had to be that: a vision produced by the odd chemistry of the brain, product of his reading, his thinking about the book, his presence here in these rainy, windy hills on the western coast of Ireland where that very sort of thing had happened all too often.

He could live with that idea. He could live with the notion that his mind, half asleep as it was just then, probably almost dreaming—he must have been dreaming—had produced that awful vision. He didn't like it, but he could live with it.

He got on with his work. By Wednesday of his second week in Doolin, he was into the second chapter of the book and had nearly forty pages to show for his effort.

On Friday, after his dinner—and he wished Father Henning would get in touch with that woman about coming in to cook and clean for him—he went to the Seafoam and spent the evening there, going easy on the lager—two pints make a quart, he kept reminding himself—and listening to the music. There were three young fellows who played the Irish uilleann pipes, both lively reels and jigs and crooning, wailing tunes, ancient as the wind; but all yielded place readily later in the evening to an oldtimer whose hands looked as if they were still shaped roughly to the plow; but when the old fellow was settled at last on a bench against the wall, in the place of honor, the pipes laid across his legs, the bag that pumped air strapped properly to his right arm, the leather pad for the base of the chanter placed just so on his right leg, and a pint of Guinness inside him and another set before him, his fingers floated and hovered and flew invisibly over the chanter as if they were first cousins to the Irish breezes themselves, indeed as if the haunting music he made were itself an independent thing, living on air alone, needing no instrument at all, and the player's fingers only flew as they did in the effort to keep up the pace.

It was near midnight when Jack, smiling and holding just enough beer to make the smile lasting and easy, drove carefully home on the dark road.

On Saturday evening, he thought he'd try Nolan's. There was music there too, but it seemed to be exclusively of a somber cast, the clientele of the pub equally somber, and older, many of them speaking only Irish, and Jack finished a single pint and left. He went on to McGlynn's and spent the rest of the evening there, listening to the music, seeing many of the same faces that he'd seen the night before at the Seafoam. The way of it, he observed, was to drift around from pub to pub in town, sharing your custom evenly among the innkeepers.

He made some acquaintances in the Seafoam and in

McGlynn's, a few people from the town, mostly men but there were women too, some from the farms in the surrounding hills, and some, mostly younger couples, who had come here only for the weekend, staying at the few local farmhouses that did bed-and-breakfast, just to hear the music. Some of them brought their own instruments, bodhrans, tin whistles, fiddles, and a few sets of uilleann pipes that might have been handed down from father to son, and joined in for a bit. Jack thought them all good and decent people, friendly for the most part, and willing and eager to make a stranger feel at home. These two, the Seafoam and McGlynn's, would be his own pubs. No one at all had spoken to him in Nolan's.

On Saturday afternoon, that second weekend in Doolin, he had braved the wet weather on foot for the first time and walked all the way to the village to buy some milk and bread. It was raining hard and he was walking on the narrow sidewalk with his head bent low when he bumped shoulders with Father Henning. They spoke only briefly because of the rain and the lack of a handy doorway for shelter, but the priest, as soon as he recognized Jack, told him he'd be speaking with Peggy Mullen in a day or two and he was certain it would all work out just fine. He'd phone, he said, or possibly even drop by to let him know the outcome, and of course Jack was not to forget that he was always welcome in the priest's house, don't be forgetting that.

He spent some time exploring this new world, a world new to him but incomprehensibly old and familiar to everyone else. The stony slopes and dizzying cliffs leading down to the ocean and the foaming, roaring surf were unfenced here as far as his eye could gaze to the south. And to the north, across a narrow crease of land, was the Burren. He drove out one day on the dirt road, little more than a rutted track between centuries-old stone walls, that led to Doolin Point, past Roadford Doolin, a tiny hamlet where a stone bridge crossed over the bubbling waters of the Aille River. A section of the Burren spilled southward here and the road ended abruptly at the edge of the rocky surface. In the distance, across the gray plain of tumbled limestone blocks worn flat by the weather, he could see the monstrous waves hovering and crashing at the shore. Twice he drove here, but each time he arrived, the rain, pounding and hissing on the stone, arrived with him. But there was no hurry. His stay in Ireland still stretched long before him: plenty of time to explore Doolin Point and the Burren.

It was all very pleasant—the work going well, the cozy pubs, the wonderful music, the promise of help with the house—and, though he didn't forget it, the windswept, nighttime vision of the deathshead face with the mouth stained green receded to the back of his mind, hidden behind the welter of new sights, new details, new rhythms of words and expressions, even new scents—the acrid-sweet aroma of burning turf was always in the air—all of it melting together to take new shape later in the book. He made scribbled notes on much of what he was taking in. He made no notes on that nightmare vision, however. If he needed it for the book, it would, he knew, be quite fresh still in his mind.

Among the better parts of those first days were his conversations on the telephone with Grainne.

She had been to the movies with a girlfriend that night he'd called, she told him, and he wondered if that information was meant to relieve his mind. She sounded as genuinely delighted to hear from him as he was glad to hear her voice. Their talk was easy and comfortable, at times like that of new friends eager to know all about each other, at other times like old friends eager to catch up.

They talked about Dublin and about New York, about the schools they'd attended, about books and friends and movies and music, and Grainne frequently interrupted to worry about the size of his telephone bill.

When he called the third evening in a row, she sounded just as pleased as she always did but not at all surprised.

It was the Wednesday evening of his second full week in the house, almost the end of September now, that he raised again the question of her possibly coming for a visit. Jack had spoken to her so much already about Doolin and the places he had yet to see that he felt she must already feel she knew it nearly as well herself. When he broached the subject, the suggestion was natural, uncalculated, and surprised him, he thought later, more than it seemed to surprise her.

"I might," she said, her voice as soft as ever on the phone. "It might be nice."

He heard in her words the familiar deprecatory tone of the Irish, forever afraid to say a thing is nice for fear it'll be spoiled or taken away. The legacy of a people long in submission to another.

"Please come," he said, before he even fully recognized the import of what they were saying. "It'd be so good to see you. I'd love to see you."

"Well, I might," she said.

"I'll come to Dublin, if you'd like, and pick you up and drive you back."

Oh Christ, he thought as he said it, and her with her Irish Catholic parents, and me the horny Yank come pounding on the door to ruin their little girl!

"Oh no," she said, "it's silly to put you to all that when I can drive as well myself."

"Then you'll come?" he said. And waited.

"I will," she said.

"Come tomorrow."

"I can't." He thought he could hear a smile. "I have to keep the shop. I'll come on Friday."

"Terrific!"

"If it's really all right."

"Grainne, please come," he said, shocked and short of breath, heart pounding, at the sudden wave of longing he felt, the stunning conviction, realized only this instant, that all would be complete the moment she appeared. "Please come."

"All right, then," she said. "I'll be there on Friday, God willing."

They were both silent for a long time after that before either spoke again, but the silence was deep and rich and warm.

Late on Thursday evening, a wall of thick gray fog rolled in from the ocean, swept quickly over the crashing waves and rocks at the shore, and hurried up the hills, wetting weeds and stones and earth, wetting the limestone blocks of the Burren, dripping moisture on the windows of houses, smothering all in a silence as gray as itself.

Jack was busily straightening up in the house. In the short

time he'd been there, it had already come to resemble his comfortably cluttered New York apartment, books and folders and piles of papers, little notes to himself, scattered everywhere. He paused for a moment, thinking maybe he'd stop by to see Father Henning tomorrow, before Grainne got here, and see if the priest ever meant to speak with that woman. Then, on further reflection, he thought maybe he'd let it go for a while. Wouldn't that be a pretty picture: the pious country widow looking from the grinning Yank to his pretty Irish sweetheart, the willing lamb being led to the slaughter. Maybe he'd just wait for Father Henning to take care of it in his own good time.

Smiling, he walked over to look out the living room window, at the fog that pressed itself up against the glass. He was humming with the record being played on the radio, the latest Cliff Richard hit—he was traitorously listening to the BBC, rather than the Irish station—when he clearly heard a baby crying outside in the fog.

It can't be, he told himself.

Cliff Richard continued singing in the background, going now for the big note of the chorus.

Jack stalked across the room and turned off the radio, then walked back to where he'd stood before.

He heard the baby again, distant now, farther away. It was crying piteously, like an animal, the wail broken only by painful sobs.

A rabbit, Jack thought, wishing he knew more about the ways of the countryside. It has to be a rabbit.

He listened, waited. There was nothing. He listened. It cried again. From down the hill?

It was not a rabbit.

Feeling suddenly trapped, put upon, but compelled outside nonetheless, Jack walked back to the bedroom, pulled on a heavy wool sweater and jacket, his scarf and cap, being grimly determined about the whole procedure, and, fully dressed now, went into the kitchen to get the flashlight. It occurred to him as he reached for it that he hadn't touched the flashlight since that other night. He came back into the living room. He was walking toward the door but, halfway across the room, he veered instead to the window and stood there, listening for the cry to come again. He waited. It was gone. It had never been.

And he heard it, just the same as before.

It was not a rabbit.

He turned to the door, pulled it open, and went outside into the fog.

The fog was pearly gray, brighter than he'd thought it from the window, as if it carried its own radiant light within the particles of moisture. It drifted and shifted about him, curled around his legs and into the open doorway behind him. The light from the room spilled into it, making it yellow at his feet, but as he stepped down to the ground and away from the house, there was only the thick and enveloping gray. It touched him with a chill, bringing goosebumps to the back of his neck and his arms, and a sudden shiver to his shoulders. It seemed to swallow sound, even the crunch and crush of his shoes on gravel.

He took several slow steps and stopped, listening again. Dimly, through the fog, he heard the dull, distant rumble of the ocean at the bottom of the slope. He glanced behind him. The wall of fog hugged the house, held it, seemed to move it back up the hill and away from him. The yellow light from the windows and the open door glowed in a yellow blur, a brighter mist, all details of rooms and home now thoroughly obscured. The damp chill slipped through his clothing and made him shiver. He waited, listening.

He switched on the flashlight with a reassuring click. He aimed it out before him. It shone only on the shifting pearl-gray wall. He turned it downward to the stony ground at his feet. It made a milky white pool in the moving fog.

The baby cried again somewhere off to his right. It was a feeble cry, but lasting, clear in the night and the drifting mist but weak and frail and barely audible.

"Hello?" Jack called. "Who's there? Does someone need help?"

His voice was drowned in fog.

Sweeping the flashlight beam slowly back and forth in front of him, he began moving to his right, across the slope.

"Hello! Where are you?"

The baby cried again, the wordless voice a little stronger for an instant, then dying away to nothing.

"Hello!"

He kept moving in the same direction. The fog, glowing bright at his feet from the flashlight, closed in dark around his head. He swept his gaze from side to side but there was only gray fog and greater darkness, nothing at all to see.

The baby cried again, still ahead of him, but now a little to his left, downhill.

Don't voices travel farther in a fog or mist? Something to do with moisture in the air. He struggled to remember but could not. He kept moving, slowly, carefully, the fog glowing around his feet and legs, trying to judge the distance and direction he'd moved from the house. He stopped, looked back uphill. The house was gone, taken by the mist.

"Hello," he called again.

A woman's voice, without age or shape or words, came out of the fog, farther away, he thought, than the baby's cry, but clearer, stronger.

He shouted now. "Hello! Where are you? Keep yelling!"

He waited to hear it again. He was panting now, mouth open. This was real, not like the other. Someone was lost, hurt, in trouble.

"Hello?"

She called again, this time from ... over there. He started moving again, the circle of light shuddering in the pearly white glow at his feet. For a moment, he raised the flashlight, shone it straight out in front of him, but it revealed only the solid wall of silent fog. He could see nothing, only the patch of ground he stood on.

"Where are you? Yell again!"

She responded and he took heart, moving a little faster on the rocky, weedy slope, feeling stones slide out from beneath his feet, muddy ground betray his step. Her voice this time had almost the shape of words.

As he continued downhill, the fog around him grew thicker, became almost a solid element through which he silently moved, and he held out his empty left hand before him as if to feel for an opening in a wall. All around him, the mist drifted like smoke, clung to his legs, his arms, his hair.

The almost liquid pool of misty light at his feet revealed a rock. He stepped to the side to go around it. The rock moved and turned toward him.

Unthinking, he scrambled backward several steps, slipped, got his balance.

"Oh, sir!" the rock cried, and turned a haggard, stricken face to look up at him.

It was a woman, crouched with knees and elbows on the ground, wrapped in a dark gray cloak all muddy and in shreds. She looked up at him from hollow eyes, eyes sunk deep and lightless in a deathshead face. The fog drifted in smoky tendrils around her body and lingered in her stringy, greasy hair.

Not wanting to, Jack took another step backward, mouth open, eyes staring. His hand trembling, he aimed the beam of the flashlight at her crouching shape. She almost glowed in its light. Her bony face, even with the beam full on it, was all shadows and hollows: eyes, mouth, nostrils, sunken cheeks and temples.

"What's happened?" Jack breathed. He knew he should do something but he could not move.

The woman lowered her head close to the ground and turned her face away. There was movement beneath the cloak, as if she gathered something into her arms. Then she lifted her head to him again, faced him, and clumsily rose to her knees, stretched her arms out—only bones, with empty, fleshless skin hanging from them in folds—and offered up toward him a filthy bundle.

It was a naked infant, a boy—Jack could see the tiny, shriveled point of the penis—and as bony and fleshless as the woman. The top of its skull and the ridge of its forehead seemed enlarged, so empty of flesh was the face.

The woman held it up in both hands, the infant stretched out on its back, limp and lifeless, the head lolling back on a boneless neck, the legs dangling loose.

The legs. Jack looked at the legs. Below the knee on each leg, from the knee to the foot, the skin was torn and bloody, shredded, tiny bits of flesh or skin hanging in tatters, the feet red with blood, torn like the legs, the toes missing, one of the feet still dripping blood.

Jack's throat was tight, choked. "You . . ." he said.

"Oh, sir!" the woman whispered, and a mouthful of dark red blood welled over her lips and spilled down her chin.

He closed his eyes, opened them. He was alone in the silence, and the light showed him only the gray and the drifting fog.

As it came on to eleven o'clock that night, John MacMahon sat with the last of a pint of Guinness before him in the dark back corner of Nolan's, the third pub of Doolin a little distance beyond the end of the one main street of the village. The light in that one back corner had burned out longer ago than any of the regulars recalled nowadays and had never been replaced. It was John Mac-Mahon's accustomed seat.

"Time," Liam Nolan called out from behind the bar. "Last orders, please. Time."

Patrick Mullen was among those who pushed their glasses forward on the bar to be refilled.

Without being asked, Nolan carried two brimming pint glasses back to John MacMahon and Brian Flynn. They'd all be there another hour at least. Why would a man be hurrying home to an empty house, Liam Nolan was always quick to say.

John MacMahon pressed his gnarly hand briefly across his stomach where the pain had come again. It was coming more often now, more often all the time. He pressed his hand harder, and waited, and after a bit, it passed.

He finished off the previous Guinness and contemplated the thick white head on its replacement. Brian Flynn did the same with his own.

"Almost October," John MacMahon murmured, and raised the foamy pint to his lips. His hand trembled ever so slightly and he had to be careful with the heavy glass.

"It is that," Brian Flynn said softly. "It is that, indeed, and no denying it."

They drank together, sipping slowly at the hearty Guinness, and continued in their thoughtful silence in the dark back corner of the pub.

At about the same time, Father Malcolm Henning exhaled a long, sighing breath as he carefully lowered his knees onto the cushioned *prie-dieu* in the corner of his small bedroom. He joined his hands before him and murmured, "In the name of the Father, and of the Son, and of the Holy Ghost." In church, he always said "Holy Spirit" where the liturgy called for it, as the new custom —he still thought of it as new—dictated for the vernacular Mass, but in his private devotions, prayers at night and the daily reading of the holy office in the morning, he allowed himself the tiny luxury of saying "Holy Ghost," the way he'd learned his prayers as a child and said them for all of his long life.

He prayed first for Ireland, that it might be a nation united once again, freed from its English oppressors who still occupied part of its land. He prayed for lasting peace in all the rest of the world. He prayed for the intentions of the Holy Father in Rome. He prayed for the village of Doolin and all the people in it, mentioning several by name, especially Peggy Mullen who had just recently buried her husband. He prayed that his own stiffening knees might not feel the cold and damp of winter quite so sharply as they had the year before. Then he added, as he had been adding each night for a while now, a prayer for the peace and protection of Jack Quinlan, newly come to Doolin.

"In the name of the Father," he finished, making the sign of the cross, "and of the Son, and of the Holy Ghost. Amen."

PART TWO

For mem'ry's the only friend that grief can call its own.
　　　　　　　　　　　　　—Sean O'Casey,
　　　　　　　　　　　　　Juno and the Paycock

CHAPTER 6

The first time Jack had said, "I'm so glad you're here," Grainne had blushed and turned her face away at once. The second time, she'd lowered her head, but not before letting him see the smile that filled her face.

The sky had been gray all day long, the air wet with a penetrating chill, until three in the afternoon. Then, in the course of fifteen minutes, the sky had brightened, the rain slowed to a drizzle and then to nothing at all. An hour later, bright blue rents had appeared in the lowering cloud cover and sunshine struck the earth for the first time in several days, glinting on puddles and greening the hills and moss and grass. The ocean turned from white-capped slate to glistening blue. The wind blowing in from the water eased its pace, became softer, gentler, though the shredded clouds continued to scud rapidly inland overhead.

"You've brought the sun," Jack said when he ran out to greet Grainne at the car.

They kissed once, out there beside the house, a kiss unpremeditated and a little startling, that lasted midway between a social greeting and the lingering touch of lovers.

Grainne had only one suitcase and a straw bag that was mostly filled with books. Jack took them from the back seat of the car and they walked together toward the house. He put the bags down just inside the open doorway.

"Let me give you the tour," he said.

Grainne's gaze took in the comfortable living room, the stone fireplace, and the sunny view from the windows down toward the sparkling ocean. "It's grand," she said.

Jack tried not to make too big a deal of showing her through the house. He was suddenly aware that they were both a little self-conscious, now that anticipation had become reality, and neither of them lingered when he showed her the bedroom. When they were done, Grainne smiled her approval of everything.

"You've even a fireplace," she said. "And I saw the turf pile outside. That'll be lovely for the evening. We have none of that in Clontrarf, you know. Dublin is entirely too sophisticated for turf fires." Smiling, she put her hands on her hips, let her gaze sweep all around the living room, taking it all in again. "You've done well."

Her bags were still on the floor near the door. Jack did not move to pick them up and carry them into the bedroom. Suddenly, he thought that doing so would represent a unilateral decision; if they were to sleep together—if they were to make love—he wanted it just to happen. Presumably, she hadn't come here with the notion that one of them would sleep on the couch, but Jack found now, rather to his own surprise, that he wasn't much interested in making any assumptions on that question. For the moment, he was just glad she was there.

"Did you eat?" he said. "Can I fix you something?"

Grainne turned from the window, where she'd been looking down the hill toward the ocean. "I'm starved," she said. "I drove straight on without stopping."

"I hope you like cheese sandwiches," he said in the kitchen. "I was waiting until you got here to shop. I figured that way I'd get whatever you like."

"Cheese sandwiches are fit for royalty," Grainne said lightly, leaning back against a cupboard. "I hear the Queen of England eats them herself."

Jack had meant to go shopping in the village before she arrived, but he'd been up most of the night, drinking tea and thinking about what he'd seen in the fog on the hill, and had slept through the morning until past midday.

"I'm sorry," he said. "I should have—"

"No," Grainne said quickly, and touched his arm with her fingertips. "A sandwich'll do me. That's not what I meant. But I wonder, is it only sandwiches and cold food you've been eating yourself?"

"I get by," he said. "But I did think maybe we'd eat out tonight. I hear there's a place not far, in Roadford Doolin. Or we could drive someplace else."

"That'd be nice. I'd like that. But only if we can go shopping, and then tomorrow I'll fix a proper meal. I'll not have you saying I left the famous writer to starve when he didn't have to."

"That'll be perfect."

They looked at each other, and Jack thought she was as aware as he of the easily achieved partnership. He moved and stood in front of her and took her hands in his.

"I'm so glad you're here," he said, and this time she came to him, laid her cheek against his shoulder, and her arms went around his body. He held her close and felt her feathery hair touch his lips. His arms slid across her slender back. He felt her breasts pressed hard and unembarrassed against his chest and, softly, with a degree of relief that nearly took his breath away, he whispered her name.

She was a gorgeous picture, out there in the warm golden light leading to sunset, with long shadows stretching away beside them as they walked toward the edge of the water. She'd wanted to see Doolin Point right away, didn't want to wait till tomorrow, and he'd been happy to oblige. They'd taken the car and parked it at the end of the road and, hand in hand, where the broken rocky surface permitted, they made their way toward the point and the crashing surf. Grainne seemed made for this, one with the light and the shore and the salty tang of the wind and spray. Jack drank her in.

Her black hair whipped out behind her in the wind. Her milky skin took on a pinkish glow. Once, when the fissures in the rock separated them, she got ahead of Jack, and he stood where he was for a moment, just watching her. He admired her long legs, like a deer in jeans, he thought, and just as graceful. She was wearing only a flannel shirt and a heavy white Aran sweater, but the cold seemed to touch her not at all. The thick bulk of the sweater concealed her figure, but when she jumped from rock to rock, arms uplifted and stretched out for balance, her breasts were full and heavy, all the richer for the slender lightness of her waist and hips and back.

"Were you ogling me back there, Jack Quinlan?" she said when he caught up.

"You're beautiful, Grainne."

"Ah," she said, "my mother warned me to beware the flattery of smiling Yanks."

He took her hand again and they made their way over the great rough blocks of stone that tumbled forward toward the ocean. All around them, the air was loud with the roar of wind and waves and lashing water. The wind was strong here, laced with salty spray, and they squinted into its cold wetness. Ahead of them, mighty waves, driven by the unbridled wind from the North Atlantic, hurled themselves in a fury of foam at the unmoved rocks of the coast. Towering eruptions of water, white and flying green, shot high into the air, paused for an instant, and dropped with deadly solid weight onto rocks still wet from the previous attack. Foam boiled up between fissures in the rock, fell back, was caught on the racing swell of an incoming wave, and boiled up, foaming, higher still, seeking the still-dry surface of the highest rock.

They sat for ten minutes, as long as the cold wet wind would let them, and watched the waves crash in and the red sun sink beyond the sea.

Jack put his arm around her shoulders and Grainne leaned against him. He thought he was as happy this evening as he'd been unhappy the night before.

John MacMahon moved slowly, stiffly, leaning on his knobby cane, down the one main street of Doolin. His cap was pulled low on his forehead as if the rain still fell, although the sun of late afternoon cast a long, dark shadow ahead of him on the cobbles of the road. The collar of his jacket was turned up at the back of his neck. He kept his free hand tightly fisted against his chest, holding the jacket lapels close across his throat to keep out the killing cold and damp.

A few people greeted him in the street, women hurrying home with a last-minute item for the husband's meal, or workmen, in their heavy boots, walking more slowly than the women.

To each of them, John MacMahon muttered, "Good day to ye," without ever slowing or lifting his eyes from the uneven ground that threatened every step.

When he reached Father Henning's house, a small stone cottage in a lane near the church, he stopped at the bottom of the path and leaned on the low stone wall for a moment to catch his breath. When his breathing was quieter and less strained, he continued up the path and used the head of his cane to rap sharply at the door.

The door was opened by Mrs. Corcoran, a stout and sturdy widow, with upper arms like hams, whose husband had been dead these last nine years. From two weeks after the husband was laid in the earth, Deirdre Corcoran had looked after the priest, who was just then beginning to have difficulty in keeping up both his pastoral duties and keeping himself and his house in order. Mrs. Corcoran took charge, kept the house, cooked most of his meals, and saw to it that he never went through the front door without his scarf pulled tightly in place. There was no saying no to Deirdre Corcoran.

She pulled the door back, planted her hands on her hips, and looked squarely at the old man leaning on his cane in the path.

"John MacMahon, is it?" she said. "Himself said you'd be along, although Lord only knows why he'd be wanting the likes of you in the house. Clean your shoes on the stone there before you come in. I've enough to be doing without you making unnecessary work. Come on. Come on. If you're to catch your death of cold, it'll not be from me keeping you out in the weather."

John MacMahon waited until she was done, as he waited every Friday evening when he came to the priest's house for supper, then carefully scraped the soles of his shoes on the edge of the concrete steps and came into the house.

Deirdre Corcoran put out her hand and John MacMahon handed her the cane. "It's more for show, to be winning sympathy," she'd used to tell him. Now he handed it over and she took it without a word.

"And the rest," she said, her hand still extended.

John MacMahon removed his cap and gave it to her. That had been the longest part of the battle, lasting almost all of the first two years of Deirdre's tenure in the house of the priest. "I don't care that you went to school with himself," she'd told him repeatedly then, "you'll not wear a hat in his house. Wear it in the pub, if you want, and wear it in your own parlor, and wear it to your bed, for all that I care, but you'll not be wearing it here, I can tell you that." When she had unthinkingly said to him one of those

Friday evenings near the end of her second year of service to the priest, "John MacMahon, you'll not wear a hat inside my house," he'd known for sure that he was beaten at last.

"That's better," she said. There was a small narrow closet near the front door and she put the cane and cap away.

"Good evening to ye," John MacMahon said, now that all that business was settled between them.

"Good evening to you," Deirdre said. "Come in and sit. I have my hands full getting your meal. He'll be out in a minute." She nodded toward the back of the house, where the bathroom was, then returned to the kitchen. The warm house was filled with the smell of roasting lamb.

"John," Father Malcolm Henning said when he appeared in the doorway.

"Malcolm," said John MacMahon, looking up from his place at the corner of the couch.

The priest settled himself in his chair and smiled at his old friend.

"So we have a bit of sun today, after all," he said.

They talked for a while about the weather, about the unusual amount of rain in recent weeks, about the oncoming winter and the cold it would bring.

"I feel it more now, I do," the priest said with a sigh, "but, God willing, I've a few more winters in me yet. If these old knees hold up."

"I feel it in the knees meself," said John MacMahon. "And I feel it elsewhere as well." He looked up and his eyes met those of the priest.

"Do you?" Father Henning said quietly. "Is the pain coming on you, John?"

"It is. I only count the hours now between when it comes. But it'll be done soon, I can tell you that. The same as it ended for Paddy."

Father Henning sighed. "Do you still feel the loss of Paddy?" he asked, his voice a little softer still.

"I do," John MacMahon said. His hand, with its large and bony knuckles, caressed the arm of the couch.

"Aye, it was a hard loss, that one."

"It was me that took the blood."

The priest said nothing, only joined his hands over his stomach, lacing thin fingers together.

"It was all done proper."

The priest remained silent.

John MacMahon waited a few seconds and then, in a low but insistent tone, said, "Will you not say a word, Malcolm? You know as well as I that it must be done."

Father Henning squeezed his fingers more tightly together. "John," he said quietly, "you do what you must do, and that's as much as a man *can* do. Don't I do the same? Well, don't I?"

He waited, and finally John MacMahon said, "Aye, Malcolm, you do."

"Well, then."

"I was hoping all this while that Paddy might be the one to take my place when I'm gone." John MacMahon made the confession as if it were being wrung from him after hours of torture.

"All this while?"

"These last few years. I'm not well, Malcolm. And, Malcolm, don't you be telling me to pray to God for the restoration of me health, because I know better at this late date than to ask for what cannot be. I'm coming near the end, I'm telling you, and that's that. And we'll need another to fill my place when I'm gone. I'd thought to have Paddy."

They were silent together for a moment, until finally the priest said, "Paddy would have been no improvement. He had the same years as you and I."

John MacMahon waved a stiff hand in the air.

"It's the truth," said the priest in a more conversational tone, "we're all the same, living relics, don't you know, dinosaurs, old men waiting—"

"Don't be going on, Malcolm, I'll not listen to it. I'd thought to name him, that was all, and now these six months I've kept it to myself while he lay dying. And don't be making light of the problem. If I drop dead in the path this night, the place will be yours, though you'll want none of it."

The priest raised a hand to silence his friend a moment before Deirdre Corcoran appeared in the doorway.

"The meal will be a little later than I planned," she said. "I'm having trouble with that stove again." She poked up the turf fire for them before she left the room.

"There was another of ours shot in Derry today," the priest said. "It came over the radio this afternoon."

"God rest his soul," John MacMahon said fervently, and for the rest of the evening they talked about the news from the north of Ireland, about their neighbors in the village of Doolin, and again about the weather. The dinner was fine, as it always was, and Deirdre Corcoran kept looking in and urging them to eat more to build up their strength against the approaching cold of winter. John MacMahon barely touched the food on his plate, eating only a bit of the mashed potatoes. After dinner, she cleaned up in the kitchen and went home. The two old men listened to the radio together and John MacMahon dozed for a while as he sat on the couch before the fire.

When he left about nine o'clock, he paused in the narrow front hall, cap and cane in place, jacket already pressed tight over his woolen sweater, and turned to face the priest.

"It's October, you know, Malcolm," he said, and his voice was almost gentle.

"October, yes, I know that," the priest murmured. There was an old sadness in his voice. "I know it."

He opened the door and they felt the cold wet chill of the night. John MacMahon carefully lowered himself down the steps to the path. The moon was nearly full and the sky clear of clouds and the pathway plain even to aged eyes.

"Safe home," the priest said. "God bless you."

"Thank you, Father," John MacMahon said, and started slowly down the path.

During dinner, at a tiny restaurant that looked like a private house in Roadford Doolin, where an ancient stone bridge arced across the Aille River, Jack urged Grainne to talk about herself. Much of what had appeared to be her natural shyness had dropped away, and she spoke, he thought, with surprising frankness. She had, after all, made something of a commitment in coming here and in agreeing to stay with him. He wondered

if she'd had to lie to her parents about where she was going for
the weekend. It turned out that she had, in a way. Her parents
had called from Liverpool where they were visiting her mother's
brother and had told her they were going to stay on a bit longer.
Grainne had persuaded a friend, Mary, to keep the shop for her
while she visited Jack. But she'd had to tell her parents something
else.

"I'm in London at this very minute, you know," she said near
the end of the meal, as they were drinking coffee, lingering at the
table.

"Are you?" Jack said, having already learned that Irish conversations were moved forward with properly inflected shows of
interest.

"I am," she said, and there was a rueful smile on her lips.
"That's what I told the folks."

"I see. And what are you doing there?"

"I'm staying with my friend, Meg. We were at school together.
She went over to London last year and she's doing very well for
herself. She's an artist and she has a flat in Chelsea that she shares
with another friend. I'm staying with her."

"Do you do that often?"

"Sometimes," Grainne said. She lowered her eyes and sipped
at her coffee. "I used to, but I don't much anymore."

Her tone had changed and Jack realized that she was no
longer talking about her fabrication to her parents. "Why not?"
he said.

Grainne sipped again at her coffee and looked thoughtful.
"Well, I suppose it's not difficult to figure out," she said. "The
times I'd go over, I didn't always stay with Meg, you see."

Jack hesitated for only a second before saying, "A boyfriend?"

Grainne smiled a little. "After a manner of speaking. I saw him
on and off for a bit. And then he threw me over." She shrugged.
"But I don't mean to be critical. I mean, I suppose I knew he
would, in the end, since I wouldn't . . . you know . . . go all the way
with him."

Jack thought it best to say nothing. He raised his cup to his lips.

"You must think me a terrible tramp," Grainne said quietly.
"Here I am, telling you about my past affairs—affair, really, there

was only the one, if you can even call it that—and all the while I'm sitting here with you, and my trusting parents' ears filled with lies. I don't know what you'll be thinking of me." She had glanced across at him for a second, but now she lowered her eyes again to conceal the blush that colored her cheeks.

Jack silently stretched a hand across the table, palm up. Grainne's hands were folded in her lap. She looked up at him quickly, then raised one hand and tentatively placed it in his. He closed his fingers gently around it, feeling the coolness of her skin.

"Grainne, I think nothing of the sort. But I'll tell you what I do think, and maybe it'll help to set both our minds at rest. All right?" He squeezed her fingers.

"All right," she said, her voice as soft as a breeze and her eyes now meeting his.

"All right," he began. "I came to Ireland not knowing a soul. Through chance, you and I happened to meet. Now, in all truth, I have to tell you, it wasn't your brains that first attracted me. The fact is, it's not a girl's brains that a man first notices from across a room."

Grainne smiled and didn't look away.

"And when we talked, I found that you sounded as good as you looked. I don't mean that to sound quite as . . . as crass as it may seem. Anyway, we talked more, on the phone, and it was only when I was here that I found I really did want to see you again. I suppose I should have gone to Dublin to see you, instead of asking you to sort of go out on a limb and come here, but—"

"It's all right," she said. "I did come, didn't I?"

"I'm very glad."

"So am I. Jack, are all Yanks so bold? Here, you're only just come from America, and it's this soon you have me telling lies to my family."

"I don't know the answer to that," Jack said. Then he put on his best Irish accent. "But I'm wondering, is it an even match between us?"

This time, she squeezed his hand.

They were silent in the car on the way home, except to remark on the brightness of the nearly full moon and the clarity of the black sky studded with stars.

"We don't often see a sky like that in New York," Jack said, laughing.

"You'll see much in Ireland that you won't see elsewhere," Grainne answered. "Is it what you thought it'd be?"

"It's strange," Jack said. "It is, only more so, if that makes any sense. Even though I was never here, I always knew pretty much what it looked like. I suppose it's from movies and books, but also from growing up in an Irish neighborhood in New York and hearing people talk. A lot of Irish-Americans, you know, try to be more Irish than the Irish."

"That's often the way," Grainne said.

Jack was driving slowly on the narrow twisting road, and Grainne was looking out the side window of the car, her eyes scanning the moonlit rocky hillsides.

"It's almost as if a knowledge of Ireland is in the air, when you grow up like that," Jack said. "But in reality, everything is even more than you've heard. The green is even greener, the coastline is even rockier, the weather is even wetter."

"Oh, the weather is terrible, isn't it? But is it what you were after? I mean, did you find what you came here to look for? For your book?"

Jack concentrated on the difficult road and didn't answer.

After a minute, Grainne turned to look at him. "Is something wrong?" she said.

"Doolin is exactly the kind of place I had in mind," Jack said after a moment. "I'd read a little about it and it sounded like the kind of setting I was looking for. It's exactly what I wanted for the book."

He could feel her eyes still on him in the darkness of the car.

"Really," he said. "It is."

"But you don't like it."

"Oh, I do," he said quickly. Then he caught sight of the view they were approaching. "Look," he said. He lifted a finger from the steering wheel and pointed ahead.

They were nearing the bottom of a hill, where the road swung sharply to the right and followed the rocky coastline a short distance before turning uphill again on the road that climbed his own slope, then passed his house on its way to the village of Doolin. To their right, the moonlit hills sloped up and away, dotted with shadowy rocks. To their left, a tumble of giant stones, and shadows just as big, fell away to the edge of the pounding waves. A streak of moonlight, stretching to the horizon, burnished the shifting surface of the ocean.

"It's a lovely place, in its way," Grainne said softly.

"It is," Jack said. "In its way."

She glanced at him for a second, then looked back toward the ocean and the white spray of waves crashing in brilliant moonlight.

Then the road turned right, uphill toward the house, and the ocean was behind them. Ahead of them was the long slope and, near the top, the house itself outlined in moonlight against the sky.

Beside him in the car, Grainne said softly, "You've brought me far from home, Jack Quinlan."

Jack kept his eyes on the road.

"I'm pretty far from home, myself," he said.

She reached over and rested her right hand lightly on his shoulder.

He swung the car to the left, off the road and onto the crunching gravel beside the house. As the headlights swept across the side of the house, glinting off a window, he thought for an instant that frightened, shadowy shapes scurried out of sight and disappeared up the hill behind the house. But they couldn't have been there—they could not—and he told himself he only imagined them.

They got out of the car and went into the house, and Jack closed the door firmly on the night.

"That new fella's brought in a girl," said Brian Flynn in the dark back corner of Nolan's pub.

"I know it," said John MacMahon. He lifted his glass and sipped at the Guinness.

"These young ones have no morals," said Flynn. "And the girls are worse than the boys nowadays. No morality at all. Have they no shame? Going about as brazen as you please, doing as they like, with no regard for anything." It was a long speech for him and he had to slake a sudden thirst with a long drink from his pint.

John MacMahon rubbed the palms of his hands on his knees. "What is it you're saying, Brian?"

There was a long silence while they both studied the worn and stained wood of the floor and the dusty black leather of their shoes.

"Were you to Father Henning's for your meal?"

"I was."

"And?"

"And what?"

Brian Flynn made a disgusted sound of impatience and turned away from John MacMahon. After a moment, he turned back.

"Did you talk with him about it?"

MacMahon raised the pint to his lips again before answering. "He'd hear none of it."

"He'd hear none of it, would he? None of it?" Flynn had lowered his voice now and leaned closer to John MacMahon on the bench they shared. "It's everlasting patience we need with the likes of him, priest and all, that's what I say. And then, don't you know, he'll be coming round again in the end, like he always done before and like he'll be doing soon again."

"That he will," said MacMahon with quiet assurance, "so don't be going on at me about it."

"But are you certain, John? Are you? It worries me to think about him sometimes, and him one of the few that knows the proper ways and all. I tell you, it worries at me."

"Brian, don't be going on so like an old woman, will you now."

Their voices were hushed in the dim light of the corner, the husky murmurings of old men nearing death that kept listeners at bay.

Flynn took a quick drink to wet his parched throat.

"But he's a priest, John," he said quickly, "don't never be forgetting that, and them priestly teachings do be getting in the way sometimes of what's needful. And we need him to be with us, you know we do."

"There's other things in his mind as well, Brian," John Mac-

Mahon said. "He'll be with us when the need comes. Now don't be going on so about it."

They sat in silence a while then. A farmer named Seamus Curtin had come into the pub a little before, carrying a battered brown case that contained a set of uilleann pipes. The pipes had belonged years before to his grandfather and were older than any soul in the pub and therefore regarded with suitable esteem. He'd had a pint by now and had done some tuning. Now he played a single long note like the cry of the wind in a fissure of rock, and the voices around him hushed to nothing. His right arm pumped the bag against his side, his thick farmer's fingers poised on the stops of the chanter; he stared before him, seeing nothing, and played. The tune was low and slow, wistful, wordless, singing of ancient hills and long-passed breezes and labors long completed and others left long undone. The crying notes slipped out of the pipes and filled the corners of the pub, as a nighttime chill might fill the corners of a house, and lamented the passing of all that was old or dead or dying.

He played the one tune, then another and another, each as sad as the one before, and no one spoke a word. It was as if the wind of the hills had come inside and filled the room with sound and terrible sorrow. There were few notes in the music, but all held long, then a sobbing rush of notes ending in another painful cry. Old Seamus Curtin held his head on the side, eyes unseeing, ear cocked as if to a distant music that was echoed in his pipes and fingers, himself but the instrument of voices only he could hear.

When he was done—he might have played six tunes or might have played only one, so seamless were they and all of a piece —he sat back on his bench and blinked his eyes.

There was silence for a while all around him. Then, "Aye," said a man, and another said it, and another and again, and some lifted their glasses toward him as if in toast to a speech that met popular approval, and Liam Nolan put a fresh pint on the low table before him.

In the back corner of the pub, Brian Flynn said nothing until after Liam had brought them two more pints. Then he leaned close to John MacMahon and said in a hoarse whisper, "I don't like it, the young fella being here at this time, in October, a stranger and all, and a young girl with him." He shook his head and leaned closer still. "I don't like it," he said again.

"Nor I," said John MacMahon. "But then again, there's no telling what may come of it."

In the silence around them, the music of the pipes still lingered in the room.

Deirdre Corcoran lowered herself to her knees before the little table in the corner of the bedroom where she prayed every night. The table was covered with her finest, most intricate, lace, and on it stood a statue, painted pale blue and white, of the smiling Blessed Virgin. Two candles flickered beside it. Deirdre Corcoran prayed every night to the Blessed Virgin and began and ended her prayers by making the sign of the cross with fingers wet with holy water from the bottle on the table. She touched her forehead, chest, left shoulder, right, and joined her hands together.

"Holy Mary, Mother of God," she whispered to the statue, "it's coming time again and himself is in need of protection."

Without speaking a word on the subject, Grainne had taken her suitcase into the bedroom to unpack. Jack had asked if she'd like a beer and she'd said yes. He lingered a while in the kitchen, giving her time to explore the bedroom, find space in the closet and drawers for herself, time to feel at home there. He sat at the small table in the kitchen, drinking from one of the bottles, thinking of her smile, her voice, her form, and pushing from his mind all thoughts of hurrying shadows. Before he realized it, half the bottle was gone and nearly twenty minutes had passed.

When he went inside, he found Grainne stretched out on the bed, one arm crooked around a pillow. She'd taken off her sweater and kicked off her shoes and was sound asleep, breathing deeply and regularly.

Jack stood in the doorway and looked at her. Leaning on the doorjamb, he sipped slowly from the bottle until it was finished.

Jack, my boy, he told himself, you're losing your mind in this strange country. First, you think you're seeing things in the dark, and now you think you're falling in love with a girl you've only just met. Whereas, he reminded himself, the harsh reality of the situation is that you're about to spend the night sleeping alone on the couch.

He strolled back to the kitchen, threw away the empty bottle, and started on the second. Then he returned to the bedroom, quietly opened the closet door and took out two of the spare blankets. He gently spread one over Grainne, settling it carefully so as not to wake her. Then he carried the other to the living room and spread it out on the couch.

He sat for a few minutes with the beer, feeling rueful at suddenly being alone but comfortable with the thought that Grainne was inside and would be there in the morning. But the thoughts of shadows were still there too, like cold air touching the warmth he felt.

He stood up from the couch and walked across to the windows. Since they faced only down the hill toward the ocean, a hill that was more often than not hidden by rain and mist and fog, he had never bothered to draw the heavy drapes across them. He stood there for a moment, but with the light of the living room behind him, could see only his own pale reflection in the glass.

He went to the door and pulled it open.

The moon was still bright, the air still clear, and he could hear the ocean roaring at the bottom of the hill. He shivered once with the cold and held his arms tightly to his sides. Light from the door and the windows spilled out and formed a glowing pool near the house. Beyond was only moonlight and rocks and shadows.

A woman's voice, somewhere beyond the light, cried in a long and piercing keening sound, "Oh, sir!"

He closed the door, locked it, leaned his back against it, and stood there, breathing hard.

After a while, when his breathing steadied, he went into the bedroom and made certain the window was closed and latched securely. He looked at Grainne for a moment, watched her sleeping, listened to her steady breaths, then switched off the light and walked back to the living room.

He sat on the couch in the dark, with only the light of the moon coming in the windows—he would not close the drapes —wrapped the blanket around himself, slowly finished the beer, and waited uneasily for sleep.

CHAPTER 7

"Father Henning, oh, God bless you for coming," Peggy Mullen cried in the doorway. She blinked in the brilliant sunlight, rubbed her hands vigorously on her apron, then pushed back a stray wisp of hair from her face. She was a strong and sturdy woman, but small, wiry, and a little pinched in the cheeks. "Come in, come in! Did you walk it all the way? Come in, Father!"

She stood back and held the door open while the priest came into the house. "I did walk it," he said, "but it's a fine day for walking. No telling how long it will last, this weather, so best to take advantage of it. It'll be full winter before too much time goes by."

"Oh, you're so right, Father," she said. "Soon it'll be nothing but cold and wet and snow. Here, give me your coat and come in and sit down." She took the coat and carefully hung it on a peg near the door. "Can I give you a cup of tea?"

"Well, I'm just after having my breakfast," said the priest, "but I suppose another cup'd do no harm."

"I'll just be a minute," Peggy said. "I have the water on for a cup myself. Here, make yourself comfortable on the sofa." She smiled and hurried off to the kitchen.

There were neither books nor magazines nor newspapers in the house, but there was a neat little stack of religious leaflets from the Paulist Fathers on the table by the arm of the couch. Father Henning flipped through them for a minute, then replaced them and contented himself with folding his hands in his lap and looking about the plain but comfortable room. Peggy Mullen had done a fine job of keeping the house through the years, he thought. She was always a great one for saving a penny without appearing to scrimp. All of the furniture was old—indeed, he thought, this very room had changed hardly at all in the four decades or so since she and Paddy had been married. He'd always felt at home here, but now, in the quiet house with only the cozy rattle of cups and saucers coming from the kitchen, he felt the loss of Paddy himself. Many's the time they'd sat together on this same sofa, talking over the old times, recalling the long days of youthful summers when they'd run free and wild on the hills and dared each other to challenge the hissing waves at the shore.

Peggy Mullen reappeared carrying a tray with the tea things and a plate of biscuits. She set it before him and poured, seating herself on a chair across the low table from him, as if the grandness of his presence forbade her sharing the couch.

After they'd tasted the tea, Father Henning put down his cup—noting that Peggy had used the good service, reserved for special occasions—and sat back, with his right hand on his knee and his left on the arm of the couch.

"Well, Peggy," he said, "and how are you getting on?"

She clasped her hands together in her lap and directed her gaze down toward the tea tray. "Ah, I'll be all right in the end, I suppose, Father," she said. "It takes some getting used to, is all, him not being here."

"Aye, it does that."

"For half a year, you know, the time he was so sick, poor thing, I had my hands full with him, needing this and needing that and not able to do a thing for himself. He had me running all the time, I can tell you, he was so helpless and pitiful there near the end. Besides keeping up all the rest of the house as usual and all. It's a terrible thing to see a man so reduced, and him so big and fine in years gone by."

"Oh, yes," said the priest, nodding sadly.

Peggy Mullen shook her head. "But I'm only saying what everyone knows, Father."

"It's one thing to know it, but something else again to go through it yourself."

"You're right there, Father, that's the truth of it."

They sat in silence for a minute, and together reached forward for the teacups and drank a bit.

"Have you made your peace about it, Peg, is what I'm wondering?" the priest said quietly at last.

The woman lowered her head further and squeezed her hands tighter together. Her head bobbed up, then down, firmly. "I have," she said. "He was a good man, God bless him, and a good husband to me, and I'm thankful I had him with me as long as I did. But we're all getting up in years now, isn't it so? It was his time, is all. It's all nature."

"That's so," said the priest. "And no escaping it."

They sat in silence for a moment again, then Father Henning reached forward with a long sigh and took a cream biscuit from the plate on the tray. He bit into it with a solid crunch, and the movement and the sound marked a new step in the conversation.

"Peg," he said, more loudly, more heartily, than he'd spoken before, "I've come today to put a proposition before you."

"What's that, Father?"

He told her about Jack Quinlan, who was renting the house on the hill facing the water, that he'd be here in Doolin for three months at the least, and was in need of a woman to cook and clean.

"I've met him and he's a decent young fellow," the priest added. "He's been to see me."

"Three months?"

"Three."

"On holiday, is he?"

"A bit of that, I understand, and a bit for work besides. He's a writer."

"Books and that?"

"Aye."

"Is he writing one here?"

"So I gather."

"About Doolin, is it?"

The priest looked significantly at his empty teacup and Peggy Mullen hastened to refill it. When he'd tasted the fresh cup, he replaced it on the tray and said, "That's my understanding."

Peggy Mullen pressed her lips tightly together and said nothing. Her own teacup sat untouched.

Father Henning took another biscuit.

"It'd be a good thing for you just now, Peg," he said. "It'd take your mind off things, and bring in a few pounds besides. It's always handy to have a little put by. And your own lads can look after themselves for a bit, though you'd not be abandoning them entirely. Don't you think it's a good plan, Peg?"

"Cooking and cleaning, both?"

The priest nodded.

Peggy met his eyes briefly, then looked away. "Well, I'm not looking to leave the house," she said slowly, "but it might be good to help fill the time for a bit. It hangs heavy on me now, not having as much to do as I did with himself laying sick inside. And it's true, I wouldn't mind having a bit of extra coming in."

"You'll do it, then?"

Peggy Mullen pursed her lips again but said, "I will, Father."

"That's good," he said. "I'm glad of it, Peg." Then he added more quietly, "And it's by way of being a bit of a favor to me as well."

"I know that, Father," Peggy Mullen said just as quietly. Then, for the first time, she looked the priest directly in the face. "I'll do the best I can to see what's what. But I can't make you no promises, Father. There's little I can be saying or doing that'll keep him off, not if he's bent on seeing what there is to see. And if he's here in Doolin at the time, sure, there's no preventing his seeing it all, that's for certain. But I'll do what I can."

The priest kept his eyes on the teacup. "God bless you, Peg," he said.

"God bless Jack Quinlan," Peggy Mullen said. Then she stood up and took the tray from the table. "Let me make a fresh pot for you, Father. This one's grown cold as ice."

When Grainne awoke that Saturday morning and found herself lying fully clothed on the bed in Jack's room, she remembered instantly that she'd been unpacking when it had all caught up with her: the long drive from Dublin, the excitement of adventure in coming here at all, the long slow dinner and drinks. She wondered how Jack would react to being left all alone in the night, without so much as a word from her.

She found him tangled in a blanket on the couch and, for a long while, she stood over him, looking at him, smiling. So he was as decent a man as she'd thought he was. She arranged the blanket a little more snugly, taking care not to disturb him.

She took a quick shower, brushed her hair, and put on fresh clothes. In the kitchen, she went through all the cabinets, checking on food supplies while boiling water for tea. With a hot cup in front of her, she sat at the table and made a shopping list. Judging from the food on hand, Jack had been surviving on almost nothing at all. When she could think of nothing else for the list, she walked back out to the living room to check on him.

He was still sound asleep and Grainne thought he hadn't moved at all since she'd looked at him before.

She returned to the kitchen and checked the cabinets again, just to be sure. There were two packages of scone mix—she smiled at his good intentions—and she took them down. She found a bowl in another cabinet and started making the scones.

After a while, when she had them in the oven, she went back to the living room. Jack was still asleep.

The wind had come up a little more since dawn and it fluttered the jackets of John MacMahon, Brian Flynn, James Brennan, and Martin Gilhooley as the four of them shuffled along, abreast of each other, in the dusty road. They wore almost identical clothes, the uniform of the Irish peasant: dark woolen suit, baggy with age and hard use, woolen sweater, its front knobby and rough from rubbing, heavy thick-soled shoes, woolen cap with a narrow peak. Scarves were pulled tight around their throats as protection from the wind, the ends of them flying in the back.

John MacMahon, walking at the right-hand side of the road, set the slow pace for the others. He planted his stick firmly on the rocky ground, leaned on it, moved forward, set it again, and the others moved with him. None of them spoke, for the climbing of the road took all their breath.

At either side of the road were stone walls, as high as a man's waist or higher, stone piled carefully, solidly, on stone, walls that might have been built, so far as any of them knew, by their grandfathers' grandfathers. Beyond the walls, grazing forever on coarse grass and such hardy vegetation, weeds and burdock, as could survive the salty winds, were muddy sheep and an occasional donkey that planted its long-whiskered nose on top of the wall and silently watched them pass.

Once, a dusty truck came chugging up a hill behind them. Flynn, Brennan, and Gilhooley moved aside, leaving the roadway clear. When the truck drew alongside, the driver called a word-less greeting above the noise of the motor, and Martin Gilhooley raised one hand. The truck moved ahead, rounded a bend to the other side of the hill, and disappeared from view. Only John Mac-Mahon ignored it. He kept moving forward, planting his stick before him, eyes fixed on the treacherous stones that threatened his shuffling feet. In the dusty wake of the truck, Flynn, Brennan, and Gilhooley fell in beside him across the width of the road, and, without a word being spoken, continued on their way.

Willy Egan was sixty-seven years of age, looked twenty years older and had the strength of a man twenty years younger. Every-thing that needed doing on the farm now took a little longer than it had in the past, but it all got done, every bit of it. God willing, he'd be able to keep the place up for many years to come. There was nothing more he wanted. There was no woman in his house, that was true—a pretty thing named Maureen Collins, from County Mayo, had thrown him over in his youth and he'd never wanted another—but he could fend for himself as well as any man alone. He had the pipe between his teeth for constant company, a roof above his head, bread on his table, the animals to talk to when he felt the rare need of speaking a word aloud, a pint whenever he wanted it, and the fine old music in Nolan's on the weekend.

The barn near his thatched stone cottage leaned away from the wind, as many did on the hillsides of Doolin. Willy was in there, tending to one of the cows that had turned up lame that morning, when the four old men appeared in the doorway and cast their shadows inside. Willy had heard them coming, shoes crushing gravel and sliding along, for a little bit before they got there, but he put off turning around and looking up and seeing them for as long as he properly could.

"Good morning to ye," he said at last, and turned around on his stool to face them.

"Morning," said Martin Gilhooley.

"Martin," said Willy Egan. Then he looked at each of them in turn. "Brian," he said. "James." And finally he looked at John MacMahon. "John," he said, "I see you've come again."

John MacMahon nodded. "Good morning to ye, Willy," he said. "Can you spare a minute to sit? We've walked the distance and need to catch our breath."

Willy Egan sighed, patted the cow on her flank, and stood up from the stool. "I can," he said, and led the way out of the barn.

There was an old wooden bench along the wall at the front of the house. They sat there, all five of them, dark huddled figures against the gray of long-ago whitewashed stone. Willy sat on the end, with John MacMahon beside him, and the others at the far side of John. All sat with their heads lowered against the brilliance of the sunshine in cold clear air. He offered them nothing to drink now, but that would come, and when the time was proper Willy Egan would provide.

"Well, you know why we've come, Willy," John MacMahon said at last.

Willy lowered his head farther. "I do," he said resolutely. "It's near time again, and thanks be to God we're all still alive to see it another year."

"Aye," said John MacMahon, "that's the way to think of it, and no mistake."

"All the same as before, is it?"

"All the same," said John MacMahon.

James Brennan suffered a coughing fit just then and the others were compelled to be silent until he was done.

"Will you want to take a look, then?" asked Willy Egan when silence had returned.

"I must, you know that, Willy," John MacMahon said.

"That's so, you must." Willy Egan sighed resolutely again, pressed his hands on his knees, and stood up. "All right, then. If it must be done, let's do it."

He turned away and walked around the corner of the house, through the passage between house and barn, and the others followed behind him.

In back of the barn, a fat old mare, her coat thick with early winter growth, stood with her hairy black nose resting on top of a stone wall. She snorted twice when she saw the men coming toward her but did not move. Her big black eye shifted slightly as she watched them draw near.

Willy Egan opened the latch on the gate and they all went in and stood beside the mare. She took her nose from the fence and turned her head a little to keep them in view. Willy went and stood where she could see him. He rubbed his hand on her long rough forehead.

The four old men came close and looked the animal over carefully. They walked to the other side and looked there too, then stood together again near Willy. John MacMahon, one hand leaning on his cane, stepped up beside her and ran his hand along her back and down her shoulder. Both the mare and Willy watched the movement of his hand.

The other three stepped back as John MacMahon looked at Willy.

"All right, then," he said.

Willy stroked the mare's nose a moment longer, then lowered his hand.

"Well, then, come and have a drop," he said. "To mark the occasion."

He led them back to the cottage and inside. They stood and waited while he bent and pulled a stone jug from the bottom of a chest of drawers. Then, in silence, they passed the jug from hand to hand, sipping the powerful poteen, brewed in the hills. When the jug came back to Willy Egan again, he took his own taste, then put it away.

He wiped his hand across his lips as the poteen burned its way down his throat. "You'll be having something for me, I suppose," he said.

John MacMahon shifted his stick to the left hand and reached inside his jacket with the right. He withdrew a piece of grayish bone, very like the color of the mare they'd just been looking at. It was a little smudged from the handling of grimy fingers, but polished smooth with ages of use. It was a comb, long-toothed and jagged in places. Without looking at it, John MacMahon handed it to Willy Egan. Willy took it without a word and put it in the inside pocket of his jacket.

"Well, we're done, then," John MacMahon said, "for the time being, at least."

"That we are," Willy said. His tone did not invite them to

stay longer. His gaze did not waver from John MacMahon's face.

All five of them went outside together and Willy Egan stood in the yard before the house, watching the others start slowly down the road.

When a bend in the road and the height of a wall had hidden them from view, he turned and walked slowly back to the barn. Inside, he took the comb from his jacket and laid it carefully on a shelf. Then he went out through the back and walked to where the mare stood, her steady eye fixed on his approach.

He patted her shoulder a few times, then ran his hand down her neck, feeling the coarse bristles of her hair even on his calloused palm. Then he stepped back and looked her over critically. Her coat and mane needed a lot of work and her legs were muddy up to well above her knees.

"You're a beauty underneath the mud," he said, "and a good cleaning up is all you need. And a combing, too, and ye shall have it every day from here on in. Ye'll like that, my old girl," he said softly, "such a nice combing ye'll have."

He came around and stood in front of the animal's face. He held her long nose in both hands and she made a sound in her throat at his familiar touch.

"Ah, my old girl," he said, and put his face close enough to feel her whiskers on his cheek.

The mare lifted one great foot, then put it down in the same place.

"Ah, Maureen, my babe," he whispered, "it'll only hurt for a bit and then it's all over and done."

"Well, will you look at the sleeping beauty!" Grainne said with a laugh when Jack finally stirred on the couch and opened his eyes.

The house was filled with the warm, sweet smell of recent baking. Sunlight was just beginning to angle into the room at one end of the windows.

Grainne was stretched out on the floor in front of the couch. She slipped a bookmark into place and got up on her knees, then sat back on her heels, facing him.

Jack stared at her groggily for a few seconds until his mind cleared.

"Morning," he mumbled.

"Well, I see you're an early riser," Grainne said brightly.

Jack blinked at her, then managed to sit up on the couch.

"And you're an early sleeper," he muttered, but there was a hint of a grin in his sleepy face.

"Oh, Jack, I'm sorry," Grainne said at once. "I just went out on you like that. I only thought to rest for a minute so we could sit up and talk. I was looking forward to it. Really, I'm sorry. And it's a shame you were put out of your own bed. That couch was never meant to be slept on."

"Grainne, stop apologizing," Jack said. He pushed the blanket from around him and stretched out a hand to help her up. They stood together and their eyes met. Jack stepped closer to her and she moved into his arms. They lingered, lips caressing, fingers spread wide on each other's back. When they drew apart, Jack held onto both her hands.

"Good morning," he said gently.

"Good morning to you. Now get on with you to the bathroom while I get some breakfast together. I made fresh scones. Will you want eggs and bacon? And do you take tea or coffee?"

"Grainne, I'll take anything you want to put in front of me."

"Tea, then. And a good meal to keep off the cold, although I don't mind saying it's a shameful hour for a man to be eating his breakfast. Now be off with you, and don't be taking all day or it'll be time for dinner before you're done with this. Here, leave the blanket where it is. I'll put it away. You just get a move on."

Over the meal, they talked about school and family and childhood and friends. Jack ate six scones.

"You'll spoil me," he said when he finished.

"Don't be getting accustomed to it," she said. "You'll be on your own soon again."

"I know. I wish I didn't have to be."

The silence hung awkwardly in the air for a moment, then Grainne rose and began gathering up the plates.

"You never answered my question last night," she said as she piled the dishes in the sink.

"What question was that?"

"About Doolin and County Clare. All the country roundabout. Is it what you were after for the book?"

Jack lit a cigarette. "Pretty much so," he said.

"Have you much done?"

"Of the book?"

"Yes."

"About fifty pages or so."

"How many do you need?"

"Three hundred. Four hundred. Depends."

Grainne turned to face him and leaned back on the edge of the sink, her arms folded lightly beneath her breasts.

"Why will you not talk about it?"

"You mean the book?" Jack said. He inhaled on the cigarette and would not look at her.

"Yes, the book. You were so excited when you talked of it before, on the telephone, and now you seem hardly willing to speak of it at all. Is it not coming out the way you wanted?"

"Well, it's going slower than I thought it would. But the beginning is always difficult."

"I don't believe you for a minute," she said. "There's something else that's wrong, I can tell from the way you talk. You don't have to tell me about it if you don't want to, but if you do, I'll be glad to listen. I've read all your books I had at the shop, you know. And I found another in a store elsewhere."

"You went looking in another bookstore?"

"Yes. And you're changing the subject. Do you not want to talk about it?"

Jack crushed his cigarette out slowly. "Let's talk about it later." He stood up. "Come on, I'll show you around outside. I could use a breath of air. And it's not often we get a bright day like this."

"Oh," Grainne said. "I was outside before, while you were sleeping, just to take a look around. Who are all your visitors?"

Jack was standing up from the table as she spoke. He paused, stared at her. Her expression was perfectly composed.

"What do you mean?" he said.

"I went outside and took a walk around the house. The dirt is all dry, with no rain, and I saw all the footprints. Have you been giving wild parties or what?"

"That's . . . That's strange," Jack said. "I don't know what they are. Come on. Show me."

They went outside and Grainne led him to the side of the house facing the road. The weather was still beautiful, the sunshine bright, the air crisp and clean, but a scattering of low gray clouds had appeared out to the west, above the ocean, and seemed to be hurrying in toward shore.

"There," Grainne said.

With his hands shoved deep in the pockets of his corduroy jeans, Jack examined the ground. It was dry here from the wind and sun, and the gravel of the makeshift driveway stopped short of the base of the house, leaving a patch of exposed earth. This was the same spot where Jack had thought he'd seen scurrying shadows in the headlights of the car the night before. It was covered with what appeared to be footprints, many of them, all crisscrossing each other, as if a small crowd of people had passed over and over the spot, milling and pacing impatiently.

Jack squatted and looked more closely at the ground. Yes, here and there he thought he could just make out the impression of a small bare foot. He rose and moved a few yards to his right, still facing the side of the house, then squatted again. He saw it again, the clear imprint in the dirt, only partially obscured, of a small bare right foot. It appeared clearly only that once, so many feet had moved over the spot, but there was no mistaking it.

Jack stood up and scowled at the violated earth.

"Do you know who it was?" Grainne asked.

Jack kept his eyes on the ground, still searching it for a clue, an explanation, something—anything—other than what came immediately to mind.

"No," he said. "Local people, probably. I don't doubt they're curious about me, since I'm a stranger here. I gather they don't see too many strangers, at least not at this time of year." He looked up at her and managed a thin smile. "I'll keep an eye out from now on. Maybe I can catch somebody at it. If I can catch one of them, it'll keep all the rest away." A thought struck him. "I could speak to Father Henning, too, if it keeps up. He's the local priest. I've met him. He's a bit of a character himself, but he probably rules like a god around here."

They strolled away, around to the front of the house that faced down the hill toward the water. Grainne took his hand and held it tight.

"You'll not have much standing with the priest when he gets a look at your weekend guest," she said.

"I can't help that. He'll just have to get used to it. And the rest of the town, too." He stopped walking and turned to look at her. "Do you go to church on Sundays? To Mass?"

"I don't go all the time but I go more often than not. I suppose it's the upbringing of the sisters. They put the fear of God into you that you'll burn in hell for all eternity if you miss Mass even once. Did you have the same training in America?"

"Yes. I had nuns in grammar school and then the Jesuits for eight years."

"Ah, the Jesuits," Grainne said, grinning. "Well, there'll be no saving your soul after eight years of that."

"I suppose not," Jack said. Then he swept his hand in an arc to cover the scene before them. "Look." To the south, they could see a little way along the coast until the hills and one sharp cliff cut off their view. The coastline itself was edged in the white froth of waves, forever curling in from the sea and striking at the rocks. The air was so clear that they could just make out, off to their left, the promontory of Doolin Point, which was usually hidden from them in a cloud of spray and wet mist. If they watched carefully, they could see an occasional crashing wave shoot a high white geyser of foam against the rocks. Before them, the hill sloped down from the house in a gradual long descent to the water. And to their right, across the cut of a valley, at the innermost point of which lay the village of Doolin itself, was the gray-white expanse of the Burren, stark, treeless, ancient and unmoved.

"Have you been there?" Grainne asked, pointing to the north. "To the Burren?"

"No, actually," Jack answered slowly. "I guess I was saving it till you got here."

"I'd like to explore it."

"Tomorrow?"

"All right."

"Grainne, how long are you going to stay?"

She was still looking at the Burren. "I'll have to see," she said. "I can't stay long."

They started back toward the house, as if suddenly conscious of the time.

"I'll go to church with you tomorrow, if you'd like."

"I would," she said. "But the priest still won't believe I'm your sister."

"Cousin?"

"Not a chance."

He didn't mean to say it, but the words were spoken before he could stop them.

"I want to sleep with you, Grainne. I want to make love with you."

"I know," she said, and her hand suddenly tightened around his. "I want that, too."

They continued climbing back toward the house.

"And when you're ready, you'll tell me what's bothering you," Grainne said quietly.

"All right," Jack said. "But I want to think about it a little more first."

When they reached the door, Jack avoided looking toward the side of the house where the footprints were pressed in the dirt.

Father Malcolm Henning was reading the *Irish Times* in the sitting room when the knock came at the door. Deirdre Corcoran was at the back of the house, changing the sheets on his bed.

"I'll answer it, Father, don't trouble yourself," she called out.

The floorboards of the old cottage creaked beneath her heavy step as she walked through the short hallway to the front door.

"It's you," she said when she pulled the door open and saw John MacMahon standing in the path.

"It is," he said, "and it's not you I've come for to see. I've come to speak a word with himself."

Deirdre stepped into the doorway and pulled the door partly closed behind her. She was wearing a short-sleeved dress but the cold never seemed to affect her.

"Speak with him, then," she said. "But see that you're quick about it and not taking up his time. He's due in the church shortly to be hearing confession, and I'll not have him coming late. And it's there you should be yourself, John MacMahon, pouring out your bloody sins and asking God's forgiveness and that of all His saints."

"Deirdre!" Father Henning said behind her.

"It's John MacMahon, come to see you," said Deirdre, ignoring the sharp tone of the priest's voice. She held the door back and the gesture was as much an invitation for the priest to step outside as it was for John MacMahon to enter the house.

"I'll be with you in a minute, John," Father Henning said past her shoulder. "I'm on my way to the church. I'll just get my scarf and coat."

She waited at the door for him and when he passed her, he said, "Now mind the time, Deirdre, so's not to be late meeting me." She was never late meeting him—he always told people you could set your watch by her—and she knew the warning was meant as a reproof for her treatment of John MacMahon.

When she'd closed the door on him and he stood with John MacMahon in the path, Deirdre hurried inside and pressed herself against the wall near the sitting room window. It was open an inch at the bottom and she could just make out what the two old men were saying.

" 'Tis done," said John MacMahon.

"Well, then, I suppose, we must," said the priest. Deirdre thought his voice sounded sad and resigned, as if he'd lost a long-standing dispute with John MacMahon and now had to live with the consequences.

"Aye."

"Well, what's your choice, then?"

"It's Willy Egan's old mare," said John MacMahon. "We seen her today. She'll do fine."

Deirdre could hear the priest's long exhalation of breath. "Has he the proper comb?"

"I gev it him today."

After a moment, the priest said, "Well, that's that, then. Till the time, at least. Now, John, don't be troubling me about it till then, will you. I'll do my bit, of course, but don't be going at me all the while. It'll be on us soon enough without rushing it."

Deirdre heard their slow steps on the gravel as the two old men moved down the path to the road.

She stepped to the window and watched them for a moment as they reached the road and turned up it toward the church. Then she walked back to the bedroom and finished the job of putting fresh white sheets on the priest's narrow bed. All the while her hands moved automatically at tucking and folding, she was praying that God would look after the two old fellows and that everything would come right in the end.

"I'll thank you to keep a civil tongue in your head, Michael Mullen!"

Michael glared at his mother across the kitchen table.

"I'll not have my mother going into service, not at your age, and you a widow, besides!"

Peggy Mullen was doing her best to face the strength of her elder son, but the argument would have to end soon or she'd lose her resolve.

"It's not for you to decide," she said.

"But it is!" he said. "But it is! Are you forgetting that himself is laying in the ground up the hill there? That leaves me the eldest, so it's up to me to see what becomes of us all. And I say you don't do it."

"And I say I do. Your father, God rest his soul, never spoke to me this way, Michael, and I'll not start listening to it now. I'm just after telling you, Father Henning was the one put it to me, and it'll bring in a few pounds besides, cash and not a penny of taxes to pay on it. And we're not so wealthy we can turn down a chance at a few pounds more. Now, Michael, there's the end of it. I'm doing it and that's that. Michael, it's Father Henning that wants it."

"At your age," Michael grumbled at the table.

"And what's wrong with my age, will you tell me that?"

They sat in tense silence for a long minute. Michael tapped one meaty forefinger on the table.

"I'm coming with you," he said, "the first time you go there. Just to look things over, like."

"Come, then," said his mother, who was short of breath with her sudden victory. "But see that you're civil. I'll not be embarrassed in front of a stranger by my own flesh and blood."

"A stranger is what he is," said Michael darkly, but they spoke no more about it after that.

The sun had climbed the sky and then started its slow decline to the ocean in the west, casting longer and longer shadows across the hills. As the afternoon advanced, so did the low-flying ragged clouds scudding in toward the shore. They were just reaching it now, appearing to pick up speed, so close to the ground did they move, as they neared the hills of Clare. The wind had picked up too, growing harsher, louder on the rocks, and colder, promising dirty weather for the night.

Willy Egan had finished other chores on the small farm and now he was in the back with the mare. He had filled a pail with cloudy water and carried it out and set it on the ground beside her.

She turned her head to look at it and snorted a couple of times.

"Ye'll like it, girl," Willy Egan told her. "Ye have my word on it. God knows, ye should have it all the time, and not only for a special occasion. I'll treat ye right, ye'll see."

He patted her nose for a minute and she nuzzled at his shoulder, her breath puffing faint white from her wide nostrils.

"I wish it wasn't so, girl," he whispered, "but this is the way of it. Now, here, let me be started."

He settled the collar of his suit jacket more snugly across his chest, then drew a wire brush from the pocket of his jacket and started to scrub her down with the water. The animal nickered in her throat a few times and shifted her feet. Then she settled down to the comforting touch of his hand on her flank and the sound of his voice as he sang her a tune from his childhood.

Jack had watched Grainne with a combination of pride and fascination as she took militant charge of the food shopping. First, she had made a quick survey of the few shops that Doolin offered, comparing their wares and prices, and assembling the meal in her mind from the best things she saw for sale.

"You'd best like fish," she told him over her shoulder, when she'd decided on a particular shop and headed back there with Jack following in her wake.

"I love fish," Jack answered dutifully.

"You will when I'm done with you," Grainne had said, smiling, as they went into the shop.

She'd gone through the place systematically, knowing just what she was looking for, and casually refused the first piece of fish offered her by the shopkeeper. "I'll have that one," she said, pointing to where the one she wanted lay glassy-eyed on a thin bed of ice. When she was done and it came time to pay, she pulled money from the pocket of her jeans and started counting it out. Jack already had a twenty-pound note in his hand, but Grainne gave him a look that clearly warned him not to protest and make a scene in the shop. Outside, as they carried the parcels to the car, he insisted on paying for the food and Grainne stoutly refused. "It's my treat," she said. "I pay my way. You bought the meal last night and I'll buy this." And she'd listen to not a word more on the subject.

"All right," Jack said at last, as they finished stowing the food on the back seat of the Escort. "I'll agree, as long as you're the one who handles that dead fish back there. It's a little out of my line."

"All you have to do is eat it," she told him.

At home, she at once took charge of the kitchen. Jack kept trying to help, reminding her that she was a guest and he hadn't expected her to be doing the cooking, and finally she shooed him away.

"Have you no work to be doing?" she said. "I heard nothing of any work you did yesterday, before I came, and you've done nothing at all today."

"I'm allowed to take the weekend off," he protested.

"That's as may be," she said firmly, "but I'll not be responsible for keeping you from your work. You can write for two hours or more before the meal is ready, and still have time for tea in an hour or so."

"Okay, okay!" Jack said, backing out of the kitchen in mock surrender.

"Go on with you," Grainne said. She was smiling, and that

same easy, mutual understanding that had touched them before was there in the room again.

An hour later, she appeared in the doorway of his office.

"I'll have tea for you in a few minutes," she said. "Can I come in?"

"Of course," Jack said, glancing over his shoulder. "Just give me a minute to finish what I'm doing."

He was sitting before the computer with a page of print on the screen. He looked at it for a few seconds, then typed another couple of sentences. Each time he completed a line of type, the print moved one line up on the screen. Jack changed three words in what he'd just written, thought about it, changed one more word, studied the screen again, then sat back in his chair.

"Can I see it?" Grainne asked. She'd been sitting on the arm of an easy chair in the corner near the door. Now she rose and came and stood beside him. "I've never seen a word processor up close."

"No!" Jack said instantly, and turned his body so that he was between her and the screen.

Grainne, startled, took a step backward.

Jack touched a few keys on the keyboard and the screen cleared, then displayed a directory. He touched two more keys and the screen went blank. A moment later, a red light before him went off. He flipped the latch on the disk-drive door, removed the disk he'd been using, and slipped it into a protective sleeve. The fans in the computer went on humming.

Grainne watched him in silence.

"I'm sorry," Jack said. "I didn't mean to jump like that. I'm just not ... used to having anyone around while I'm writing. I'll let you read it when I'm done, I promise."

"All right," Grainne said a little doubtfully. "I didn't mean to intrude. I'm just curious, that's all, about the computer and about what you're writing, too." She tried a little smile on him. "I'm one of your greatest fans, you know. I buy all your books. Why, you're probably getting rich on me alone."

"Well, that won't be so any more, because you'll be getting them all for free from now on. Anybody who's willing to handle a dead fish like that deserves something in return."

"Don't be disgusting," Grainne said. "That's your own meal you're talking about. You should be glad there's food on the table."

He smiled too, and they silently agreed to close off the tiny awkward episode.

Grainne sent him out to the living room while she fixed the tea. He smiled when he smelled fresh-baked scones again, but his smile faded instantly when he realized that he'd been so lost in what he was writing that he hadn't smelled them before. What he'd been writing had nothing at all to do with scones and hearty meals.

He went to the radio and tried the few stations it received, but both the Irish and British stations were broadcasting little more than American country and western music. He settled for something soft and innocuous from the BBC.

When Grainne came in carrying a tray with the tea things, she found him standing at the windows, looking out at the dark clouds that were just now starting to fly inland past the shore. Out over the water, the sky had darkened. A thick bank of fog was heading toward the coast.

"There'll be rain tonight," she said as she set the tray on an end table by the couch.

Jack came and joined her and Grainne poured the tea.

"This is nice, having tea like this," Jack said after a moment. He turned to look at her. "It feels . . . very homey now that you're here."

"I'm glad of that. And I'm glad I came."

"Put down your tea."

"What?"

"Put down your tea."

There was a smile playing at the corners of his lips now. Grainne put her cup on the tray.

Jack put his arm around her shoulders and drew her close. Grainne slid sideways on the couch and came into his arms as if she'd been waiting weeks for his touch. Their lips came together in sudden longing, hungry for the taste and feel of each other, eager to explore. His tongue touched hers and hers quivered in return, questing against the tender inside of his lips. His right hand went to the back of her neck, tangled in her hair, and pulled her closer still. Her fingers curled tightly at his shoulder and back.

Then they drew apart, each breathing heavily, each still holding the other. Grainne curled in close against him, her face on his shoulder, and kissed him on the line of his jaw. Jack brushed the hair back from her face and kissed the top of her head.

"You smell like scones," he whispered into her hair.

"Hmmm," Grainne murmured.

After a moment, still without moving, she added, "I thought you'd never take me in your arms, Jack Quinlan."

"I thought Irish Catholic girls didn't fool around."

"Ah, that's where you're mistaken," she said comfortably, snuggling closer still, her arms around him tight. "It's only that we don't talk about it so much as some others."

He stroked the side of her face tenderly with his hand, stroked her temple with his thumb, felt her silken skin.

"You're beautiful," he said softly, "did I tell you that?"

"You did, I think," she said, "somewhere along the line, but don't let that stop you from telling me again."

"You're beautiful."

"Hmmm. And you."

He kissed her forehead and she turned her face up to him. Their lips met again, more slowly this time. He cupped her face gently in his hand and kissed her chin, her cheeks, her nose, her eyes. When she settled back against his shoulder, he lowered his hand and placed it on her breast, sighing at the touch of its wonderful softness, its firm weight against his fingers. Grainne moved her hand and placed it over his, pressing it tightly against her.

There was a knock at the door.

"Oh, Jesus!" Grainne cried and jumped away from him.

"Oh, God, what perfect timing!" Jack groaned. "I've been alone here since the day I moved in and somebody has to pick *now* to come visiting!"

"I'm sorry I jumped like that," Grainne said breathlessly. She pressed one hand over her heart.

Jack strode across to the door and opened it with a harsh, "Yes?"

"God save all here," said Father Malcolm Henning.

Jack saw the priest's eyes at once pass beyond him to the sight of Grainne sitting on the edge of the couch, but the old man's gaze immediately came back to Jack. "Good day to you," he added to his greeting.

"Hello, Father," Jack said. Behind the priest, standing on the gravel at the foot of the three steps up to the door, Jack could see a gray-haired older woman who clutched a dark blue winter coat around her thin frame and seemed to be looking anxiously at him. Beside her stood another, much bigger, woman who was peering at him and into the house with open curiosity. And, behind the two of them, stood a big man in heavy boots, coarse woolen pants, a badly worn and faded plaid wool jacket, and a peaked cap pulled low on his forehead.

The priest was still looking at Jack, his eyebrows slightly raised.

"Yes, well, uh . . . Won't you come in?" Jack said. He held the door open and stepped aside. As he did so, Grainne rose from the couch and came to stand beside him.

Jack quickly introduced her to the priest, and Father Henning introduced Peggy Mullen, Deirdre Corcoran, and Peggy's son Michael. They all bobbed their heads politely and shook hands. Father Henning and the women, Jack thought, were very busy looking *not* surprised at Grainne's presence in the house and her obvious right of place, standing there beside him at the door. Only the big fellow, Michael, frowned a bit, his face darkening, but then he remembered to doff his cap along with the frown.

"Please," Grainne said with a charming smile, "won't you come in and sit? Here, Father, let me take your things. Come in and sit, all of you. We're just at tea. It'll only take a minute to put on more."

While Jack was helping the women off with their coats and Michael was hanging his own on a peg he'd searched out and spotted near the door, Grainne was already leading the priest to the sofa and pressing him to take a freshly buttered scone.

While they were settling themselves on the sofa and chairs, Grainne found a moment when the others were all looking else-where to flap her hands at Jack, indicating he should make talk while she went to the kitchen for more tea.

As soon as they were seated, Father Henning told Jack he'd

brought Mrs. Mullen to introduce her in the hopes of coming to an arrangement about keeping his house. Deirdre, he said, kept his own little place and had been good enough to drive them over in her car, and Michael was coming in this direction anyway. Jack had already decided he didn't like the sullen look of Michael and that the man hadn't been coming this way at all, but the two women seemed pleasant enough. He resented the crowd a little, since it was now neither suitable nor possible to interview Peggy Mullen, but there was no reason to doubt the priest's recommendation. Jack explained what he needed, and at his request, Father Henning suggested a wage. He thought Mrs. Mullen looked a bit startled at the amount the priest named, but Jack thought it was quite reasonable. By the time Grainne returned with a new tray and enough cups from the kitchen, it was agreed that Peggy Mullen would start on Monday and everything was settled satisfactorily.

After that, the conversation was very general, although Jack found that Father Henning was just as adept today at drawing information out of him as he'd been the other time they'd met. Grainne easily took a leading part in the conversation, asking questions about Doolin, about the most scenic views in the area, and where were the best meat and fish to be had. Michael Mullen drank down his tea, then joined his big hands together, and confined his conversation to appropriate nods. No one asked about or even hinted that they'd like to know Grainne's relation to Jack or what she was doing there or how long she'd be staying. It was all very pleasant. The visitors finished their tea without hurrying, stayed a polite few minutes afterward, then took their leave.

Jack and Grainne, by mutual consent, waited until they heard the car drive away before they spoke. They were both grinning.

"Well, the tongues'll be wagging this night in the village of Doolin, I can promise you that," Grainne said.

"I don't doubt it. Your coming here is probably the most exciting thing to happen in Doolin all winter."

"It may be. Well, I hope you're as impressed as you should be."

"What do you mean?"

"Ah, Jack, you have a lot to learn about the ways of the Irish. When the priest of the village sees fit to set his foot inside your door, and just at teatime to boot, it can mean but one of three things. First, it could mean that you're terribly important and of a class with the priest himself. Second, it could mean that you've done something perfectly awful and he's come to save your soul, or at least to put things right on his own. And the third reason for a priest's visit to the house is that you've passed on to your eternal reward and he's come to pay his respects."

"Well, I don't think I'm dead, not yet anyway. Which of the other two do you think it is?"

"There's no telling," she said with a hint of a sly smile. "We'll just have to wait and see."

They had another cup of tea together, but the visit of the priest and the others had taken up time and now Grainne had to get back to the kitchen and fix the meal. They had earlier agreed to visit the pubs after eating and sample the music.

Jack went back to his office to work until the meal was ready. He inserted the disk in the computer and got the last page he'd been writing on the screen. He read it through twice, then sat there for the rest of the time, staring at it. When Grainne came to announce that dinner was ready, she stood in the doorway and didn't enter the room.

Deirdre Corcoran remained in the car, but Father Henning got out with the others in front of the Mullen farmhouse. They had all been silent on the drive back.

"Well, it's done, then," the priest said. "And good luck to you, Peg."

"Thank you, Father, for your time and trouble," she said. "I'm sure we'll all be grateful to have a little extra coming in. And it'll be taking my own mind off my troubles and the loss of himself, God rest his soul."

"I'll be off, then," Father Henning said. "I'm just glad it's all settled." He looked at Michael Mullen and the two men exchanged a stony look, which was not lost on the woman.

"Goodbye, then, Father," she said. "We'll see you at church in the morning."

"Father," said Michael Mullen quietly, and touched the peak of his cap.

"God bless you both," said the priest.

"She's a nice girl, that Grainne," said Deirdre Corcoran when he got back in the car and they'd driven away in the direction of the priest's house. "Will the two of them be living here permanent-like, do you suppose?"

"I'm sure I wouldn't know about such a thing," said the priest, and his tone cut off any further comments.

Willy Egan came into Nolan's, got a pint of Guinness from Liam at the bar, wrapped his big farmer's hand around the glass, and carried it toward the back of the pub, nodding to acquaintances on the way.

John MacMahon and Brian Flynn were in their accustomed place in the murky rearmost corner, and the others, James Brennan and Martin Gilhooley, were with them too. Willy Egan pulled over a low backless stool and set it before the small table, beside Brennan and Gilhooley and facing MacMahon and Flynn who had the bench against the wall. He took a slow drink from the pint, licked the foam from his upper lip, and set the glass before him on the table.

"Good evening to ye," he murmured, his glance including all four men.

"And to you," said John MacMahon. He lifted his own pint in a manner that appeared in no way special, but the others all lifted their own pints at the same time, as if at a signal, and all drank together in salute.

They sat in common silence for a while, lost in Celtic contemplation, and there was always one or another of them lifting a pint to his lips.

Around them, Nolan's gradually grew busier, more crowded, as the local people filtered in. The benches along the walls filled up first, and then the stools facing them across the low tables. There was some changing of seats, and the murmur of low greetings, and movement to the bar with foam-streaked glasses and returns with freshly-filled pints.

And after another while, the music started. A farmer from over Ennistymon way, a little man who seemed swallowed by the size of his coat and whose cheeks were as hard and red as berries, pulled a tin whistle from his pocket and played first a lively reel to get attention and draw a smile, then settled into the sad old songs of his youth.

While the farmer was in his third number, a thickly-bearded young fellow who'd been sitting alone in the middle of the room lifted his fiddle case from the floor and carried it to the back of the pub, where he found a place on a bench not far from Brian Flynn. He took out the fiddle and, with it held up close to his ear and his head bent over it, plucked softly at the strings until they were properly tuned. Then he returned to the front area of the pub, seated himself facing the old man with the tin whistle, and waited until that number was finished. Liam Nolan took his bodhran from beneath the bar and loosened his wrist with a fast run of the beater against the tight goatskin. Old Seamus Curtin had meanwhile been putting his pipes together and getting himself settled as well.

They played another reel together, taking turns skipping through the notes and watching each other's fingers. And then, as before, they went back to the sadder tunes, the whistle sounding a note of long-lost hope, the fiddle sighing with it, and the pipes lamenting.

During the second of those, Father Malcolm Henning came into the pub.

There was some shifting around on the stools and benches at the front near the bar, making a place for the priest to sit. Heads bobbed all around in respectful greeting and, without so much as a word, Eddie Toner, who sold dry goods to the people of Doolin and the whole surrounding area, went round behind the bar to fetch him a pint and not disturb Liam's playing of the drum.

The music floated in the air like bitter, wispy smoke—the breathy piping of the whistle, the cry of the strings, the keening of the pipes, the hollow mutter and rumble of the bodhran —music of foundered dreams and sorry partings, music from ages long gone by, tunes to which no man in the place could put a name in either of his languages, Irish or English, but to which all could nod in keeping to a melody known from birth or before.

When the number was finished, there was some scattered applause and murmurs of approval. The musicians laid down their instruments in deference to the priest, and pints were handed out to them from the bar. Now, with the music stopped and low conversation resumed, some of the oldtimers rose stiffly from their stools and gathered round Father Henning for a quiet chat.

The pub was cozy already, but someone went to the fire and added more peat and stirred it all up to a sizeable blaze, adding to the warmth of bodies. The place was warm now, snug and closed away from the bleak night outside, filled with the murmurs of familiar voices, in English and in softly lilting Irish, together with the heavy thump of glasses on scarred wood tables, and the sweet and acrid smell of the burning turf cut from the bogs between the hills.

"Did Father Henning mean anything special," Jack asked suddenly, "when he came into the house? Do you remember? He said, 'God save all here.' I know it's a traditional expression, but I wonder if he meant something by it."

"I can't think why he'd mean anything special by it," Grainne said. "It's just a thing you say when you enter a person's home. You'll not hear much of it in the heathen city, to be sure, but the old ways linger in a place like this, out here in the wild places. Why do you ask? Did you think it had some double meaning?"

"I was just wondering, that's all," Jack said.

The night air had grown damp and chill, penetrating clothes with sharp-edged icy fingers. Their breath plumed whitely from their mouths in the diffused and dim light of the moon. They had been to the two other pubs of Doolin and heard some of the weekend music in each, but then Grainne had said she wanted to see Nolan's and try it out. She loved these old country pubs.

"I'm not so sure you'll love this one," Jack had said as they started down the road toward it. "Do you remember Mrs. Mullen's great hulking son, Michael, this afternoon? The strong, silent type? Well, I was in Nolan's once, when I first got here, and every last one of them in there looked just like that. I didn't exactly feel that I'd found the Ireland of a thousand welcomes."

"Jack, there's something terrible troubling you about this place, isn't there?" She said it slowly and quietly, not as a challenge for him finally to give in and talk with her about it, but as a notice that she understood.

They had taken ten steps farther along the road before Jack at last said, "Yes."

But they said nothing else and in a few minutes more they reached the pub.

It was crowded now, at a little after ten o'clock, with only an hour or so left to the evening. Liam behind the bar lifted his chin at Jack slightly in what Jack, if he were inclined to be generous, might have taken for a nod of recognition from his one visit before. He got two pints and handed one to Grainne. There was no place to sit, so they pulled their jackets open and remained standing near the bar. Grainne looked perfectly content, but Jack thought the two of them looked like outsiders here, with their city clothes and soft hands and their educated accents.

"Do you see anyone you know?" she asked him.

"Nobody."

Seamus Curtin, over near the wall, was settling his pipes again for one last tune. They stood and listened to the music, the pipes, the long, slowly-shifting notes floating sadly round their heads.

When the tune at last wound down to an end, Grainne leaned close to Jack and whispered, "Jack, isn't that Father Henning? Back there, near the corner? Oh, and see the country-looking lot he's with! Come on, let's go talk with him. Come on, let's. I promise you, in twenty minutes or less, we'll know everyone in the place."

Michael Mullen was drinking beer at the table in the kitchen.

His brother Patrick sat across from him. He was still on his first bottle and it was only half empty.

"Will you not come at all, then?" Patrick said again. "Just for a pint or two and a bit of a tune?"

"Must you always have me to watch over you?" asked Michael. "Are you not able to find your way home from a pub alone? Follow your feet, man, and they'll bring you here safe, and if they don't, I'll make you my solemn oath to comb every ditch and boreen in the morning."

"It's not for you to lead me home that I'm asking. It's that it's no good for you sitting here with the drink by yourself." He pushed his chair back and stood up from the table. "Well, I'm off, then," he said, "with or without you."

He waited but Michael only took another drink from the bottle and replaced it on the table without looking up.

"You're a hard one, Michael Mullen," Patrick said as he finally turned away.

Peggy Mullen was sitting on the couch in the living room, listening to the whisper of the radio as her knitting needles flew. Patrick said goodnight to her as he took his coat from the peg and shoved his arm into it.

A minute later, Michael Mullen followed his brother out the door. He closed it quietly, but from the way he walked and held himself, his mother knew he'd really meant to slam it.

"Give us a tale, Father, will you?" someone said. Others repeated it, saying, "Aye, Father, a tale. It's not every night that you honor us."

The priest demurred briefly but it was all for show and they all knew it. Father Henning was renowned in the region for his tales.

"Well, then," he said, "I know a good one, but 'tis as dark in its meaning as it is rich in the telling."

"That'll do," John MacMahon said suddenly in his hoarse voice, leaning forward and looking closely at the priest where he sat opposite Brian Flynn. "That's the very sort that'll do, Father."

A few people glanced at the old man and nodded. Grainne secretly dug Jack in the ribs.

The priest took a mouthful from his glass and then cleared his throat.

"Well, it's a tale that starts about an old woman who lived a while ago in the County of Mayo. And it's about her two sons as well, great fine big lads, the both of them, and faithful to a fault to their dear old mother. I had the tale from the brother of the woman, the uncle to the boys, so I can vouch for its veracity. Now, I'll not be telling you the name of the village where she lived, for she still has relations alive there and it would bring some pain to them if the story ever came back, and tales have a way of growing and twisting in the telling from one to another.

"The elder of the two sons, let's call him Johnny Mac, and the younger by no more than a year, let's call him Tim. Now there was no man in the house to help in the rearing of the boys, for the woman's husband, God rest his soul, had been a good man —his name was, let's say, James—but a bit of a drinker, and one night on his way home he'd taken a notion to go for a ride on the one horse he owned. So off he goes, clinging on for his dear life, and yelling in the night. But he urges the horse off the road, you see, for some reason known only to himself, and in no time at all the horse is uneasy and trembling, what with a rider up there not exercising the authority the horse expects and has a right to. So the next thing is, the horse stumbles and there goes drunken James tumbling off his back with his head aiming right for a rock and, before even the rest of him had hit the ground, the man was dead and done. There's a lesson in that but I'll not be preaching at you here and now, I'll leave it for yourselves to discover."

Father Henning took a slow drink from his glass. A few in his audience ventured a smile but none took their eyes from his face. The priest cleared his throat again and resumed.

"So here's the old woman—McKeon, we'll say her name is—here's old Mrs. McKeon left to her own devices, with little more than stirabout and praties to be feeding the lads, a few old chickens in the yard, and the weight of the whole thing falling heavy on her shoulders. She's only a little bit of a thing, not a strong woman at all, and it's a burden to her, not to mention the loss of her James. But she thinks and thinks and prays for the help of God and before long she devises a solution.

"'Johnny Mac,' she says to the elder of the sons, 'you must up and away now to make your way in the world, for I can no longer be putting food enough on the table to feed us all. It's a hard thing I'm telling you, but it's in the way of harsh necessity.'

"The son, Johnny Mac, is not entirely surprised by the news, for he's been seeing the mother looking funny at him for a while since the father's passing, and pushing the extra egg on him of a morning, as if to build up his strength for a journey or a trial.

"But he's been thinking closely on the subject as well, and he puts down his knife and his potato, and he says firmly, 'I'll not be going off and leaving you only with the one lad here to be looking after you, and him even younger than meself.'

"'Ye've much of your father in ye, may he rest in peace,' says Mrs. McKeon, 'but I'll say the same to you as I had often to say to him. Ye'll do as I say, Johnny Mac, and that's an end of it, for I'll not discuss it further.'

"Johnny Mac was silent after that, for he knew that tone in his mother's voice. But the other side of it was, that his father had told him often while they walked of an evening at the edge of the bog, that should ill fortune befall him, the care of the old woman would all be upon his head. 'Ye're the eldest,' his father had said, 'and it all comes to you in the end.'

"As you may imagine, there was much discussion back and forth in the course of the next few days, and some of it heated, I can tell you. But in the end, as they all knew he would from the start, Johnny Mac conceded and the mother won the day.

"So, without going into some of the details, I can tell you the arguing was often unseemly and loud, and some of it not fit for repeating. The heart of it, the reason that Johnny Mac struggled so hard with his fate, was that he was torn, you see, pulled almost in two, by a pair of equal necessities. On the one hand, there was the image of his dead father, a good man whom he'd loved in despite of his faults and his untimely death, shaking a finger at his nose and telling him to stay on and look after the mother, and no matter what. And on the other hand, there was the mother herself, telling him to be off. But in the end, as I said, Johnny Mac yielded to his mother's insistence and gave in.

"And once he'd done that, he wasted no time at all in taking his leave, vowing the while that he'd find work somehow, some-where, God willing, and send back the spare pound or the extra penny as often as he could, and that young Tim should now fill the place of the two of them in seeing to the mother's well-being.

"Well, the day comes for him to be off, and just as he goes out at the door, he turns back for a second and says, as he's in the habit of doing, and his father before him, 'God save all here,' and the mother smiles and nods.

"And don't you know, Johnny Mac finds work in little more than a week's time, just as the bit he's taken from the purse as a stake is about to run out and leave him high and dry.

"He's come to a town, you see, where the railroad comes

through. It's not a fine and grand city, mind, but a respectable place that looks, to his eyes, accustomed as they are only to the village of his birth, like the farthest end of the earth. Not being used to the ways of the town, he walks up to a decent-looking man in the street and enquires where he might be asking after work. The man takes one look at the bulk of him and directs him to the railroad station. Well, this is Johnny Mac's lucky day, for the station-master takes a good hard look at the width of his shoulders and the breadth of his chest, and tells him to take a seat until the supervisor comes along.

"So Johnny Mac sits there waiting, with the stomach growling inside of him with the hunger and the thought of his mother in his mind, until along comes the supervisor. Well, this one does the same as the other, shaking his head over the bulk and brawn of the lad, and before the day is out, they've hired him on to stoke the furnace on the engines. You see, one of their boys is just after leaving them flat while he recovers from injuries suffered in an unfortunate altercation with another fellow bigger than himself. So there's the railroad supervisor in need of a healthy lad who's willing to work, and there's old Mrs. McKeon's Johnny Mac before him twisting his cap in his hand."

Father Henning paused a moment to wet his throat with the Guinness.

"It was almost as if things were just naturally falling into place with a will of their own."

He took another drink for good measure, then set the glass on the table.

"So. The particulars are all arranged and agreed right there and then, and Johnny Mac is set to work on the spot, that very evening, and he goes at it with a will, all the while thinking that, after all, the old woman was right. In no time at all, he expects, he'll be getting his first pay envelope and sending home to his mother and his brother as much as he can, with only as much kept back as he needs himself to hold body and soul together. His father's wish and warning is fulfilled in its essence, she still has the one son by her, and Johnny Mac figures to return to his place of birth and his mother's hearth one of these fine days like the grandest of conquering heroes.

"Now you may wonder at this point how the mother and the remaining son Tim are getting on back at home, but I can tell you that the tale, in this part of it, has no dealings with them. They're getting by as well as may be, with no overabundance, to be sure, and only just fending off the ravages of hunger. No, the tale at this part is all about Johnny Mac and what became of him, but we'll be going back to the village to take up the rest of it when the time comes, never fear.

"So here's Johnny Mac stoking and stoking and the furnace of the engine burning and burning and the train roaring along as proper as you please. Now it's hard work the lad is doing, but he's a good soul and the labor is all for the benefit of his old mother and he can already feel the weight of the coins in his pocket and so he minds it not a bit."

Father Henning lowered his voice.

"But then, you see, the lad's luck took a turn for the worse. A very serious turn for the worse, and no mistake about it."

The priest raised the glass again and sipped slowly while his listeners leaned forward and waited.

"You see," he resumed in the same sad, lowered voice, "Johnny Mac was only a country lad, with no experience or knowledge of the wider world, and here it all was just rushing past him on the train in a blur so as he could hardly make it out. He'd lift his head between the shovelfuls from time to time, with the salty sweat stinging at his eyes, and cast a glance to the side of the train, and there would be towns and villages and monumental great big cities the like of which were beyond all his dreaming.

"And so after only a while, not a long time at all, the driver of the train took pity on him and said he could rest his arms and his back for a minute and look about him if he wanted. Well, Johnny Mac jumped at the chance. He wiped the sweat from his face with the tail of his shirt and stared in wonder at sights he'd never laid eyes on before. There in the distance was a great church with a steeple higher than Johnny Mac had ever imagined, and over there was a house with more windows to it, he thought, than there were in the whole of his village. Everything his eye fell on was different from what he'd known, even the sheep on the hillside were a different breed and every lass in a field far prettier than those he'd seen at home. Every sight was a thing of wonder and he marveled at the wisdom of his mother and the good fortune that brought him to this state, money promised for his pocket and the wonders of the world laid out before his feet and not a penny charged for the looking. Here, he told himself with the deepest satisfaction, was the greatest day of his life, and he had no hopes of ever seeing a greater.

"And the sorry part is, there was truth in what he thought, for as it turned out, that was the last day ever his wondering eyes looked on the earth.

"He was still hot, you see, from the heat of the furnace and his own labors in keeping it fed, and when he felt a bit of a breeze on his face, he thought he could need nothing more than that to complete his happiness. The speed of the train, of course, made the wind seem to rush all about it. So the lad grabbed hold of a handle and swung himself out from the side of the train to get the fullest benefit of the breeze. The sad thing, as you will have realized, is that he had no knowledge of the dangers in such an exercise, and it was those very dangers that brought him to an end as untimely, and even more bloody, than that of his deceased father. The driver of the train said after, in his remorse at being unable to prevent it, that the lad had no knowledge of what to expect and, when it did happen, just as quickly as that, he could have had no time to realize that his time was up in that instant.

"It was done and over in a second, no time to prevent it, no time to cry out a word for help, no time to call out to his mother and say he was thinking of her to the end, no time to ask God's forgiveness for his sins, as few as they may have been, no time for any of that.

"You see, what happened was this. Alongside the tracks of the railroad just in that place, there was this great old tree that had been felled by lightning and now had fallen against another tree. Its limbs were bare of life and it was only waiting for some enterprising soul to come along and break it up for the fire. But as it was, it was all bare spiky limbs, shattered and blasted and pointing like threatening fingers very close to where the train rushed past every day.

"Now here I must put in a warning. As you may gather already, the tale is not pretty from here on out, so if you're unwilling to hear the terrible details of the lad's unhappy fate, then I'm giving notice here and now that this is the time to withdraw."

He drank from the pint again without meeting anyone's gaze. Shoes scuffled softly on the worn wooden floor, but no one moved away.

"Well, then," he said, "we'll go on with it, all the way to the end."

He lifted his glass again and drank from it, as if fortification were required to see this tale all the way through.

"You might almost have thought this tree knew our lad would do that, leaning out as he did from the side of the train. You might almost have thought it. So there's the tree, its dead and broken limbs, bare of any hint of green, just pointing fiercely along the track in the direction from where the train was coming. And there, rushing along with the dizzying speed of the engine, was poor fated Johnny Mac.

"Now I don't have to tell you they came together with terrible force. It was a terrifying sight indeed, and thanks be to God that none of us here were there to see it. The only witness was the driver of the engine and it's from him that this part of the tale is known, although, God help him, the poor man has never been easy in his thoughts a single day since seeing that terrible sight.

"It took his head off. That's what it did, it took young Johnny Mac's head off, ripped it clean from his body in less time than it takes to speak the words."

"Lord ha' mercy on his soul," murmured someone at the back of the crowd, and others nodded their heads in agreement.

"What happened was this. He was leaning way out, you see, and grinning at his good fortune and taking in all of the land-scape, and then, just a second before it strikes him, he turns his head to face forward. A branch catches him, like so, under the chin, and jerking his head back sharp. At the same time, when it's pulling at him, and this all in the wink of an eye, mind, his body catches on a projection of the train itself and it's held fast there. But his head is held by the point of the branch, like in a vice, as you might say, and so his body rushes on with the train while his head remains caught on the tree. The driver of the train is only just in time to see the blood shooting from the lad in a great red fountain and, looking back down the line, to catch a glimpse of the lad's poor head where it's speared on the branch like a potato you might roast over the fire.

"He was a good lad, Johnny Mac was, and it might be easy to assign his soul a place in heaven with the saints, for wasn't he brought to that place by his desire to do the good and right thing? He was, and that's where he met his end. But the tale is not over yet. There remains still another episode you must know before you have the whole of it, and it's for that that we'll return now to the village of Johnny Mac's birth.

"Nothing has changed in the village. The mother and young Tim are getting by as best they can. The old woman, being sickly, is hard pressed even to take in a bit of washing for a few pence, having all she can do to keep up her own place. And Tim is handy for nothing but the odd job, such as he gets from time to time. It's going hard for them, very hard, and little their friends and neighbors can be doing for them, so little do they have themselves.

"Well may you imagine the grief and wailing when the kindly supervisor of the railroad arrives, having gone all that far out of his way, at the old woman's cottage door, and delivers the news to her and Tim. Don't the neighbors from up the hill and down the road all come running across the fields to see what the yelling is for?

"And then comes the worst of all.

"The supervisor of the railroad has been carrying this parcel beneath his arm, you see, like this, and never once during the telling of his tale did he set it down out of his hands. Now, when the woman is a little recovered from the dreadful shock she's suffered, he comes out with the news that he's brought her the son's dear head in this parcel, and places it gently on the table.

"And it has full the opposite effect from that you'd imagine. The woman quiets at once, and all the others in the cottage, and it's crowded by now with neighbors from that part of the valley, seeing the example of the bereaved mother, grow quiet as well.

"The old woman, with scarce a hesitation or a tremble in her fingers, lovingly pulls back the wrappings of the parcel and exposes the head of her son for all to see. She takes it in her hands, just like this, and holds it aloft, her left hand at the back of the head with its hair all caked with blood, and her right hand cupping the chin. She holds it up high and turns it all about the room so all there should have a good look.

"'D'ye see?' she says to Tim and the friends and neighbors. 'D'ye see? My Johnny Mac's come back, just like he promised.'

"The supervisor from the railroad, not knowing what to make of it all, and even more eager to be on his way now than he was a minute before, reaches inside his coat and pulls forth a paper in which, he quickly explains, the railroad company announces that, in deference to Johnny Mac's service and in view of the accidental nature of his death, they've seen fit to arrange that a small amount of compensation should be paid monthly to those he's left behind, commencing with the sum herein enclosed.

"The mother only smiles a bit, as if to say she's not the least bit surprised. And with that, the man from the railroad hastily takes his leave.

"All in the place turn back to look at the mother as she stands before them, still holding aloft the head of her poor dead son.

"'D'ye see?' she says to them. 'D'ye see? It's just like he promised.'

"And it's then, with the mother herself still smiling that little smile, that the gore-crusted face of her son—for someone at the railroad had been less than thorough in cleaning it up for its return—gives a little tic, as you may say, a little twitch in a muscle of the cheek, and don't you know the two dead eyes open wide and stare all about at those in the cottage. And not a second later the lips give a twitch as well and the mouth opens up and out comes the unmistakeable voice of Johnny Mac, as attested by all those present to this very day, the voice of the lad himself, saying, 'God save all here.' And then the eyes closed and the mouth, and the head was still then forever after.

"Some, in relating the tale, tell as how Mrs. McKeon kept the lad's head in a wicker basket on a shelf near the door for years after, and perhaps it's still kept so today, but I'm not in a position to vouch for that and I'll say nothing more about it.

"And there's the end of the tale."

There were several murmurs of "God help us," but no one around the priest moved for a long while.

Jack had been staring at the table. Now, with the story ended, he became aware that Grainne's hand was clutching his arm, her fingers digging hard into his flesh. He turned his head to look at her. Among the faces in the crowd behind her, he saw that of Michael Mullen, staring at him coldly.

It was raining now but the temperature had dropped, making the rain more like chilling sleet. It coated the road to a slick and slippery surface, making the walking slow and cautious in the dark. Heads were bent forward both to see the road itself and to keep the sleet out of faces and eyes. Caps were pulled low, collars turned high, coats held tight. The wind gusted willfully, slapping faces with icy rain and snatching at the breath, whipping coats against legs and scarves against backs. It drove the sleet at them and pattered noisily on the road and the rocks and the stone walls.

As they drifted in small groups from the pub, daring the night for the walk or the ride home, a dog, a spaniel, half drowned and frozen with the sleety rain, whined and scanned their faces, paced anxiously a few steps this way, a few steps that. It did this until the last of them were gone, then it waited a few minutes longer by the door, its head hanging low, and whined with worry. Then it turned and trotted down the road to the village, its ears wet and plastered flat against its head, to seek its master at the next pub in line and see him safely home.

The pain was bothering John MacMahon again, the pain that was eating up his guts, and he had to be supported on the road homeward in the wet weather between Brian Flynn on one side and Martin Gilhooley on the other, each holding onto an elbow to keep him upright, with James Brennan walking in the rear.

The wind pulled at them and threw sleet in their faces, and they kept their chins buried tight against their chests, all except John MacMahon himself. Although his body at the moment lacked the strength to keep itself upright, he faced the pain, dared it to bring him down before he was willing to go, and kept his face held up boldly against the storm. Sleet coated the top of his cap and a little found its way under the peak and clung like crystals to his thick eyebrows. His thin lips were pulled back from his teeth with the pain inside him, but he said not a word as the others helped him along the road.

When they finally reached the cottage, James Brennan hurried ahead a little and unlatched the door and pushed it back. He reached in and switched on a dim light near the door as Flynn and Gilhooley helped John MacMahon into the one chair in the room, an old wooden frame thing with sadly worn flower-print cushions. He clutched at the arms of the chair, the hard knots of his knuckles standing out white with the pain that seized him. But after a minute or two, with the familiar safety of his own home around him, the pain eased a little and he was able to speak.

"It's coming on stronger all the time," he said, the breath wheezing in his throat. He had to clench his hands and suck in his cheeks for a moment as it passed through him again. Then it receded once more. He looked up and his gaze met that of each of the three of them in turn.

"Pray God, I'll be strong enough to see out the month," he managed to get out on a long exhalation of breath.

"You will, John, you will," said Martin Gilhooley at once. "We'll be with you all the time, the three of us, so you'll want for nothing."

John MacMahon shook his head. "No, no," he said, "that's not the way I'm thinking." He drew in a long, slow breath, as if testing treacherous terrain, but it was all right this time and he sat back a little easier in the chair, his head resting against a cushion.

"If I'm not here to do it with ye, ye must promise me to see it through proper. Will ye make me that promise, each and all of ye?"

The three glanced at each other, but even as they did so, Brian Flynn was already saying, "John, I give ye my word on it."

"And mine," said Martin Gilhooley.

"And mine as well," said James Brennan.

Flynn reached forward and put his knuckly old hand on top of John MacMahon's where it rested on the arm of the chair. Then Gilhooley stretched out an arm and put his hand on top of Flynn's, and James Brennan made a fourth, placing his hand on Gilhooley's.

"That'll do, then, that'll do," John MacMahon said, and wearily closed his eyes.

The others straightened up and looked at him.

"Here, we must have you out of them wet clothes," said Martin Gilhooley. "Give a hand, will ye?" he added quietly to the others, and moving with practiced ease, they helped John Mac-Mahon out of his wet shoes and jacket and trousers, and then eased him tenderly into his bed.

"Ah, that's a relief," the man sighed when they were done pulling at him and he was lying down at last.

Brian Flynn, his arthritic old fingers twisted into claws by the cold and wet of the night, pulled the blanket up to John Mac-Mahon's chin.

"Sleep well, John, with the help of God," he said softly, "and we'll be here for ye in the morning."

By the time James Brennan was switching off the light and pulling the door closed behind them, they could hear John Mac-Mahon's breathing change as he slipped into merciful sleep.

Jack and Grainne had to leave the car where it was in the village. Most of the other patrons of Nolan's and the two other pubs had done the same when they saw the condition of the roads. Even the walking was treacherous, with the road like a sheet of glass and more sleet coming down. The cars, if any had risked driving them, would surely have ended up in the ditches.

With the wind whistling in their ears and blowing straight in their faces off the Atlantic and hurling the icy sleet in their eyes, they were forced very often to stop and turn their backs into the wind to try and keep off the worst of it. The walk home took more than half an hour.

As they were nearing the top of the hill that, once crested, led past the house and on down the slope to the sea, the wind seemed to grow in ferocity, howling and lashing at their heads. There was no one else on the road here with them, all the others having turned off into narrow paths and lanes near the village itself. And it was dark, as dark as Jack could ever remember seeing a night, and the wind and the freezing rain kept coming at them. Grainne clutched tightly at his arm for support as the wind battered against the slope, scattered to every side, then gathered itself for a race across the hill. When at last they reached the top of the rise, they felt suddenly isolated, naked and abandoned, unprotected, in the face of the fiercely roaring wind. It buffeted their chests, snatched away their breath and left them gasping, longing to be home and dry and warm and safe.

They started tentatively down the icy slope. Below them they could just make out the house. Jack had left the lights on and the yellow glow from the windows flickered dimly through the chilling rain.

When they were midway between the top of the hill and the house, Jack heard the music.

It was the same tune of sadness and longing that they'd heard the old man playing in the pub, in Nolan's, just before Father Henning had started his tale. Jack knew a fair bit about traditional Irish music, from records and from a few places in New York where Irish musicians often played, and he'd heard a few familiar melodies and songs tonight in the first two pubs, the Seafoam and McGlynn's. In Nolan's he had heard nothing that was familiar, and for that reason this particular tune had stayed in his head. It was made of long sighing phrases, broken only by catches that might have been sobs, and seemed to speak of all the saddest things in life, want and fear and death and love. He knew that what he heard now on the hill, floating at him out of the night, its sound only a little muffled by the icy patter of the rain, was the very same tune.

"Wait!" he said urgently to Grainne.

They stopped and stood there on the hill. Grainne, still holding onto his arm, looked anxiously at him.

"What is it, Jack? What's wrong?"

"Listen!"

"I don't hear a thing," she said after a moment, "only the rain."

"The music," Jack said. "The same tune we heard in the pub. Listen." His head was cocked on one side, trying to determine which direction it came from.

Grainne's eyes swept the dark hillside and the road before them, but there was nothing to see or hear but the darkness of the night and the icy sputter of the rain.

"I don't hear a thing," she said.

"*Listen!*"

She was startled by the intensity of his voice. She gripped his arm tighter and listened again.

"I don't hear it, Jack," she said. "Did you leave the radio playing in the house maybe?"

Jack turned his head to look at her. "No," he said. "It's not the radio."

"Well, in any case, come on. We'll catch our deaths standing out like this." She pulled at his sleeve and took a careful step downhill.

"You don't hear it," he said. He hadn't moved. The rain was streaming down his face.

Grainne turned back at the strange sound of his voice. "Jack, I don't," she said. "It's just an odd trick of the memory. Will you come along now?"

"All right," he said, almost meekly, and they walked the rest of the way together.

Jack said nothing more while they were in the road, but the sad and lonely tune was still there, being played somewhere on the hill, and the rain and the wind and the music followed at his heels all the way to the door.

When they got into the house, she didn't question him about the oddness of his behavior. Instead, she announced that she was going to make them tea, and left him by himself in the living room.

"Yes, all right," he said, but it was as if he'd hardly heard her.

While she was in the kitchen, she felt a sudden cold draft blow through the house and smelled the freshness of rain. She came to the living room and saw Jack standing at the open door, his hand still on the knob, as if he were ready to slam it closed at a second's notice. He was staring out at the rain and gave no sign of knowing she was watching him. Silently, she went back to the kitchen and finished with the tea.

When she came back, bearing two cups that she'd already fixed with milk and sugar, he was at the window, in a studiedly casual pose, looking out toward the Atlantic and the storm that rattled droplets against the glass.

She called his name and they sat together on the couch. Jack drank the hot tea gratefully.

"Will you tell me, Jack, what it is that's bothering you?"

He lifted his gaze from the cup and met hers. "You're going back to Dublin tomorrow?" he asked.

"I am," she said gently. "I must, I told you that. I'd stay if I were able, really I would."

"Will you come back?"

Grainne dropped her eyes from his with a touch of the shyness that brought a twinge to his heart. "I will," she said quietly, "if you'll have me."

"Please come back."

"All right."

"Grainne," he said after a moment, "it's true, something's been bothering me. And I guess it still is. In fact, I know it still is. I'm afraid it's been distracting me a bit, and this weekend hasn't been quite the way I'd planned it. But when you come back, I'll be in a better frame of mind, I promise."

He put his cup down on the table but he was still toying with it, turning it around and around on the saucer.

"Is it the book?" Grainne asked. "Are you having some difficulty with it?"

"Yes, in part, it's the book."

Watching him closely, Grainne thought he seized on that as something to talk about, rather than the thing that bothered him most.

"I did some research on the Famine before I came here. I told you that. I'm writing a novel, not a history book, so most of what I read were secondary sources. And I came here—besides just coming for the trip itself—to get the local scene, the details, to find out how people here think and talk and live."

He hesitated at that point and Grainne said, "And you don't like what you've found."

"No, that's not it, not exactly. I *do* like it here. It's beautiful, like nothing else I've ever seen, and in some ways I can even imagine myself living here. At least," he added, attempting a smile, "I think that way on the rare occasions when the sun comes out."

Then his face grew serious again. "But there are other things, other aspects of the place, that bother me."

"Couldn't it just be that it's all so strange to you?"

"I suppose that's part of it. But it's not all."

Grainne waited, and finally asked, "Do you want to tell me about it now?"

"No," Jack said, and it was the only thing he'd sounded sure about in the whole conversation. "I've been thinking about it, and I've decided that there's no reason to bother you about it any more than I have already. It's probably nothing anyway. I'll figure it out or settle it in my mind or whatever, and that'll be the end of it. It'll be better the next time you come, Grainne, I promise."

Grainne composed her face to make it clear that she was agreeing to drop the subject, whatever it was, only reluctantly.

"When can you come back?" Jack asked. "Can you come next weekend?"

"I don't know. It depends on my friend Mary. I'll have to see. I'll tell you during the week."

"Will you try? For next weekend, I mean."

"I will. I promise."

The conversation drifted along, slowly growing back toward a more normal, less anxious, tone. When Grainne said she'd make more tea, Jack insisted that it was his turn to get it.

"What did you think of Father Henning's tale?" she asked when they were settled again.

Jack tasted his tea. "Sort of gloomy," he said. "I thought pub tales were supposed to be, I don't know, more jolly than that."

"Oh, not always. And even less so, I suppose, in a country local like that. We're a strange people, Jack, we Irish. We cry as much as we laugh."

"Yes," he said thoughtfully, not looking at her. "I gather that."

"Did the tale put you off somehow?"

"In a way. It was pretty gruesome, after all. And I wouldn't have thought Father Henning would tell something like that. I would have thought he'd tell something more pleasant. And, for that matter, something that was rather less ... well, less pagan than that. You have to admit, it was a pretty crude story."

"Heathenish," she said, a faint smile playing at her lips.

"Yes, exactly. That's what it was. A primitive, heathen tale in a Christian setting."

Grainne nodded in agreement.

"Doesn't it strike you as odd, that a priest would tell a tale like that?"

"Not really, it doesn't," she said, her tone now as serious as Jack's. "You know what the seanachie is, don't you?"

"Yes. The storyteller."

"Yes, but it's more than that, really. And you must multiply everything all the more because this is such a small village and remote from the cities. The seanachie is the taleteller, yes, but it's a very old, a very ancient, position in a village. In olden times, the seanachie was treated with all the highest regard and never lacked for a meal or a roof over his head. It was almost a sacred function he performed, preserving stories as he did. As he does. We still hold poets and writers and singers in that same way in Ireland, as if they were both a little blessed and a little mad, both. And there's still a lot of the old ways alive in some of these more remote parts of the country. It was a hard and dark sort of a tale he told, that's true, but you were probably the only one put off by it."

"I wasn't really put off by it. I was more surprised." He was silent a few seconds. Then he said, "What did you make of the story?"

"Are you using me for research, Jack Quinlan?" Grainne said, offering her smile again to lighten the mood.

"A little," Jack said very seriously. "What did you make of it?"

"Well, it was a little moralistic in its way," she said slowly, "almost as if it was a truly Christian sort of story about obligations to keep promises, that sort of thing, and duty and responsibility, whatever the personal sacrifice you might have to make."

"All right. But what about the rest of it? The primitive part?"

"You mean about the head speaking at the end?"

"Yes. And about the woman keeping it in a basket."

Grainne thought about it. "This is a remote part of the country," she said at last. "I guess I keep saying that, don't I, as if you didn't know it? But it is. That's why you came here in the first place, isn't it?"

"Yes. Go on."

"The old ways linger long in a place like this. Jack, you've seen the people. They're poor, for the most part, farmers with only a bit of land, and that bit more rocks than dirt. Or fishermen. Women who knit sweaters. The sweaters may sell in Grafton Street for forty pounds but don't think the women are getting that. You've seen the way they live. Most of them have nothing more than stone cottages. They may have electricity and they may have plumbing, but you may bank on it that they're living, most of them here, the same as they lived a hundred years ago or more, maybe two hundred. Jack, they haven't come along very far, a lot of them. And the old, dark stories are in their blood."

She smiled, a little ruefully. "Listen to me, will you?" she said. "I'm talking as if I'm different and not one of them myself. But I am, Jack. I'm just the same as them, and that despite my highly regarded university education. The city and the university polish off a lot of the roughness, but not all, by any means. I'll warrant you, there's many a banker in O'Connell Street who goes home of an evening and, with no one looking on but the wife, will rejoice to eat a baked potato out of his hand and sip at his tea from a saucer."

She paused, glanced sideways at him. Jack said nothing, almost as if he knew what was coming.

"And you're another, as the saying goes," she went on. "You're the same too. Maybe less so, for being born in America, but you were reared, you said, by a woman born here and you grew up surrounded by Irish. You know the rhythms of the language and the words of the songs and the taste of the food. I already know that you don't think you're eating a meal unless there's a potato on your plate. That may be the least part of it, but it's part of it, nonetheless. You know the habits of mind, the attitudes and assumptions. You may have less of it, but you have it, even so. You may have paid it no attention all your life up to now, but here you are, just the same, drawn back to the hills and the strand and the farms and the bogs. There's no denying the blood, Jack. No denying the blood."

They did not sleep together that night.

After Grainne's lengthy speech, they sat on the couch in

silence for a while, until finally Jack reached over and drew her close to him.

"Will you come to bed now?" she asked a little later.

Jack, without meeting her eyes, said he wanted to stay up a while longer. He started to explain, awkwardly, that he knew it was her last night there and that he wasn't avoiding her, but she cut him off with a finger placed gently across his lips.

"That's all right," she said with a sad smile. "I understand, Jack. So long as you know I'll be looking for a warmer welcome the next time I come. And so long as you understand that's not an easy thing for an Irish girl to be saying."

They kissed, held each other for a minute, and Grainne went in to bed.

Jack waited until she was quiet in the bedroom. Then he went to the window and stood there, looking out at the night and the storm that was still lashing the coast. After another while, he opened the door a few inches and listened, but the only sounds were the rain and the wind. He sat on the couch and tried to make sense of the things he'd seen and, now, the music he'd heard, and to put it together with what Grainne had said. She was right, of course, but that still didn't account for the other things.

Without realizing it, he dozed off. When he stirred and woke for a minute—his watch told him it was four-thirty in the morning—he found that Grainne had come out to the living room and tucked a blanket all around him.

CHAPTER 8

The rain followed him into the church. He'd been bent over double, making a smaller target for the lashing anger of the storm, but his clothing was soaked through anyway and his hair was dripping. He could hear the wet squelch of his shoes on the stone floor and feel the icy coldness of his feet. He had not been heading for the church, certainly had not been heading for the church in the dark, in the middle of the night, but the storm had become too much for him out in the slippery road and the church had been right there, he'd pushed at the door and found it open and he'd ducked in at once, seeking shelter.

The church was in darkness and he cautiously slid his hand along the clammy stone wall, following it around the perimeter of the vestibule. Behind him, sighing with its own weary weight, the heavy door swung closed, and though it seemed impossible, the darkness of the church grew darker still.

He came to a halt, one hand still on the wall, and stood there, breathing deeply through his mouth. The cold and the rain and his dash for the door had taken away his breath. Water ran out of his hair and down the side of his face, down the back of his neck, and he shivered.

Then he heard the hollow shuffling of feet against ancient stone.

He stood still a moment longer, then cautiously, blindly, followed the wall around to the doors into the church proper. His hand groped for a moment, flailing in air, chilled by sudden panic, when the wall disappeared and left him nothing to hold. Then he realized that the inner doors must be open. He took a deep breath, felt the doorjamb and, beyond it, the door pushed back against the inner wall. He shuffled forward, thinking to sit in the church a few minutes and wait out the worst of the storm. He could hear it rattling furiously at the wooden door behind him.

They took hold of his elbows when he was three steps inside the doorway.

Firm hands gripped his arms in the darkness and silently led him forward toward the altar. He heard nothing, only his own unsteady steps on the stone floor and the rattly breath of someone wheezing in the dark. Gradually, as he was propelled forward, he began to hear other sounds—more breathing, something that might have been a cough or a catch in the throat, a sniffle, perhaps, and the stealthy movement of feet—but he could see nothing, nothing at all, and knew only that the hands that held him moved him forward and would brook no opposition.

They belonged here somehow, he knew that, but the fright and shock and confusion, abetted by the chill of the air and the cold stone floor beneath his feet, numbed his brain, his thoughts, as it numbed his knees and made them weaken with his weight.

He would go with them for the moment—they insisted and, at least for the moment, he had no choice, hardly any will of his own—and then his mind would clear and he would know who they were and what they were doing and what it was they wanted of him.

The hands supported him toward the altar and, just before the stone step of the altar itself, they moved to his shoulders and gently but insistently pressed him downward to his knees. His weakness was suddenly so overpowering that he was grateful for the little rest the kneeling offered. He knelt and slumped heavily but the hands insisted that he kneel upright. His chin fell forward on his chest, in weariness, in vague fright at what he might see —as if, miraculously, he might be empowered to see in the hellish dark—but other hands, or the same hands, gripped his face with bony fingers cold as stone and lifted his head toward the altar. He could not tell if his eyes were open or closed. He knew only that the church and all those who moved in it were entombed in a darkness that was palpable—it pressed relentlessly at his back and shoulders and on the top of his head, pressing his weight against the stone—and that the night had made him blind.

"God save all here," said a voice above him, and he looked with his blinded eyes and saw his father, long-dead, standing in priest's vestments at the altar.

Behind him, in the hollow expanse of the church, a hundred voices murmured, "Amen."

"In the name of the Father, and of the Son, and of the Holy Ghost," his father intoned.

And they murmured again, "Amen."

He closed his eyes, or thought he closed them, and opened them again, or thought so, and saw not his own father but the priest, Father Henning, and he was lifting the golden chalice in the consecration of the Mass.

"This is the cup of my blood," he said, holding it aloft, "take and drink of it."

They came forward all around him, great waves of people moving and breaking on either side of him, and the chalice fed them all. They drank deep from the cup, but it flowed with a bounty of blood that was endless, and when at last the priest stood before him, bent close to him and offered the chalice, the cup was still full to the brim. He took it from the priest's hands —all this in the dark—and held it to his lips, feeling the warmth of the gold in the icy church, and drank to the bottom of the chalice, but when he handed it back to the priest, the chalice was once again filled to the brim with blood. The priest then drank himself —his throat moved clearly with each swallow—and as he drank a little blood ran from the corner of his mouth, down to his chin, and dripped onto his white vestments. It spattered there but left no visible stain.

The coppery taste lingered in Jack's mouth and a muscle in his cheek would not stop twitching.

The church was still again, except for the breathing.

The priest was gone now and the tall old fellow from the village stood at the altar, holding aloft something that his strength would barely support. It was a child, an infant, and he saw the old man hold it forward, then turn from the altar and come toward him, holding out the bloody bundle.

He took it in his arms and cradled it against his chest. The infant was naked and filthy and smelled chokingly of earth and death, but he held it tight because there was nothing else to do. All around him there was only the breathing, though now it seemed tense and waiting. He lowered his unseeing eyes in the darkness and looked into the dead face of the infant and saw at once that it was Grainne.

They took the infant from him and turned him around. There was nothing to see, only the empty, pressing darkness, and nothing to hear, only the breathing. But they were all there, all the people of Doolin, every face he'd seen, every voice he'd heard, all watching him now as other hands propelled him from the altar and led him to the middle of the empty church.

They stood in a circle and he was one of them. The figure on his left—whether a man or a woman, he knew not—leaned heavily against him and kissed him coldly on the cheek. He turned to his right and there was Grainne beside him, waiting, her dark soft eyes searching his, waiting still, waiting forever, knowing he would come to her in time, and then he leaned forward and kissed her cheek in turn, and watched as her eyes lingered on his for a lovely, warm moment before turning away to pass the kiss of peace around the rest of the circle.

The crowd around him grew and he was lost in the midst of those he could not see. He caught only glimpses of faces that were familiar, the priest, his father, the old man, a child he thought he knew, and Grainne, her face drifting among the others and her eyes sometimes meeting his own.

Then Father Henning was in the middle of the circle, his black raincoat gleaming wet and flapping at his legs, and he was reading the prayers for the dead. At his feet was an open grave, here in the middle of the pitch-black church, and Jack could see water running down the sides of its crumbling dirt walls. The priest read aloud the names of the dead, naming every name in Doolin, and prayed that their souls, and the souls of all the faithful departed, would, through the mercy of God, rest in peace, amen.

But it was not a burial after all, because four old men went forward from the circle and knelt at the edges of the grave, leaned into it, almost hovering above the hole, and began hauling something out. It was an exhumation, Jack saw that now, and the memory of Grainne's face on the infant in his arms made him seek her face now in the crowd. He did not see her and panic rushed through him for an instant, but then someone gently squeezed his hand and he looked and saw that it was her.

When he looked back at the grave, the body was almost in view. All around the circle, every one of the faces buried in the impenetrable dark was turned to him. He returned his gaze to the grave and they showed him the body now, its flesh rotted away in trailing wisps, its eyes deeply sunken in the skull, and of course the face was his own.

He peered through the pressing dark as the corpse was set on its feet and turned in his direction. He squeezed at Grainne's fingers but found that she was no longer there. A space had opened up around him in the crowd, and now he was alone, the others all silent and watching.

The corpse that was himself, unburied, denied its eternal peace, came toward him, stretching out a yellowed hand toward his arm. It took hold of his elbow and pressed it, held him in place, and he thought that, somehow, its touch was gentle. The corpse of himself came closer still, stood for a moment before him, searching his eyes, then leaned forward slowly and tenderly kissed him on the cheek.

Jack stared back at his own dead face, searched it in turn as the corpse had searched his. He moved his gaze away and scanned the other watching faces. They were solemn, all watching him closely—he saw Grainne among them, and the priest, and the four old men—and as he looked at their eyes in the dark he knew that they were waiting to see if he would—that they wanted him to—return the kiss to the corpse of himself.

CHAPTER 9

The church was in the valley, on the far side of the hill, and the sound of the bells ringing for Mass on Sunday morning reached the house only dimly in waves, on the caprice of the wind, like the tolling of the bell of a ship in danger at sea.

The storm had eased off but it was still raining at dawn, a slow, steady drizzle that could keep up all day. A heavy layer of gray clouds hung low above the hills, threatening them with its weight.

Jack awoke first, stiff from sleeping on the couch, and went out to the kitchen to fix breakfast. When he finally went into the bedroom, carrying a tray to surprise Grainne with breakfast in bed, he found her sitting up and wide awake.

"You knew I was getting breakfast," he said, trying to sound accusing.

"I did," she said, grinning and reaching for the tray. "Far be it from me to interfere with a man in his kitchen."

They ate together in the bedroom, talking about the sights they hadn't visited but would definitely get to next time Grainne came.

"Do you know what time is the Mass?" she asked.

"Ten."

"We'd best hurry, then. And I must be off right after it, Jack."

When he carried her bag to the car, she held an umbrella over his head while he tossed it into the back seat. Grainne drove. Jack still had to retrieve his car from where they'd left it in the village.

"This should be interesting," he said as they drew near the church. "I imagine we'll turn a few heads, if not cause an outright scandal. Here we are, obviously sleeping together, as far as anyone knows, and then boldly walking into the church. We'll be the talk of the town."

"Well, it could go either way," Grainne said, a hint of a smile touching her lips. "One of two things could happen. For one, Father Henning, for all that he seems a nice enough man, could point his finger and denounce us by name from the altar. They used to do it all the time in the old days, you know. Or for another, he could offer up a special prayer of thanks. Here's Jack Quinlan coming to Mass, you see, after being in Doolin a couple of Sundays already and never a foot set inside the church. And who's to thank for it? I am. I've taken upon myself the salvation of your soul. All you'd have to do to settle it once and for all is go up and receive Holy Communion with the rest. Do that, and Father Henning will be putting in for canonization for the both of us."

By the time the priest appeared and the Mass began, they were all there in the church, all the people of Doolin, it seemed, all the familiar faces from the shops and the roads and the town's three pubs.

The people from the grocery store where Grainne had done her shopping were there, and the three owners of the pubs, two of them with their wives and three children apiece, only Liam Nolan appearing by himself in the company of some of his cronies.

Deirdre Corcoran was there, head bowed as she said her beads up near the front, as if she had a proprietary interest in being close to the altar and the priest. Peggy Mullen came in, followed by her two big sons who kept their eyes on the floor before them as they genuflected and took seats on either side of their mother.

Eddie Toner was there with his family, a skinny, dark-skinned wife and two matching children, a boy and a girl. And there was the man Jack recognized from the town's one garage, and several farmers he'd seen in front of their houses or barns as he'd driven around the area, and some of the blue-capped fishermen he'd seen sitting in a doorway near the inlet just beyond Doolin Point, waiting for calmer seas before taking out a boat.

Jack and Grainne had taken seats on the left side of the church, near the back, silently agreeing not to draw too much attention to themselves. The church was built of gray local stone, damp and cold and drafty—Jack noted that some of the windows were broken and covered over with tin in a few places and only sodden cardboard in some others—and they sat with their coats on and their collars turned up high against their necks. They had a view from there, with only a little turning of the head and craning of the neck, of most of the people in the church ahead of them and those who followed after. Hard, dour faces they were, almost all of them, pinched by poverty and wet weather.

When the four old men came in together, Jack recognized them at once as the same four the priest had been sitting with in the pub, the same four he'd seen that other day at the grave.

They moved slowly, feet shuffling beneath them on the worn stone floor of the church. Two of them, one with great gray tufts of hair projecting from his ears, were trying unobtrusively to lend a supporting hand beneath the elbows of the one who appeared to be the eldest, the one Jack recalled thinking was the leader each time he'd seen them. The old fellow was long-limbed and tall and brittle as a bone, and was clearly making his best effort to walk upright without help and get into the seat by himself. But when he was seated, Jack clearly saw him puff out his thin lips with a sigh of relief.

Then a bell was rung at the altar and Father Henning appeared from the sacristy, followed by two little boys.

"In the name of the Father, and of the Son, and of the Holy Spirit," intoned the priest, and the Mass had begun.

Jack noted that the old women and many of the old men rattled their rosaries, which had nothing at all to do with the Mass, just as loudly and devoutly as their counterparts in the parish church of his childhood in New York. It was only a rare and brave-hearted priest, he recalled, who had ever dared to challenge them on that point and try to get them to pay attention to the ceremony itself.

The old folks liked and needed the firm and weighty feel of the talisman in their hands.

Jack had not been a regular churchgoer in more than a dozen years, except for Midnight Mass on Christmas Eve, which he liked, he readily admitted to himself, for the traditional hymns and the convivial spirit. His failure to attend church and actually belong to a neighborhood parish was one of the things that had long kept him from taking an active part in the Irish community at home.

But as he looked around him, while Father Henning said the prayers of the Mass up at the altar and the people murmured the responses that Jack no longer knew, he was struck with the vivid reality of something he'd only been aware of intellectually until now. For these people, the Catholic faith was at the center of their lives. For them, being Irish and being Catholic were one and the same thing, so central an element of life that it required no thought at all. The church and its priests had long held Ireland together, forced the people to survive, in the face of invasion, disruption, oppression, and famine. And, perhaps most important of all, their faith promised them a life hereafter that was endless and joyous and rich, a fine and grand reward for a lifetime of hardship and struggle in a land as harsh as it was beautiful.

He stole a look at Grainne beside him. For all of her liberated modernism and free-thinking attitudes, unfettered by old morality, here she was, sitting in rapt attention at Mass, listening to the priest. Father Henning was coming near the consecration of the Mass, and Grainne's eyes were fixed on his face and hands. When he raised the chalice aloft for all to see and spoke the words that transformed the wine it contained into the blood of Jesus Christ—"For this is the cup of my blood; take and drink of it."—Grainne rapped her fisted knuckles lightly over her heart with the ringing of the bell along with everyone else in the church.

Contradictions, he thought, and—

Something else, a chilling wave of cold, swept suddenly through him, a memory buried deep in his mind, far beyond recalling, but in his thoughts nonetheless. What was it? Something triggered by the words of the consecration. No, he couldn't retrieve it. He shivered and pushed it from his mind.

Contradictions, the Irish are nothing but contradictions, and Grainne Clarkin—with her milk-white skin and jet black hair—not least among them.

And you're another, he heard her saying again as she'd told him last night. . . . *You may have less of it, but you have it, even so. . . . There's no denying the blood, Jack.*

When Father Henning walked over to the stone pulpit at the side of the altar, Jack expected a lengthy sermon. Well, at least, he thought, it'll be better than the ungrammatical ramblings of the priests he'd always heard at home. But Father Henning was brief—Jack surreptitiously timed him at a little over four minutes —and said, in effect, only that the oncoming cold and wetness of the winter should serve always to remind the faithful of the welcome warmth of God's love.

Almost everyone in the church climbed out of their seats and shuffled up to the altar to receive Holy Communion. Jack and Grainne remained where they were, heads bowed in prayer or, at least in Jack's case, a reasonable imitation of prayer.

After that, the remainder of the Mass went quickly.

"Go in peace," said Father Henning at the end, and blessed them. "In the name of the Father, and of the Son, and of the Holy Spirit. Amen."

Head bowed, and followed by the two little altar boys, the priest disappeared into the sacristy.

Jack and Grainne had to wait a few minutes at the side of the church for the rest of the people to move out slowly through the doors. When they finally got outside, they saw that the rain had eased off further, leaving only a chill dampness in the air and a low-ering sky that was struggling grimly toward brightness. Almost everyone from the church was still standing around outside, the women gathering in the roadway and the men near the side of the church. This was the great social event of the week and they weren't about to see it end any sooner than they had to. As Jack and Grainne emerged from the church, Father Malcolm Henning came around the corner of the building, wearing a black overcoat now, and began greeting people. He knew everyone by name.

"We'd best wait and say hello," Grainne whispered. "It wouldn't be polite just to go off without saying a word."

"Okay," Jack said. "Sinners in the hands of an angry God, and all that."

"Don't be disrespectful. And by the way, it's very irreligious of you to be timing the priest at the pulpit."

"I didn't think you saw me."

"I did," she said, and shook her head in mock irritation.

While they waited for the priest, Mrs. Mullen bobbed her head at them from where she stood talking with some other women, and they both smiled and nodded at her in return.

Father Henning was gradually moving toward them. When at last he turned to face them, he came forward with his hand extended to Jack.

"It's good to see you," he said. "And Miss Clarkin," he added warmly, looking at her. "I hope we'll be seeing more of you from now on."

Jack felt Grainne's hand digging at his back. "Thank you, Father," he said. "You will."

"Well, that's good," said the priest. "And I'm sure it'll all work out fine for you with Peggy Mullen. She'll take good care of you, she will." He took hold of Jack's arm for a moment. "Come and see me," he said confidentially. "Anytime at all. I'd be glad of a visit."

He smiled at them both again and moved on to another little group.

Jack and Grainne moved away toward where they'd left her car, within sight of his own, a little distance down the road. Grainne got into hers and waited while he walked to the Escort. As Jack walked around it, making a long detour to avoid a monstrous puddle, he glanced back toward the church. Father Henning was standing near the doorway, deep in conversation with the eldest of the group of old men who had sat with him in the pub and who had sat this morning at the back of the church. Just at that moment, another old fellow with the look of a farmer about him joined the others. The six old men, in their dark clothes, stood like hunched black ravens against the light gray stone of the wall.

Jack thought for an instant that the priest and the tall old fellow glanced in his direction at the same time. He could almost have thought their eyes met. He got into the car and closed the door.

"Well, I'm off, then," Grainne said.

"I'm sorry to see you go."

"I'll come again."

"Next week."

"If I can."

"Will you try?"

"I will."

"Please try."

"I will. You get your work done."

"Yes."

They held each other for a minute and kissed, standing there in front of the house, with the motor of her car running and the door open, waiting for her.

"Drive carefully."

And she was gone. Jack watched the car as it went down the hill toward the water, diminishing in size, then disappeared around an outcropping of rock.

He stood for a while, with his hands shoved deep in his pockets, near the concrete steps to his door. It was almost as if she'd never been.

He hardly knew her.

And he hardly knew this place. He'd come here to be a part of it, at least for a while, to get to know it. But he was still the outsider, the mere observer.

And he was still that with Grainne too.

His hand felt oddly cold where she'd squeezed his fingers.

Contradictions everywhere, he thought.

He stepped up to the door, unlocked it, and pushed it open. Behind him, as if it floated on the damp wind from the ocean, came the same faint tune the old fellow had played in the pub and that had followed him across the hills the night before.

PART THREE

The battle is not as fearsome as the waiting for it, nor is the sword as terrible as the fire in the eye that guides it.

—Liam O'Flaherty,
The Black Soul

CHAPTER 10

But things looked better to him on Monday morning.

He'd spent the rest of Sunday, after Grainne's departure, reading a book he'd promised himself he'd read for almost a year. He told himself grimly that he was giving himself a treat, a *treat*, and he should be glad of it and take advantage of it. For the first hour, he had to force himself, remind himself constantly to concentrate, but then he got into it and it was better.

He'd thought, as soon as he was in the house with the door shut stoutly on that melody that came out of nowhere—nowhere but his head, he told himself firmly—that he'd call Grainne that night. Give her time to make the long drive back to Dublin, get into the house, have a cup of tea and something to eat, and then he'd call her.

But then the music got to him. He didn't hear it any more from outside, but it was fixed clearly in his head now, almost as natural and normal as the rhythm of his own breathing. On and on it went, lamenting lost loves and early deaths and painful partings, as if it spoke a language he'd never heard before but that now came to him with perfect clarity, rich in concrete meanings and subtle connotation. And he decided to deal with it himself.

He'd deal with it himself—whether he made sense of it somehow or just managed to banish it from his thoughts—and not lay the weight of it on Grainne. He'd made the weekend difficult enough, a weekend that should have been wonderful for them both, and he wouldn't start that same shit on the phone. He wouldn't do it. He would not.

He read the book. At some time in the evening, he went out to the kitchen to get something to eat, and found that, when he wasn't watching, Grainne had laid in a supply of eggs and cheese and some other things that were easy to whip up into a meal. Until then, he'd been a little worried, beneath the surface of his thoughts, that she had no intention of coming back, that she'd probably be out every time he called from now on, that she was put off by the strange way he'd been acting and he'd never see her again. The food in the refrigerator changed that. He relaxed, ate a meal, felt better, finished the book, and went to bed early.

He slept for nine and a half hours and in the morning, Monday morning, viewed the whole world differently. The sun was shining brightly, the air looked crisp and fresh, and he was going to call Grainne in the evening to see if she'd checked with her friend about next weekend. A scene in the book that had been troubling him for a month, just not taking shape in his mind, suddenly jumped into place, out of nowhere, while he was shaving. If he worked all morning, he could have lunch at McGlynn's, maybe, or the Seafoam, and spend the afternoon exploring. He'd hardly seen anything of the area since he'd gotten here, and that was one of the things he'd come for. It was high time he started doing it. Maybe he'd even call on Father Henning around teatime, just for a chat. Yes, maybe he would. And Mrs. Mullen was due today —thank you very much, Father—so he wouldn't have to give any more thought, for the most part, to cooking and shopping and cleaning and laundry. Work, work, work, a three-month tax-deductible vacation, and a beautiful girl coming to visit again in just a few days. Okay. Yessir, okay.

Mrs. Mullen arrived at a quarter to ten.

She came in carrying a net bag filled with packages of cleaning items, soaps and sponges and various specialized cleaners, all with names he didn't recognize and functions he didn't understand, and an itemized receipt for her purchases.

She'd only gone ahead and bought them, she said, so as to save them both the time. Jack agreed that it was an excellent idea and immediately paid her what he owed her for the things. He gave her a quick tour of the house by way of orientation. He could tell from the look on her face that she was marveling at the number of books he'd brought—it occurred to Jack that he should make up a list of more titles and ask Grainne to bring them on Friday if she could—and she regarded the computer with a combination of respect and silent suspicion. She inspected the kitchen by herself, obviously relieved to be in her own domain again, took inventory of the refrigerator and the cabinets, and enquired about his eating habits and preferences.

"Just put a meal in front of me in the evening, and I'll be perfectly happy," he told her. "And I'll be out in the middle of the day today."

"Seven o'clock, then, for your supper," she said firmly, and set to work on the dishes he'd left in the sink.

Jack left her up to her elbows in suds and went into the office to work.

The scene in the book that had been troubling him and that had only made sense that morning was out of sequence with what he'd been working on, but he opened up a new data document and went ahead and wrote it anyway. Later he could just fit it into the book in its proper place.

Two hours later, he'd written the equivalent of eight manuscript pages—his fastest pace at the best of times, he knew from past experience—and he was feeling just terrific. He decided to use the time he felt he'd gained by writing a few letters, one to his agent in New York to assure her that he was working every day and that the book was going well, one to his British agent in London, saying that he might be able to get over for a few days, a brief note to his accountant who was handling his bills and such in his absence, and a couple of personal letters to friends.

As he was finishing the last of the letters, he heard Mrs. Mullen in the living room, talking to someone. His first instinct was to go out and see what the problem was. Then he reminded himself that Mrs. Mullen could no doubt take care of whatever it was —probably some friend of hers who'd dropped by just to gawk at the house and at him as well—and he went back to finishing the letter. When he was done, he set the computer to print two copies of each letter, and strolled out to the living room.

Mrs. Mullen was in the bedroom, changing the sheets on the bed.

"Who was that at the door?" he said.

"The post," Mrs. Mullen replied as she tucked the covers beneath the mattress so tightly that he wondered if he'd be able to get into the bed that night.

"The post! There was mail?"

"There was," she said without looking up. "I gather from Mr. Hegarty, he's the one that brought it, it's the first you've had."

"Yes, it is," he said. "Where'd you put it?"

"Well, I didn't want to be disturbing you at your work, so I just put it on the table in the kitchen. Was that all right? There was a couple of big parcels too."

"Yes, fine. But you can bring it into me from now on."

He hurried off to the kitchen. He knew from all of his friends who were writers that they all felt the same way he did: the daily arrival of the mail was often the big event of the day. Besides the mundane things like bills, the mail brought checks, books for review, manuscripts from publishers seeking praise-filled quotes for their covers, new books by friends whose work he admired, copies of the newspapers containing the reviews he wrote, magazines with his own short stories, and letters bearing news and gossip.

The pile on the kitchen table was a little battered from its transatlantic journey, but it was impressive. There were two packages that obviously contained manuscripts—some publicity departments were ingenious at tracking him down—four letters from friends to whom he'd given his Irish address, a book to review for the *Washington Post*, and a big envelope from his agent that he suspected contained more letters and, with a little luck, a contract on a film option that needed his signature.

He opened the package from his agent first. The contract was there, along with her usual hastily scrawled note saying that she hoped he was having a good time and *working hard* and not getting notions of becoming a recluse and writing nothing but (uncommercial) sensitive poetry.

He slapped the contract on his left hand and grinned.

"Are you sure I can't fix you something?" Mrs. Mullen asked from the doorway behind him.

Jack jumped at the sound of her voice. "Oh! Yes, well, a cup of tea would be great. Thanks."

He sat at the table and began opening the mail.

It was terrific. It was just terrific. There were letters to be answered, a couple of decisions to be made, a contract to be signed and returned at once, manuscripts to be read, a book to be read and reviewed. There was even a letter with Irish stamps on it containing an invitation to address a literary society in Galway. That was probably the doing of his British agent, but the letter had inexplicably gone to New York, and his agent had scribbled on the top of it, "That's what you get for being famous. Have fun!"

Everything was normal. Everything was fine. The rhythm of his life had been changed, interrupted for a couple of weeks by the trip, the dislocation, even by the excitement of meeting Grainne. But now he was busy again, feeling the pressure of work he enjoyed and the comfortable squeeze of deadlines, no longer cut off from all the rest of his life.

"Mrs. Mullen," he said happily, "you've brought me luck!"

Peggy Mullen was making potato salad and didn't look up from what she was doing.

"I'll have chicken for your supper," she said. "And I'll see can I get some soup out of the bones."

As soon as he pulled the letters from the printer, he realized that he'd forgotten to buy envelopes. With the letters and the signed contract in his hand, he asked Mrs. Mullen which of the shops in Doolin would have them.

"Fanning's," she said at once. "They keep all that sort of thing. You can buy stamps there as well." The implication was clear that there wasn't much call in Doolin for "all that sort of thing."

As he went out the door, he impulsively stopped, then went back and took the book he had to review from the kitchen table. The weather looked bright and clear, at least at the moment, and not too cold, and he was planning to take a long drive this afternoon. Maybe he'd find a pretty spot to sit and read for a while.

He got into the car and started the motor, then glanced down at the book beside him on the seat and, grinning, tapped his knuckles on the cover.

"You lucky fellow," he said, addressing the author of the book, "your chances of a good review have already gone up a couple of notches."

He was humming the Irish national anthem as he drove up the hill toward the village.

Fanning's did indeed sell "all that sort of thing." He bought what he needed, then wrote out and stamped envelopes for the letters and the contract.

McGlynn's, he thought, when he'd tossed the other things into the car. Lunch at McGlynn's today, then at the Seafoam tomorrow, and then I'll alternate after that. Spread my custom around a little, get to know the people. It didn't occur to him to include Nolan's in his plans.

He had sausages and mashed potatoes for lunch, with a pint of lager, and he thought he'd never eaten so well. While he ate, he pulled out a pocket notebook he'd bought at Fanning's—he always carried one at home—and jotted down a couple of things he needed to remember to do. At home, his desk was always littered with lists and reminders. Oh, and call the people in Galway about addressing the literary society.

Everything was fine.

He went sightseeing, feeling as excited as he ordinarily would on the first day of a normal vacation, with no research to do and no distractions of setting up housekeeping and an office in a foreign country. He felt suddenly liberated, almost high, and the car fairly flew over the roads.

His eyes drank in all the sights, all the rich profusion of details that mark a place, a land, as being different from what we know: the color of the sky, the shape of the clouds, the contours of the earth. And more than that: the narrow twisting road, lined on either side with unmortared walls of stone, the muddy sheep that speckled the hillsides, the occasional abandoned hut, its stone walls crumbling, a tangle of ancient thatch still clinging to the gable at one end. Even the perspective of driving on the left side of the road, which he'd gotten used to after only a couple of hours on the road from Dublin to Clare, seemed to give him a fresh, new angle of vision on everything.

On a distant hillside he spotted a ruined church or abbey with daylight showing through its glassless windows and hollow interior. He made a mental note to put it on his list of things to explore. He slowed his speed as the car neared a blind curve and then had to halt as twenty or thirty sheep, unimpressed by the vehicle, came ambling toward him. They were quite on their own, no farmer in sight, and Jack sat there grinning at them until they had strolled past the car and left the road clear again.

The road began climbing into the hills south of Doolin and, at one point, he was presented with a stunning view of the majestic Cliffs of Moher, their sheer rock faces staring impassively at the gray-blue Atlantic, while the ocean heaved and boiled against the rocks at their base.

He pulled the car off at the edge of the road and took in the view for a few minutes, breathing the clear air and feeling the wind toss his hair. That did it. The Cliffs of Moher would be the feature attraction for today. At the next junction in the road, a weathered little sign pointed the way and he turned the car in that direction.

He spent an hour and a half there, climbed the path to the top of the hill, stared at the tower on the crest that Yeats and Lady Gregory had loved, admired the view of the cliffs, and resisted the temptation to buy souvenirs at the tourist shop adjoining the now empty bus parking area. A good place to stay away from in tourist season, he thought, but wonderful now with only a few people besides himself and the hills and the cliffs and the wind.

The fact that he was not here as a tourist but as a resident —three months was a long time, after all—made him feel even better, and he was humming again as he drove out of the parking lot and turned left toward Doolin.

"Well, how do you like it?" said Father Malcolm Henning when the two of them were comfortably settled in his sitting room. Deirdre Corcoran had gone off to fix the tea.

"I like it just fine, Father," Jack said.

"You're all settled in, then, I take it?"

"Oh, yes. And the book is going fine. I got off to a slow start, but it's going just fine now."

"You certainly sound happy about it. Is Doolin everything you wanted for your research?"

For an instant, it occurred to Jack that the otherwise innocent question carried a double weight of meaning. And although there was nothing specific to remind him, Jack suddenly found himself thinking of the strange story the priest had told in the pub on Saturday night.

"Oh, it is," he said. "In fact, in some ways, it's almost more so." He kept the pleasant look on his face but waited to see how the priest would respond. He didn't want the conversation to become the same mild-mannered sort of contest the first one had been—he was feeling too good, too friendly, for that—but he did want to ask about the tale.

"How's that?" asked the priest.

Jack almost shook his head in wonder at the old fellow's conversational expertise. Ask everything, say nothing, that was his technique. Well, okay then, Jack had a few gambits of his own, not as subtle perhaps, but just as effective.

"Well, for one thing," he said casually, "I was very interested in that story you told the other night in the pub. It didn't strike me as a very Christian sort of tale, especially for a priest to be telling."

"In what way did it seem unchristian?"

Jack had to grin openly at that.

"Talking heads?" he said.

That simple response must have done the trick, because the priest's face crumpled into a thousand wrinkles as he returned Jack's grin.

"It is quite a tale, isn't it?" he said. "But, sure, that's the way I heard it told to me, and I was only passing it along. You know, don't you, that the tales must be passed on just exactly the way they come to you."

Now Jack had an opening of his own, one the priest had unwittingly given him—that, combined with Grainne's prompting the other day.

"Are you the seanachie here?"

The priest's eyes were fixed on him and he was still smiling, but he said nothing for so long that Jack was beginning to feel the need of filling the silence with words. But he held out and, at last, Father Henning spoke. When he did so, the tone of his voice was changed, more serious, and again carried what appeared to be a double burden of meaning.

"I am," he said, and the hard, clipped way he said it made it almost into a challenge. He stared at Jack. He hadn't moved, hadn't changed the expression in his face or his eyes, but everything about the sound of his voice speaking those two monosyllables made it clear that he'd offer nothing more.

Jack watched him for a minute, but finally, against his will, he had to drop his gaze.

"Listen, Father . . ." he began, trying to recapture the easiness of the first few minutes of their talk.

Father Henning said nothing.

"All I—"

But just then Deirdre Corcoran came in with the tea.

People are always coming in with tea in this damned country, Jack thought, no wonder they're so slow with everything, tea always comes first, but he instantly pushed back his irritation. When in Ireland, do as the Irish do, he told himself. I am not going to let this old man, priest though he may be, spoil my day. He can help me out with the book by telling me stories and providing local color and local history, or he can tell me nothing, in which case I'll simply make it all up if I have to. If Doolin, in the person of Father Malcolm Henning, wants to close itself off from me, then so be it. But he's not going to play his little games with me. I won't have every conversation turned into a contest. But why in the goddamn hell won't the old codger talk to me?

"You'll be putting on weight with Peggy's cooking, I can tell you that," Deirdre Corcoran said to him as she straightened up from the tray.

"Yes," Jack said a little too quickly. "Yes, I suppose I will. I'm looking forward to it. I'm not much of a cook myself."

"Didn't your ladyfriend put a meal on the table for you?" she asked, still pretending to be fussing with the tea things.

Father Henning shot her a glance. Jack caught it and thought he saw that hint of amusement return to the priest's face.

"Yes, she did, but she'll only be here on weekends, whenever she can manage."

"You're engaged to be married, are you?" said Deirdre.

Frontal attack, Jack thought. And a solid wedge driven into his line. Time to fight back with a frontal attack of his own.

"No," he said casually, leaning forward to take a cream biscuit from the plate on the tray. "No, we're not. Just good friends, that's all."

"Oh, I see," Deirdre said from the doorway.

"Deirdre, I do believe I smell something burning in the kitchen," the priest said mildly.

Deirdre retreated, and Jack imagined her quizzing Peggy Mullen closely later that evening. The whole world, at least the world of Doolin, would know what color his underwear was by the time the sun went down.

"You have a very direct sort of way of speaking, Jack," the priest said when they were alone, and Jack knew instantly that, in some odd way, maybe because of his boldness, the priest had moved a little closer. And he'd called him by his name, for the first time, Jack thought. Given the way this not-so-budding acquaintance was going so far, that could mark a new plateau.

"So does everybody around here, it seems."

"Not everybody," the priest replied. "As you'll learn when you've been here a bit. Are you still planning to stay three months?"

"I am." Don't sound too Irish, Jack told himself at once. That mimetic tendency could make them think you're making fun of them. And that thought raised another: these people deliberately seemed to cut him off, forcing him to regard them as if they were some sort of primitive savages, guarding their secret rites and customs from the intruding, prying eyes of a stranger.

"You'll be seeing a great deal, then, as the time goes by," said Father Henning. And then, as it had before, his manner suddenly changed. "I was so happy to see you at the church yesterday. I hope you'll be coming regularly from now on. Now I won't be lecturing you and trying to tell a grown man what's what, but it would be a good thing for you and I think you'd feel better for it." As he spoke, the words rolling so easily off his tongue, he was indistinguishable, Jack thought, from all the hearty Irish priests he'd known in his childhood and youth.

But, still, there was something different here, something distant.

"I expect I'll be there, Father," he said.

They sipped at their tea.

"So you're the seanachie," Jack said, and watched for a reaction.

The priest set his cup down carefully. From seeing them in action, Jack was beginning to realize that the Irish used the tea-cup or the pint glass of Guinness the way George Burns used his cigar, for punctuation and pacing and making the most of a point.

"I am, in a way," Father Henning said, but now he was staring at his teacup and not watching Jack's face at all, not measuring anything, as he'd done before. "In the old days, you know, the seanachie was treated almost like one of the lower gods, so important was his function of preserving history. But you must remember too that among an illiterate people he preserved more than the tales of kings and battles. In remote areas, it was he who preserved the history, say, of a village. He was the records office, as you might say, and often he was the only one who recalled the exact boundary of a bit of land, or whose cousin, twice or thrice removed, had married so and so."

The priest paused, but he was looking for no response, Jack knew, just thinking ahead to the next part of what he was going to say. "In the old days," he had begun. To an Irishman, that phrase didn't mean what it meant to an American. When an Irishman says "the old days," he might mean his own youth, or a time a hundred years gone by, or a thousand.

"The seanachie today is more of an entertainer than anything else, just another one getting up at a ceili and doing his turn between the dancing. But, still, you know, it can be more than that too. Every priest is a kind of seanachie, isn't he? Keeping alive a way of life. Preserving a body of teaching in such a way that it makes sense to ordinary people. Upholding long tradition."

"Do the secular and the clerical often come together in the role?" Jack asked.

The priest was silent a long time before he answered.

"Yes," he said. "Sometimes they do."

"Where does your tale in the pub fit in? Is that secular or cleri-cal? Or both?"

"Maybe a little of both," the priest said. Finally he looked up. "Now, Jack," he said, and reached across the low table and took hold of Jack's arm, "you've got me going on here like some senile old fellow whose mind is half lost in the bogs." He sat back and poured hot tea into his cup. "Let's talk about more pleasant things. It's not often I get to talk to someone with your education, you know. Tell me all about the books you've written."

Half an hour later, Jack left, promising to bring over copies of his books for the priest to read. But he still couldn't make up his mind if he liked the old man or not.

"It was great," Jack told Grainne that evening on the phone. "She made chicken and potato salad and peas, just the way my grandmother did when I was a kid. She'll work out fine. And I feel almost like a stranger in my own house, she has everything so shiny clean. . . .

"I did. I went to the Cliffs of Moher. They're fantastic. Not quite as good to look at as you, but they're beautiful. You've never been there? No, I don't mind going back. Of course. . . .

"Eight pages. Eight *terrific* pages of my patented deathless prose. My agent's going to love me even more than she does already. Oh, and I got a bundle of mail today. Books, manuscripts, letters. I feel like I'm back to normal. Oh, and a speaking engagement in Galway, if I want it. I don't know. I was going to call them this afternoon, but I forgot. . . .

"Which reminds me. I visited Father Henning today, the village witch doctor. Oh, come on, if it's so disrespectful, why are you laughing so hard? I went for tea. Well, it wasn't as lively as the Mad Hatter's tea party, but it was interesting. He's a sly old fellow, that Father Henning. He's got his secrets, I'll bet, and I'd love to know what they are. Yes, I know it's my turn. I'll ask him over next week. If I can fit him into my busy social calendar. . . .

"And I miss you, did I mention that? I do. Yes, really. Can you come on Friday? Well, let me know as soon as you do. Yes, very much. Good. I'm glad to hear that, Grainne. Okay, well, I'll call on Wednesday, then. Remember I miss you."

He stood in the open doorway, as he had several times before in his stay, but this time it was to taste the fresh, clean air on this surprisingly mild night. Overhead, the sky was deep and black, with pinpoint stars that twinkled. In the distance ahead of him, down the hill, he could hear the steady, dull roar of the Atlantic, waxing and waning like a gigantic, neverending heartbeat.

He lit a cigarette and smoked it slowly, leaning against the doorjamb. Behind him in the living room, RTE, the Irish radio station, was playing a Crystal Gayle record. Her voice floated out past him into the stillness of the night.

No visions here. No spirits. No men dying of starvation in the road. No women holding out the bodies of their—

He would not think about that. He'd had a brief bad spell, yes, that was true, but he could account for it. The dislocation, the strangeness of the place, the book weighing on his mind and some of the stark scenes he'd read about in his research on the Famine, the coming to Ireland at last, after all these years. All that, combined with a rampant, and frequently lurid, imagination.

He blew out a long stream of cigarette smoke and watched it dissipate in the clear night air.

It was fine. Everything was fine.

The Crystal Gayle record ended and one by Shelley West and David Frizzell began, "You're the Reason God Made Oklahoma."

Listening to it, he smiled happily. He hadn't come such a great distance, after all.

Singing the lyrics along with the record, he closed the door on the night and went inside.

CHAPTER 11

On Tuesday, he started the book all over again. He'd thought at first he could work directly on what he'd done so far, just getting the pages up on the computer screen and revising them as he went along. After two pages, he decided it was too confusing that way. He took a fresh disk and started all over again. He had a whole new way of beginning the book in mind now, and the words just flowed from his fingers into the keyboard and appeared in front of him on the screen as if they were coming in from someplace else, someplace beyond him. This was better, this was the right way. The characters in the story were alive now, talking, working, doing things, as they had not been before. He revised the setting he'd had in mind, making it even more like Doolin and the sur-rounding area, adding details, and everything fell into place as if this were the one and only way to write the book. He finished seven pages in the morning—not bad, since he'd been starting all over again, with a whole new approach—while Peggy Mullen did whatever it was she did in the rest of the house.

He had lunch at the Seafoam, although Mrs. Mullen—she promised meatloaf for the evening, and fresh bread—had urged him to eat a sandwich of the leftover chicken. In the Seafoam, he got talking with two lorry drivers who were making deliveries in Doolin and the nearby area. They each bought a round of pints of lager, and by the time they left, Jack thought it best to walk off some of the beer before driving on these Irish roads . . . and, besides, it would give Andy and Tom a chance to be far away with their lorries and their quart-and-a-half of beer apiece.

He ended up spending the afternoon poking through Doolin's few shops, buying a couple of odds and ends, just to give himself a chance to look around more than he had and possibly meet a few people. He found that, with his own changed and more open attitude, he did meet some of the people. He chatted with the shopkeepers, quickly realizing that they already knew a few things about him and were only too eager, in their quiet way, to learn more. Before he realized it, the afternoon was drawing on toward evening. He stopped at McGlynn's—only a half-pint this time—before heading home to Mrs. Mullen's meatloaf and the book he had to read.

His days fell into that easy pattern and, to his pleasure, he found he was feeling better, eating better, sleeping better, a walking advertisement, he thought with satisfaction, for the health-giving properties of living in Ireland. The regular routine was fine for his work and the pages accumulated easily each morning. Mrs. Mullen willingly kept him supplied with tea while he was in his office, and she put a hot meal on the table every evening, just minutes before Deirdre Corcoran arrived outside in her car to take her home, herself having just put a meal in front of the priest. Jack felt an odd sort of kinship with the priest through that.

He was usually out and around in the afternoons, getting fresh air and exercise. And in the evenings, he did his reading and made notes on his work for the next day. By the end of that week, he'd sent off the book review to the *Washington Post*. The day before, another book review assignment had arrived from the *Cleveland Plain Dealer*. He called the literary society in Galway. In typical Irish fashion, they were not yet certain of the exact date of their next meeting, let alone the one after that, but they were delighted to hear from him and were very excited to know he'd be addressing them. As soon as their schedule was set, they'd call, now that they knew where to reach him.

Everything was normal. Everything was better than normal, and he was feeling just fine.

The only dark spot in his life was that Grainne couldn't come for the weekend.

Her friend Mary couldn't fill in for her, and her parents were still in Liverpool, so Grainne was stuck keeping the shop open herself. Jack immediately said he'd come to Dublin for the weekend, but Grainne firmly said no to that. She'd be much happier if he just went on with his work and got as much done as possible, because she knew he'd fall behind in it while she was there. But her parents would be back soon, probably in a week, and maybe then she could come for more than two days. And were there any books he wanted her to look for while she could?

The days went by. Mrs. Mullen wasn't to come on Saturdays or Sundays—that was the arrangement—but she saw to it that the refrigerator was well stocked with food that was easy to heat up.

On the weekend, Jack decided to skip the pubs on Friday night in favor of reading the new book he had to review. On Saturday evening, he opted for McGlynn's and found, to his pleasure, several young musicians who played a good number of tunes he recognized. Even when the words were in Irish, he at least knew the English sense of them and the melody.

On Sunday morning, he went to Mass, waited to shake hands with Father Henning afterward, and invited the priest to tea on Wednesday. Father Henning said he'd be there. Jack was pleased to find that there were now quite a number of people in the crowd outside the church to whom he could nod or speak a greeting and who greeted him in return. He did see that same ominous-looking little group of four oldtimers, but they didn't seem to notice him and, besides, who cared anyway?

The pages piled up, slowly, steadily, pleasantly.

The house and the kitchen, under Mrs. Mullen's silent control, ran without his giving them a thought. There was a hot meal on the table every evening and Jack thought he might be putting on a pound or two.

Another couple of letters arrived and he was now answering each one the day it came.

He talked to Grainne on the phone at least every other evening, and began counting the days till she'd arrive.

He knew people in the village now and always had a remark to make, as they did, about the weather.

The weather was, day by day, moving closer to winter in this northern latitude. Over a couple of weeks, he noted that dawn was arriving later all the time, and that evening darkness came earlier. The mornings were uniformly gray, and a heavy cloud cover, thick and rolling and massive, pressed down on the land. There might be a couple of hours in the afternoon—shorter all the time, it seemed—when the daylight was brighter, but for most of the day the air itself seemed the stonegray color of rocks. It rained for a couple of hours at least, each and every day, and the gray air had a nasty, biting, icy feel.

Father Henning came for tea on Wednesday.

He arrived at the door with Deirdre Corcoran standing at the bottom of the steps just behind him. She had driven him over and, if Mr. Quinlan had no objection, she'd take tea with Mrs. Mullen in the kitchen and then drive the priest home after.

Peggy Mullen had outdone herself in preparing the tea. It was a full, old-fashioned tea, with hard-boiled eggs, cheese, and a variety of light sandwiches, fresh-baked scones, almost a meal itself. Deirdre lent a hand in the kitchen and with the serving.

When the two men were finally alone in the living room, Jack quietly ventured the opinion that Mrs. Mullen seemed to be enjoying her work. Father Henning wiped his mouth delicately with a napkin, and when he took it away, his lips were turned up in a smile.

"Oh, I'd say so, yes," he said. "Well, it's no surprise, is it? You can bet safe money that they'll be telling all the details of this tea, the two of them, for weeks to come."

"This?" Jack said, indicating the food.

"Not so much the food as the occasion," Father Henning said. "You and I, you know, make up the entirety of Doolin's gentry."

It struck Jack instantly that maybe that was the reason he'd felt like such an outsider with the people of the village. Americans weren't accustomed to thinking that way, so maybe that was why he'd missed it. Gentry, eh? Well, of course. Doolin had no professional people, no lawyers or doctors—you had to drive to another town for those services—so it was only natural that the local people would regard a stranger like himself as something special: a writer, who made his own hours, worked if and when the mood was on him, and had money in his pocket to boot. Of course the people of Doolin would look at him with a mixture of respect, curiosity, and suspicion.

"I suppose you're right," he said pleasantly. Then another thought struck him, the darkly shadowed memory of the visions —they *were* only visions, that was all they could be—that he'd seen in the road and on the side of the hill and that seemed almost to remind him of something else. And as he thought of them, the remembered melody of the tune from the pub, the wordless song that had followed him from the village all the way to his door, floated back into his mind, as clear and as haunting as it had been that night.

"I suppose you're right," he said again, more slowly this time. Father Henning, deeply involved with the fresh scones, looked up at him and nodded. "But, you know," Jack pressed on, his voice casual, "the Irish have a long history of, shall we say, resentment of the gentry. I wonder if my presence here has provoked any resentment."

Father Henning sipped his tea and helped himself to a fresh cup. Jack hadn't touched his yet. The priest sat back comfortably on the couch, one arm stretched along the back. He looked very composed and Jack noted the youthful way in which the elderly man moved and held himself, fully at ease with his body. "Have you felt any resentment?"

Another question, Jack thought. Doesn't this man ever give any answers?

"Yes, I have," he said, watching the priest's face. "I have, and

I thought maybe you could explain it. I'd like to be done with it, frankly, and I hoped that you could tell me what to do." Okay, priest, he added silently, go to it. Let's have a straight comment.

"How long will you be staying here?"

Jack had to smile. "Father," he said, "I've got to hand it to you. I really do. Do you realize that you never answer a question? Except to ask another one? Do you realize that?"

"Really?" the priest said. "Do I?"

They looked at each other for a minute, then both burst out laughing.

When the brief laughter subsided, Jack said, "What does the length of my stay have to do with it?"

Father Henning pursed his lips and looked thoughtful. Jack thought he looked much more pleasant when he was smiling. Now, with deep creases across his forehead and dark lines around his mouth and eyes, he looked somehow sinister, like a man who carried a secret that he wanted to, but could not, reveal.

When he answered at last, he spoke slowly, carefully. It struck Jack that the priest was weighing every word, attempting to convey to him some unspoken message that was infinitely more important than the actual words he was speaking.

"Jack," he said, "you've come here as an observer, you might say. And no one likes to be looked at as an object of curiosity, least of all the . . . relatively unsophisticated people you find in a place like Doolin. These are decent people, Jack, living by their lights as best they can, keeping body and soul together and asking little more. It's a hard life. For many of them, it's no easier a life than they might have had a hundred years ago, or three hundred, or even more. They're good people, mind, I'm not saying otherwise, but they have a strong preference"—the priest lowered his head and looked at Jack over the tops of his glasses—"for being left alone."

Jack exhaled slowly, never taking his eyes from the other man's face. What the priest had said was clear enough, and made sense, in a way. But the things he had *not* said, Jack thought, seemed even clearer.

"Am I in some danger?" he asked, his voice dry, almost casual.

"What makes you ask that?"

"Father, listen," Jack said, finally letting the impatience show, "I asked you here for a pleasant afternoon, a nice little visit, and not to grill you with questions. It wasn't my intention to get into a debate with you or to play rhetorical games. That was a serious question. A *very* serious question, in fact. Am I in danger?"

"Has anything happened that makes you feel threatened?"

"Oh, for God's sake, cut the questions, okay?" Jack's impatience now boiled over, its tide swelled by the memories that he had, for a while, pushed out of his mind but that now were back in all their deathly, bloody clarity. In his thoughts, the mouth of the dead man in the road yawned open and a worm crawled over the chipped and broken teeth. The woman on the hillside, shrouded in fog, her lips and chin slimy red with blood, stretched out her thin arms and offered up the sacrificial body of her dead infant child. The child's head dropped back, loose and lifeless as the twisted neck of a chicken. Blood dripped steadily, almost ran, from the torn and shredded flesh of the child's feet. A corpse with his own face walked toward him, reaching for his arm. And blending with the pictures, floating out of the fog of memory like the ghostly soundtrack of a movie, was the yearning, sobbing music of the pipes.

The priest was still watching him. The lines were still cut deeply into the dry skin of his face. He took his arm from the back of the sofa and joined his fingers together as closely as arthritis would permit. The joints stood out in hard bony knots.

"Okay?" Jack's sudden wave of anger grew bitter with the fright that had lurked quietly at the back of his mind, and in the face of the old man's seeming calm. "Okay? You're supposed to . . ." Jack cut himself off sharply as he realized he'd raised his voice. "You're supposed to help people," he said more quietly, trying to filter some of the accusatory tone from his words. "You're supposed to answer questions, not respond with only more questions. I asked you something very serious. Do you have an answer?"

"I am answering your question," Father Henning said very softly, his voice little more than a whisper of wind over gravel. "Has anything happened that makes you feel threatened?"

Jack stared at the man. He could do one of several things. He could throw him out, and to hell with the consequences. He could tell him what he thought of all this bullshit, this game-playing. He could try to get the priest's friendship and confidence. Jesus, he could ask the priest to hear his confession, make up something, and get to him that way. He could tell a carefully constructed version of the truth, another one of his many fictions, and goad the priest into commenting on it. They went on staring at each other, each man searching the other's face for a clue to the thoughts behind it.

"Yes," Jack said at last.

The silence hung between them. In the kitchen the women were talking. There were no distinct words but the rhythm of their voices reached Jack's ears. He heard a teacup rattle faintly against a saucer.

"Do you want to tell me?"

"I don't think so."

They were almost whispering, neither of them moving, neither releasing the other's gaze.

"If you don't tell me, I can't answer your question."

Jack was silent.

"I'm trying to help. Please believe me." Father Henning's voice sounded more gentle, but Jack suddenly thought that the change came in spite of the priest's effort to remain impassive. And that awareness instantly confirmed in his mind that the priest did indeed have a secret, something that worried him, worried him about *Jack*, worried him as if he were now merely getting confirmation of what he'd suspected all along: somehow he'd known that Jack had been seeing . . . visions.

"You know, don't you?" Jack said.

"I only know what you tell me."

Jack took one long slow breath. "What if I told you about . . . a woman and a child? An infant. What if I told you about that?"

"Go on."

"No."

"But there are others?"

"What if I told you about that?"

Father Henning was the first to drop his gaze. "You'd do better to leave here, you know," he said.

"I will not. What's going on?"

The priest shook his head slightly. "Nothing new," he said.

"But you know," Jack said. "You know about the woman and the child. You've heard that before."

The priest raised his head to meet Jack's gaze, and his eyes were wet with a terrible sadness.

"You've heard that before," Jack said again, but this time there was a puzzled wonder in his voice. And suddenly, for the first time, he and the priest were on the same side, no longer—at least for the moment—opponents. "Father, what is going on here?"

"You've seen other things as well?"

"Yes."

"Will you tell me?"

Jack thought a moment. "No. Not until you've told me something. You have heard that before, haven't you, about the woman and child? Haven't you?"

"I have."

Jack sighed, longing to ease the tension a bit. "Well, if I'm not the only one, then maybe I'm not crazy after all. Or at least I have plenty of company."

"Did your young lady see anything?" the priest asked suddenly.

"No," Jack said. "Not that I know of."

Jack's heart pounded faster when he saw a look that he thought was relief on the priest's lined face.

Father Henning straightened up and made an effort to sit back on the sofa as casually as he'd been sitting before.

"We'll not talk further about it now," he said, and his voice was stronger, resonant with his more normal firmness. He held up one hand as Jack began a protest. "We'll not. This is neither the time nor the place. But we will talk again about it."

"All right. When?"

"When the time is right," said the priest. And before Jack could reply, Father Henning turned in the direction of the kitchen and called out, "Peggy! Deirdre! Is it cold tea you'd have us be drinking?"

Almost instantly, the two women appeared in the doorway, filled with apologies from Mrs. Mullen and mutterings from Deirdre Corcoran.

"And maybe just one or two more of your lovely scones," the priest added, his smile beaming over both the women. "And, Jack," he said, turning and winking at him, "it's a lucky man you are to be treated so well as this. Paddy Mullen, Lord have mercy on him, went to his grave praising Peggy's food."

"God rest his soul," Peggy Mullen murmured as she took away the tray and went to fetch more scones.

The rest of the visit, another hour or so, went more easily. In fact, Jack reflected when he was once again alone in the house, the rest of the afternoon was very pleasant indeed. The tense, heated exchange early in the conversation had at least—if it had done nothing else—broken down some barrier in the priest's mind, had overcome whatever it was that had made him keep his distance from Jack before. They talked casually, the priest telling anecdotes, laced with considerable wit, of his visits to America, and Jack talking of the schools he'd attended and some of the books he'd written, although he said nothing of the book he was working on now. Father Henning showed great interest in Jack's writing and turned out to be quite well read. "The nights are long here in the winter months," he said by way of explanation. Jack was reminded that he'd promised to give the priest some of his books, and he went to get them from the office.

Then the conversation had come to a natural end and Father Henning had called to Deirdre and told her they were leaving. Mrs. Mullen quickly straightened up in the kitchen, telling Jack she'd left something for him for later.

And then they were gone, with no opportunity for Jack to quietly arrange another meeting with the priest.

As he stood outside the house and watched the red lights of Deirdre Corcoran's car disappear through the darkness up the road, Jack felt both the satisfaction of a host whose guest has enjoyed his stay and the uneasiness that follows a confession that may have touched deaf ears.

It was the uneasiness that stayed with him for the rest of the evening, and instead of fading with the passing of the hours, it only grew worse.

He was restless, pacing around the house, making tea and

forgetting to drink it, opening books and staring at them without reading, changing stations on the radio and growing quickly impatient with the music.

He never should have said a word about all this nonsense to the priest. Not a word. It was all his imagination—mysterious, unaccountable, like the stories that welled up from his unconscious and poured out through his fingertips into the keyboard, rich with color and detail and dialogue, coming from God alone knew where. He'd been through all this before and that was it, his imagination, he was sure that was it, the source of everything he'd seen. How could he tell such things to an Irish country priest over afternoon tea and have the priest not think him mad?

But Father Henning had not thought him mad.

He as good as admitted he'd heard it all before. And heard more besides. They'd talk again, he'd said, although they'd obviously do it only when the priest was good and ready.

"Christ," Jack said softly, and tossed the book he'd been holding open onto the couch beside him.

He stalked into the kitchen, looking for something to eat. Mrs. Mullen had left cold chicken and potato salad but, as soon as he looked at it, the thought of eating suddenly turned his stomach. He went back to the living room and sat on the couch, elbows on knees, kneading his hands together, tapping one foot on the carpet.

Then he was up again, going around the room and switching off the lights. Hands shoved deep in his pockets, he stood at the windows, as he had so many times before, looking out at the pitch black night and straining for the sound of the sea. It came to him in dark, blurred waves of sound, distant but powerful, waves of sound crashing at the shore, audible only at the edge of his mind.

"Christ," he muttered again.

It was after three o'clock before he slept that night.

He felt better in the morning. Not good, he admitted to himself frankly, but better. He started work very early, wrote two pages, felt better still, drank the cup of tea that Mrs. Mullen brought him as soon as she arrived, read over the two pages, and decided they were shit. Okay, so he'd take a couple of days off from the book, clear this nonsense out of his thoughts, and go back to it with a fresher mind. He turned the machine off and walked out to the kitchen.

Mrs. Mullen was sitting sideways at the kitchen table, peeling carrots, the long orange strips of skin falling into a pan on her lap.

"Mrs. Mullen," Jack said, "who's keeping up your own house while you're here? You have two sons, don't you?"

"They look after themselves, they do," Peggy Mullen answered without looking up. "They're well able."

"And I'm not?"

"Oh, no," she said quickly, her hands poised over the pan. She glanced up at him and instantly away.

"I hope they don't resent me," Jack said.

"Oh, no." Her hands were unmoving in her lap.

"I mean, here I am, eating your good cooking and having my house cleaned and run so well for me, and the two of them doing without." Jack remembered her son the day he'd come to the house, a fellow about his own age, he guessed, but silent and dour, his bulky farmer's body ill at ease in a polite living room, resentful of all he didn't know.

"Oh, no," the woman said again, "not at all. They're as glad as I am of the extra bit of money coming in. And with himself lying yonder in his grave, God rest his soul, it takes my mind off of troubles, you might say. The two of them can look after themselves well enough for this bit of time."

"Three months is a long time," Jack said. There was something in the woman's voice—little more than nervousness, perhaps, but something, some secret or purpose she was keeping to herself, but she was unpracticed in lies and it showed through the fabric of her voice and words.

"Not such a long time in a life," Mrs. Mullen said stolidly. Her hands started in again on the carrots. "Will you eat the potato salad again or would you like a couple baked for your supper?"

There was nothing to be had there and he wasn't about to challenge an old woman. He dropped it. Now he was really imagining things. The poor woman was probably afraid he'd let her go and she'd lose out on the money. That explained her nervousness.

But an hour later, when he pulled on a parka to walk to the

village for an early lunch, he thought her eyes followed him out the door. Even as he walked up the road, chin buried deep in his collar against the cold wind, he thought her eyes followed him still.

Well, he'd talk to Father Henning again. He'd let a couple of days go by, take it easy, clear some of the nonsense out of his mind, then talk to the priest.

And Grainne would be coming to visit again, maybe for longer than before. That was a pretty thought and, in spite of the chilling wind, he managed a smile.

It was mid-October now, with the days growing short and crabbed, reluctant to yield any grudging light at all, and the air cold and bitter with damp. Now the Atlantic winds came in every day, like savage raiders making a flying foray for treasure, hunting here, striking there, searching everywhere they touched, finding nothing of value and rushing away, angered, with a promise, a threat, to return and strike again.

The ground had grown hard, the dirt tight-packed, the gravel frozen, and when the dark and bitter rains came, the water pooled in black or slate-gray puddles on its surface, reflecting only the lowering weight of steely clouds above. There was no yellow sun, no blue of sky, only gray pressing down from above and stonegray rocks below.

The shore seemed the edge of the earth. Beyond it and far past the limits of sight, there was only the green and seething sea, rolling and heaving beneath the winds, flecked with white foam like the writhing lips of a monster. Controlled by nothing, it hurled itself at land, resenting the barrier of stone and soil, enraged at the check to its thrust, howling outrage at impediments of rock. Waves crashed, foamed, billowed, split apart in fury, and flung their crushing weight at the stones of the shore. Nothing moved, and the ocean, like a furious undersea beast, backed off, swelled once again, and hurled itself anew. The crashing grew louder as the month of October advanced.

CHAPTER 12

But he did not see Father Henning after all.

On the Friday morning of that week, he awoke with the idea fully formed in his mind of going to Galway for the weekend.

Yes, absolutely, that was just the thing he needed. He rejected the notion that needing a vacation from his vacation was silly and self-indulgent and extravagant. He could do it and he would. Why not? There was nothing to stop him. And hadn't he come here to learn about Ireland and the Irish? And there was more to Ireland than Doolin. So what if he'd be going back to Galway another time to address the Literary Society? And that thought gave him another idea. He'd call the president of the society and see if he was free for dinner on Saturday night. God, he was tired of eating alone, walking alone, sleeping alone, *being* alone. He'd be talking to himself soon, let alone seeing things in the road and in the fog of the hills. Galway was just what he needed.

It took him less than half an hour to get ready.

He called Grainne at the shop in Dublin, told her he was going, and laughingly reassured her when she told him to be wary of those wily girls he'd no doubt be meeting in Galway. He called the president of the Galway Literary Society who was instantly delighted with the suggestion of dinner and offered to book a room for him at the Skeffington Arms Hotel in Eyre Square. Jack happily accepted. He told Mrs. Mullen to call Deirdre Corcoran to pick her up whenever she was ready. He packed a bag quickly, ate two eggs, three thickly buttered slabs of brown bread, and a bowl of lamb and barley soup that Mrs. Mullen quietly forced on him, and he was on his way.

His Geographia map indicated that it was only a little over fifty miles to Galway, but he knew from his one other long drive, from Dublin to Doolin, that no auto trip in the country was as easy as it looked on paper, with the roads twisting and turning in the paths made by cows and sheep that had wandered there a millennium ago, and many of the major routes, even those designated grandly as national highways, were little more than narrow two-lane country roads, a strip of concrete laid along the edge of a bog or a ribbon flung across a hill. Terrific. There was no rush and he was looking forward to it. He should have done this long before. The radio in the car played loud and strong and he sang along as he drove.

He headed north toward the village of Knockfin, skirting part of the limestone slopes of the Burren as they rushed downhill to the sea, then connected with a better road, heading east toward Lisdoonvarna. He turned north again, this time on the N67—the very fact that the road had a number was a joy, incontrovertible proof that he was heading once again for civilization—and drove the relatively easy eighteen miles, again crossing part of the inland Burren, through the towns of Toomaghera and Doonyvardan, and on to Ballyvaughan. East then again, along the southern shore of Galway Bay, to Kinvarra, then Kilcolgan, then north again to Oranmore and at last to the city of Galway. He took it easy, no need to rush, and the hills and the Burren and seashore and slate-gray sky drifted past pleasantly with the easy flow of time.

He loved the drive and when he got to Galway, he loved the small but pretty city even more.

His room was waiting for him at the hotel, along with a note from Brian Dunphy of the Literary Society, promising to meet him for dinner at six o'clock on Saturday. The shops were still open and he strolled around happily for a couple of hours. A big bookstore near Eyre Square had the British editions of two of his books. He found a cinema, decided to go, and still had time for a pleasant dinner. He bought a small pocket guide to the city, selected a promising restaurant from the "Upper Class" listing, enjoyed his meal and two drinks immensely, saw the movie, went back to his room at the hotel, read for twenty minutes, and fell asleep thinking of Grainne. He dreamt of making love to her and slept soundly through the night.

The whole weekend was a huge success. On Saturday, he drove out to Salthill and spent an hour strolling along the beach, enjoying the sand and the scent of the ocean. Here the salty air reminded him of the New Jersey shore in winter, something the damp winds and rocky coast of Doolin had not done.

He drove back to Galway in time to change out of jeans and into slacks and a jacket for dinner and his meeting with Brian Dunphy. When he was dressed, he just had time for a quick phone call to Grainne. He called from a telephone kiosk in the hotel lobby, but there was no answer.

Brian Dunphy turned out to be a teacher of high school level literature classes. He had, he quickly revealed, an unrequited passion for popular fiction and, so God was his witness, had actually read all of Jack's books as they'd been published. He even had all the American editions, and, sure enough, he'd brought them all along for Jack to sign. They got along famously, and before the dinner, in the Skeffington Arms dining room, was half over, Jack was already looking forward to his return visit.

While they drank coffee after the meal, Jack said he'd read about a pub called the King's Head in High Street that had music on the weekends. Dunphy asked if he was interested in the genuine article, traditional Irish music played on authentic instruments and songs sung in Irish. With yet another common interest strengthening the bond between them, they hurried off to Dunphy's car and drove at breakneck speed through Claddagh and Salthill again, then out on the twisting coastal road as far as the village of Spiddal. There, Dunphy took him to a pub called An Cruiscin Lan, in the heart of the Connemara Gaeltacht, an Irish-speaking area, and the only English he heard spoken or sung for the rest of the evening was their own.

By the end of the evening, he'd learned two dozen words in Irish, plus a few lines of one song, and he and Brian Dunphy were fast friends for life. He'd been planning to try Grainne again when he reached the hotel, but by then he was too tired and the lager was buzzing too loud in his head. He slept until eleven o'clock Sunday morning, but a sympathetic waiter in the dining room saw to it that he got his breakfast anyway.

If Brian Dunphy had been free on Sunday, Jack would have stayed another day, but Dunphy was tied up and Jack decided he should go back to Doolin and be ready to start work, refreshed and renewed, on Monday morning.

He left Galway at two o'clock, and as he retraced his route from Friday, it felt good to be driving roads that were already familiar. Somewhere between Kinvarra and Ballyvaughan, a weak sun even appeared for twenty minutes or so, as if to light his way back home.

In Ballyvaughan, he stopped to find a toilet in a pub, and when he came out he decided not to take the N67 south across the Burren, the way he'd come on Friday, but to stay on the L54, out to Black Head jutting into Galway Bay, then south, passing through coastal towns named Cregg, Murroogh, Fanore, Craggagh, and thence back to Doolin. It still wasn't too late, the route was only twenty miles or so longer, and if he kept moving, the daylight, thin as it was, would last him nearly all the way.

The coast road was narrow and twisting, clinging sometimes to the crumbling edges of cliffs, but it was almost empty and often provided a sweeping view of the coast and the darkening sea. Just south of Craggagh, as the road skirted the seaward edge of the Burren, he could see off to his left the dark peak of Slieve Elva brooding over the wild and untouched landscape.

Ten minutes later, as thick fog was rolling in from the sea to envelop the hills, the L54 turned inland and came to a junction with an unnumbered local road leading south to Doolin, a road Jack knew now even in the dark. He swung right at the junction, feeling secure in his knowledge of the road and his nearness to home, and a few minutes later he saw the pale young girl for the first time.

He saw her out of the corner of his eye, off to his left. In that first instant, he hardly reacted at all, so strange was the sight.

She could not have been more than eleven, and that was a generous estimate, allowing for the thinness of body and gauntness of face that made her look older than her years. She was wearing what might once have been a nightgown, but was now worn and thin and shredded in places, revealing a bony flash of arm or fleshless thigh. She was barefoot and, hardly more substantial than the fog that drifted across the road in the headlights, she was running along beside the car.

Her knees and elbows, pumping points of bone almost devoid of human flesh, arrowed, bent, folded, pumped and continued running, one long motion, neverending, running in the road. Her face was grim, unchanging, eyes fixed forward in her head, the only sign of the effort of running a flaring of nostrils that were almost transparent. Her eyes were dark, sunken beneath ridges of bone, in a face shadowed further and grimed with dirt. She ran and spoke never a sound, made never a cry. She stayed just to the left of the car, just behind the fuzzy cone of light cast back from the headlights, glowing almost as the cloud of mist and drizzle engulfed the car. The shadows of her body shifted, now here, now there, with the pumping of legs and arms, the coiling of the mist, the bouncing of the light on the rough surface of the road.

"Jesus Christ!" Jack cried when her pale image reached his conscious thought. He hit the brake and the rear end of the car slewed a bit on the road that was now slick with rain and dust. For an endless moment, he was horribly confused, disoriented, sitting on the wrong side of the car, driving on the wrong side of the road. One instinct told him to pull right, away from her, another warned him against going off the road, another told him there was room, another told him the child who ran there beside him simply could not be. He pressed down carefully on the brake, and held the trembling wheel with suddenly damp hands. The car, mastered again, rolled to a halt.

The child was gone.

He swung around in the seat, looked back into the misty dark behind him, but she was not there. He snapped his head around, looked ahead—she had run ahead as he'd stopped the car, she must have—but she was not there. There was only coiling, smoky fog, glowing gray-white in the lights at the front of the car, glowing red in the lights at the back.

"*Goddamnit!*" Jack roared at the night, and punched a fist down on the dashboard.

"Where the *hell are you?*" he yelled again, his voice husky with anger and fright. But the windows of the car were all closed and his voice boomed back at him in the tight space. The fog was condensing on the windows, sending rivulets of moisture running down the glass, blurring his view of the night.

"*Shit!*" he snarled. He slammed the side of his fist down on the console.

Seconds. It was still only seconds since he'd seen her and stopped.

He snatched at the door handle, shoved the door open, and flung himself out. Light spilled from the car to pool and glisten at his feet.

The cold touched him and he shivered, standing there in the middle of the road.

He heard the hum of the car, he heard his own breathing, and nothing more.

He shook his head. "Shit," he said sadly, barely whispered the word.

There was no other sound and nothing moved.

"Is there somebody there?" he called, not too loud.

The lights of the car illuminated only a short stretch of wet and silent road, gleaming with the rain on its surface.

"Who are you?" he asked of the silence.

The only reply was the beating of his heart as he noted the difference in his question, noted the shift in his own belief.

He stood there a while, his hand on the top of the car door for security, looking ahead down the ribbon of misty road and occasionally looking back the way he'd come. Only the fog was moving.

He got back into the car and turned on the heater. It blew hot air on his legs and into his face until he felt his body growing clammy beneath his clothes. He turned the heat off, rolled down the window beside him, stretched over and rolled down the other. The fog, like dry ice pumped onto a stage, reached smoky tendrils into the car.

Without knowing he was going to do it, he shivered again. He rolled his shoulders to drive it away and exhaled a long slow breath.

"Okay, okay," he said aloud, not knowing why.

He shifted the car and pressed down slowly on the gas pedal. The car began to move. He left the windows open, hoping the cold air would clear his brain and dry the sweat on his face and the back of his hands.

Nothing happened. He drove very slowly, waiting, watching, but nothing at all happened.

The road was like a ribbon laid across the land, following its every curve and bump and contour. No houses, no trees, no shadows, no light, only the road gradually revealed before him as the glow of his headlights touched it. Once he looked back quickly through the rearview mirror, but saw only the black of night, touched with red by the lights of the car.

He was alone. He reached over with his left hand—it was the only thing he found awkward about driving from the right side of the car—and switched on the radio. It roared with static for a few seconds, the sound wavered, then cried out suddenly with the yearning wail of the uilleann pipes, with the tune from the pub, the melody that had followed him across the hills—across the centuries, it seemed, as if it waited just for him—and filled the car with its sorrowful sound.

Gooseflesh crawled coldly across the back of Jack's neck and under his hair, across his shoulders, down his back and his sweaty arms. His shoulders writhed, trying to ward it off, but the goose-flesh only crawled again.

He slammed down on the brake. The car slid and lurched to a halt.

He stared at the radio. The sound of the pipes swelled and died and swelled again, as if with long-drawn sighs and sobs, reaching palpable hands of sound to touch his face and draw out tears.

He knew before he reached for it that he could not shut it off.

He pushed the button on the radio. The sound of the pipes went on, yearning, sighing, dying away and swelling again to cry once more.

His body pleaded with his mind, every muscle begging, to get out of the car, get away, get away.

He made himself stay where he was.

He trembled, a part of him wanted to cry in terror and hide his face, but he made himself stay where he was.

He pushed the button on the radio again. Pushed it again. Pushed it again. Pushed it again.

A voice deep in his mind, a perverse little voice that told him to thumb his nose at danger, to laugh in his fright, whispered now from far inside and told him to go with the music, to go it one better and join in the tune.

He sat in the car, hands clamped tight on the wheel, eyes staring at the mist drifting out of the night, and hummed, tried to hum, with the tune that rose and fell, rose and fell, calling to him still. He hummed, he was short of breath with the pounding of his heart, but he hummed, and after a little, when he'd slipped into the ancient metre of the music, he sang with it, sang out loud, no words, only sounds, meaningless sounds that were filled with the music and the keening for the dead.

Aware only as if the hands that did it were another's, he reached out and started the car again and continued, so very slowly, on the road.

After a while the car picked up speed and his voice, in its single-minded determination now to join with the song, the wordless song, and not be afraid, sang out the melody, filling the night, now loud, now tender and soft, now calling to the freshly dead and wishing them back, now longing for their touch.

And after another while, the child, the girl who was only bone with a covering of skin, who was only pointy cheekbones and dark-shadowed eyes, who was only running bony legs and pumping elbows, who stayed just at the edge of the moving lights from the car and looked at him not at all, reappeared and ran with him, stayed with him, ran there with him to the unseen rhythm of the tune of the sighing pipes.

She followed him on the road, on every curve and dip and rise of the road, through every swirl of fog and mist and spray of rain, down the last long slope of the hills into the village of Doolin, sleeping behind its stone walls and shadows darker than night itself on this wet and nasty evening, through the narrow main street of the village and out the other side, climbing again, and dipping into a narrow glen, then climbing, always with him, always running with him, staying always at the edge of the light, pale and white and shadowed.

Only once, as he topped the last rise before the slope ran down to his house, did she turn, never ceasing to run, and let him see her face. The music was fading and dying as he caught the movement, the shift in the shadows, and turned to look upon her. She was running still, but now her face was turned to him, turned so he could see her, and her mouth and chin were red with fresh-dripping blood.

She was there when he pulled the car in beside the house and brought it to a halt. She was standing still as he turned off the lights and the motor. She was moving again, coming toward him around the front of the car, as he opened the door and stood on the crunching wet gravel. She floated beside him, her pale and soundless face turned up, as he walked slowly toward the steps and the door. She stayed with him as he reached into a pocket and pulled out a key and stretched a hand toward the lock.

Then her hands touched him, hands cold and wet with the rain and the fog, hands that clung, that pulled at his sleeve, that brushed pointy nails across the backs of his hands, that reached and grasped at his face and the back of his neck. She floated before him, her face right there before him, her bloody lips open and drooling red slime, and she cried in the terrified voice of Grainne Clarkin, "Jack! Jack! Jack!"

CHAPTER 13

John MacMahon awoke, alone in the chill stony silence of his cottage, about an hour before the thin gray light of dawn touched the hills. The damp night air had penetrated the uneven spaces around the door and the single small window and laid a cold finger on everything inside. Even the soiled blankets that still covered him up to the chin were cold and clammy against his skin.

His hands were knotted into hard fists, clutching at the top blanket, when he came awake. As his eyes opened on the darkness, he was conscious only of the pain that chewed relentlessly at his insides. It was a beast gnawing his intestines, and it had grown fiercer and hungrier in the last few weeks. Sometimes it seemed to sleep for a while, a day, sometimes even several days at a time, but then it returned, after a while it always returned, its hunger greater than ever, its teeth sharper, its bite more piercing. It bit down and chewed and he came awake in an instant, eyes wide on the dark, face covered with sweat, body shivering in the chill.

He closed his eyes again. Lips trembling, he tried to form the words of a prayer.

"Holy God," he muttered, and his shivering, chattering words might have been the only sound in miles and miles of hills, "won't you help me now when most I need you? Dear God, please hold my hand. Only . . . Only for a while now. Only just a bit longer. Till your work is done and then I can sleep easy."

He had slept only a few hours through the night. His body, crying for rest and surcease, drew him back down into the depths of the dark and he dozed again for a while, hands still knotted in the blanket. Every now and again, his lips moved but he made no sound. Every now and again, his hands twitched, but the covers kept him no warmer. Every now and again, his eyes opened, blind in the dark, unseeing, then closed again and he slept.

Then a hand touched his face, fingers caressed the side of his face, scraped lightly on the white stubble of his jaw, touched gently at his sunken temple. He opened his eyes, searched all around him as he struggled to bring the darkness and streaky light into focus, and saw at last an angel hovering at the side of his bed. He turned his head a little on the pillow and looked the sad-eyed angel full in the face.

"Ah, you've come," he sighed, and let his eyes fall closed again. "You've come at last, have ye?"

He felt the fingers of the angel stroke his face once more and then sensed it drifting away. His eyes remained closed. He remembered the pain from before and waited for it to well up again inside him. It was still there, but only dull and distant. His clenched fists relaxed a bit on the blanket. After a moment, he thought he heard the splashing of water and wondered, in confusion, how it could be that the sound of the River Aille carried all the way to here.

"Here, John," said the angel, and he slowly opened his eyes. The angel's face floated above him. A hand slipped beneath the back of his neck and gently lifted his head from the damp pillow. A wet cloth wiped at his forehead and eyes and the stringy wattles of his neck.

"You've soiled yourself again in your sleep, John," the angel said.

He forced his eyes wide, forced them to focus on the angel. There was flickering light from a candle on the rickety table beside the bed. He stared and stared and saw at last the face of Deirdre Corcoran.

"Ah, Deirdre," he whispered, and sighed at last with relief. "Ah, woman, may God bless you for helping me through this last. 'Tis only a bit more and then 'twill be done."

"Here, John," she said, "let me help you off with that nightshirt and get you clean, for then I must be off to look after himself."

He yielded without a word to Deirdre's pushing and prodding as she pulled the soiled nightshirt from his body and got him clean again.

"Thanks be to God for ye seeing it through," he told her, his voice a little stronger now. She had him nearly dressed and sitting on the one chair in the room.

"It's true enough, you'd be lying here, rotting," said Deirdre, but she said it very gently. She put a cup in his hand and held it tight until he grasped it. "Now see can you take a bit of buttermilk and bread."

He raised the cup to his lips and drank slowly, and Deirdre stayed until he'd finished it all.

The gray mare twitched her ears when she heard Willy Egan moving about in the yard. She pawed in the dust at her feet, stamped a couple of times, then stretched her head over the boards of the stall, her left eye watching the door for the first sight of him. She snorted in anticipation and her breath made twin plumes of white before her long black nose.

Her appearance had changed in the last few weeks. Her stringy mane, once greasy and knotted with burrs, hung straight and smooth now against her curving neck. Along the straight line of roots, it showed white, then, as the thick hairs lengthened, it turned gray, then a sleek, almost shiny silver. When she tossed her head, the mane flopped easily against her neck.

Her coat too was different, washed and curried now, lying flat against her body, showing the ripple of muscle and tendon beneath. Where scars had blotched her hide before, salves had evened out the surface somewhat and the new glossy coat was already beginning to hide them. Bright white showed at her four fetlocks and she had four good new shoes.

Where before she had shared the barn indifferently with three silent cows, she was now beginning to show signs, Willy Egan had noted, of regarding them with impatience, as if irritated at the proximity of such dull and lumbering beasts. Each time he had thought that, a smile had played at the corner of his lips. And each time it had faded instantly away.

He came through the doorway now and headed straight for her. The animal snorted and tossed her head, making the silver hair on her neck flip up, then down.

"Good morning to ye, my girl," he said, and patted her firmly on the neck. Her eye on that side floated around in its socket and watched him. She lowered her head and rested it on the top of the stall. Willy rubbed the clean gray hair on the front of her face.

"Ah, I know, I know," he said. He gave her one last pat on the neck and went off to tend the cows.

He was just getting back to her an hour later, with the light of the morning turning from black to icy gray, when he heard footsteps on the gravel outside. He looked up and saw Brian Flynn in the doorway and Martin Gilhooley standing just behind him. Willy stretched his neck a little, looking past them, but there were only the two.

"Good morning to ye," said Flynn, and Gilhooley behind him echoed it.

"It'll be good, God willin'," said Willy. "Is it just the two of you then?"

"It is," said Flynn. He raised his right hand and pulled at the hairs in his ear.

"And himself?" Willy asked. His hand was still on the stall. "It's not bad news you're bringing me and it still early in the day?"

"It is not," said Brian Flynn. He dropped his hand and shoved it into the pocket of his jacket. "But John is in his bed again. The pain come on him bad in the night."

Willy Egan shook his head. "May God ha' mercy on him, and him suffering so," he breathed. "Will he last it out, d'ye think?"

"He will," Gilhooley replied solemnly, "if it's any of his own doing."

"Which is to say, he will," said Flynn.

"Ah, he's a strong one," Willy said. "The strongest I've known. Pray God he's with us still when most he's needed."

They were all silent a moment, not looking at each other.

Willy Egan lifted his eyes from the straw at his feet. He patted the mare on the neck and she nuzzled his shoulder.

"Come look at me beauty," he said. "Now, I ask ye, won't she be just fine when the proper time comes round?"

Father Henning had owned the typewriter, a monstrously heavy black Remington, for forty-nine years. Several of the keys stuck badly and usually required an extra hit or two to make them go, and the space bar responded erratically to his touch. Whenever he used it, the priest invariably ended up muttering to himself that he'd need to hear his own confession when he was done. And, considering the savage nature of his thoughts and the vileness of his wishes for the blasted machine, he wasn't all that certain he'd even grant himself absolution.

He had a little room just off the foyer, big enough only for a desk and one filing cabinet, that he liked to call his office. He was in there now, banging away at the machine, typing his bimonthly letter to his superiors in the city of Limerick, begging for funds to make "absolutely essential" repairs to his little church before the winds of winter blew it completely away and left him no place to house his flock. Every now and again, he pounded his fist on the table and muttered dire threats. Each time he did it, Deirdre Corcoran appeared in the doorway, apron still around her wide middle, and gave him a long hard look.

Finally, sighing with relief, he sat back and read over the product of his labors.

"It's done now, woman," he called out. "You can take the cotton from your innocent ears, without fear of your being scandalized."

A minute later, Deirdre appeared and set a cup of tea on the desk beside the typewriter.

"Drink your tea while it's hot," she told him. "Have you typed the envelope to put it in?"

"Ah, dear God, no, I haven't," he said.

"Well, drink that down, then, to fortify yourself, and I'll bring another when the job is done."

Looking very much the martyr, Father Henning gulped down the tea and went to work on the envelope.

Deirdre swept away the empty cup and returned with a steaming fresh one just as he finished licking the envelope and pressing it closed.

"I'll attend to the stamp," she said.

"Deirdre Corcoran, there's a cozy place waiting for you in heaven, I'm sure."

She was still in the doorway. The edge of her apron was crushed in one hand.

"John MacMahon was took especial bad in the night," she said.

The priest's head snapped up to look at her.

"I told him to keep to his bed for the day at least," she added. "Here, won't you even take the tea before you're off?"

But he was already pushing past her into the hall.

"Well, he's acting strange, I can tell you that much," Peggy Mullen said. She looked across the kitchen table at Deirdre Corcoran, then lowered her gaze to the cup of tea that was growing cold in her hand. "But, mind, he could be coming in any time now, so best keep an ear cocked for the sound of the car."

"Is he out much?" Deirdre asked. "Isn't it work he has to be doing? A book to be writing?"

"It is, and he's in there, in his office, of a morning, but I couldn't tell you if it's work he's at or not. Sometimes he takes a meal in the middle of the day and sometimes he goes out for it, but he's always out of an afternoon now."

"Does he say where he's going?"

"I've asked once or twice, just curious-like, you know, and he says only that he's driving about in the hills." She raised her eyes to the other woman's face. "It's hard, I'll tell you, to be spying on a man like this, and me an old woman!"

Deirdre sighed heavily and pushed herself to her feet. She took their two cups and set about making a fresh pot of tea.

"I couldn't say for sure," Peggy Mullen said softly to the other woman's back, "but it wouldn't surprise me at all if he thought he was seeing things. I don't think he's sleeping well at nights, neither."

"What's become of the girl?"

"She'll be here again. He's only waiting for her to be free. She owns a shop, a bookshop, in Dublin. I think he'll be in a better state when she's here."

Deirdre poured boiling water into the teapot. The top rattled when she put it on.

"But you think he's seeing them, do you?" she said without turning around.

Peggy Mullen was silent a moment. Then she said, "I do."

"And the girl?"

"I don't know. She was hardly here, you know, and only the once. But him and her is closer, I think, than many a husband and wife I've seen. If he's seeing them, then she'll see them as well, when she comes. All right, then, that's what I think, if you ask me."

"We'd best be telling himself, then," said Deirdre.

"Father Henning?"

"And John MacMahon as well."

Sometimes Father Malcolm Henning thought it was all too much for him. Here were the winters getting colder and wetter, the nights darker and longer, and the hills themselves growing steeper. Lucky thing he'd thought, in his rush from the house, to take his fine old stick to lean on as he climbed the hills to the cottage.

And another old friend so soon to be lost. First it was Paddy Mullen, and now John was on his way out, and soon it would be his own time. All the years that had passed, all the long evenings and the dark nights, all the rainy days, and the three of them always together, always knowing the others were nearby and knowing the others knew the same. All nearly ended, all coming to the close.

Did it matter, as he thought of his own death, that he was a priest? His mouth twisted as he walked. He'd done what he could, served as best he was able, trusting more in his conscience and his heart than in theology and canon law, and he'd honored his God to the limit of his strength. All these years, and he'd done what he thought his God wanted of him, on Saturday afternoons and Sunday mornings and at all hours of the nights in between.

And—thanks be to God, and with the help of Paddy and John, the three of them together—he'd preserved the other as well.

And did it make it any easier now, this satisfaction that he'd served both light and dark, both the open practice and the secret, to know that his own time was coming, perhaps before this very year was out, or the next, or the year after that? Was it any easier for the knowledge? He wasn't sure, but he thought— trusting, as he always had, his conscience and his heart—that only great age brought resignation within reach.

The light and the dark, they were always so bound up together.

He had to stop, halfway up a hill, and lean against a stone fence until he caught his breath.

He should have had Deirdre bring him in the car. No, no, of course not. Hadn't John MacMahon passed his entire life now and never once ridden in a car? And, besides, it was true, he still liked to walk the hills.

He looked around him. The moon had appeared between the clouds that drifted quickly overhead. It was still low near the earth, and shining brightly on the silence of the hills, its edges made crisp by the clear, brittle air he breathed. From above him, higher up the slope, he heard the low bleating of a sheep. He listened until the animal did it again and then was still.

Nothing changed here. The sheep themselves might have been those that lived a hundred years ago, or a thousand. The very shadows on the hillside, rocks or sheep or jagged cuts in the earth or the distant dark shape of a cottage, might have been the same.

The priest sighed, wiped a cold hand across his face, leaned on his stick for balance, and stepped back onto the road. He'd taken only a few steps when his foot touched something soft.

The priest stopped and looked down and sucked his breath in hard.

The man lay in the road, his body clearly visible in the moonlight. He lay on his stomach, his head turned to the side, one cheek on the ground, and his arms stretched out straight before him as if in supplication. He wore only a torn and filthy white shirt, gray in the shining moonlight, and pants held at his waist by a length of hempen rope. His waist was almost the size of a healthy man's arm, and the ankles and bare feet that protruded from the pants were more bone and blackened skin than flesh. His body might have been dropped there from a great height, crashing to earth in that spot, so still did it lie.

A cloud passed before the moon just then, and the hill and the road were buried in darkness.

Father Henning stared down at the spot where the body lay.

"God rest your soul," he murmured and, joining the tips of his thumb and index finger together, made the sign of the cross above the body. "In the name of the Father, and of the Son, and of the Holy Ghost."

He stood a moment longer and then, slowly, leaning on his stick, he made his way around the body and continued up the road. The moon came out from behind the clouds again and shone brightly on the hill, but the priest did not look back.

Finally, with his heart hammering in his chest and his mouth open to take in as much air as possible, thin and icy as it was, he came in sight of John MacMahon's old cottage. From where he stood in the road, he could see the orange-yellow flicker of candlelight and a turf fire through the single window in the end wall of the tiny house.

He stood there in the road, catching his breath so that he'd be able to speak when he reached the door. Then he went ahead, more slowly than before and leaning heavily on his stick.

He reached the cottage and pushed the door open. He saw John MacMahon, his face pale and drawn with pain, lying in the bed. The candle, on the table beside him, left his eyes in dark pools of black. Brian Flynn sat on the one chair, at the foot of the bed, facing John. James Brennan and Martin Gilhooley sat on the hard dirt floor, their backs against the wall. Gilhooley had his knees drawn up to his chest and his arms wrapped tight around his legs. Brennan's legs were stretched out straight before him. In the fireplace, a turf fire burned brightly and heated the room. The air was thick with the warm and acrid scent of the burning peat.

They turned to look at him and John MacMahon's head turned a bit on the pillow.

Father Henning ducked his head beneath the low lintel of the doorway and entered the cottage.

"God save all here," he said, and crossed the room toward the bed.

Liam Nolan warmed up the last of a piece of pot roast in the tiny kitchen at the end of the bar, and served it to Michael Mullen with four thick slices of bread. Mullen finished off the pint he'd been drinking, then bent forward over the food and went at it as if he hadn't eaten in a week.

"You'll not have your mother back in her own kitchen for a bit yet," Nolan remarked impassively as he watched Mullen eat. He carefully drew another pint of Guinness and set it on the bar before him.

"Not for a bit, no," Mullen said quietly between mouthfuls.

The pub was not yet filled. Doolin had no rush hour traffic, no swell of office workers stopping off for a pint on the way home. Only a few of the shop owners in the village were there and a few farmers who'd finished up early or had a strong son to see to things at home, and the inevitable oldtimers for whom the pub was restaurant, club house, and parlor. On a week night such as this, the customers were like family, people who had lived all their lives in close proximity and for whom each other's deep-lined, weathered faces were as much a part of the brooding, ever-present landscape as the rocks and the hills and the cliffs of the shore.

"Not for a bit," Michael Mullen said again, more quietly still. He drank from the fresh pint, swallowed the hearty Guinness with obvious satisfaction, then returned with less urgency to the rest of his meal.

Two new customers arrived and Nolan went to get their drinks. Then he returned and stood before Michael and dried glasses with the corner of his apron. "Will your brother be along for a bite to eat as well?" he asked.

"He will, I think," Michael said. He pushed away the empty plate and lifted the Guinness to wash down the last of his meal. "He's not much good in the kitchen, no more than me."

Nolan set out a dozen glasses, one after the other, on a towel spread on the bar.

"I've a nice pair of lamb chops put aside," he said. "I'll give him them."

Michael turned sideways on his stool and rested an elbow on the bar. His eyes scanned the faces in the pub, then glanced at the clock on the wall.

Nolan, still drying glasses, was watching him closely.

"The old fellow's sick," he said, his lips barely moving, his eye on the glass in his hand. "Kept to his bed all day, so I hear, and the pain that terrible it's twisting him up inside."

"No," said Michael Mullen.

" 'Tis so. You don't see none of them about, do you?"

"Will he last out the time, d'ye think?"

"He will," Nolan said in the same quiet voice, eyes still downcast, hands still moving, polishing the glass. "He will, with the help of God."

"With the help of God," Michael murmured.

There was a little silence between them. A man at the far end of the bar signalled to Liam and he went off to refill the man's glass. When he came back, he said, as quietly as before, "It could all fall to you, you know, if it came to it, being the son of one of them."

"I know it."

"Ah, but can you carry it on, a thing like that?" Nolan asked. Now he was looking Michael straight in the face. "Can you carry it on, and you with so many years still before you?"

"I can," Michael said. He stared at Liam Nolan for several seconds, then lifted his pint of Guinness and took a long, long drink from it. When he put the glass down, he had to take a deep breath. He wiped his mouth with his hand. His eyes found Liam Nolan's again.

"I can, I tell you," he said.

Liam nodded and was silent for a bit. Then he said, "But I wonder does the priest have another notion in his mind." He lifted his eyebrows a fraction of an inch.

Michael wiped his mouth again. "He might," he said. "He might. It's what I've been thinking myself."

"I'm near ready for the grave, Malcolm," John MacMahon said when he recognized the priest. "Nearly done and ready."

Brian Flynn rose at once from the chair and offered it to the priest. As Father Henning took the chair and moved it up near the head of the bed, Flynn joined his fellows on the floor. He rummaged among some parcels near his feet.

"Father," he said, "will you take a bite of something? There's not much, only a bit of bread, but there's currants in it. It's a long walk you've had up the hills, and another the same way back, and the wind blowing in cold from the sea."

"I will," Father Henning said.

Brennan broke off a generous hunk of the bread and passed it over to the priest. As he took it, he had to suppress a thin smile. The instant his fingers touched the hard golden crust, powdered with white, he recognized Deirdre Corcoran's own baking.

They all sat in respectful silence while he ate the bread.

When he was done, he brushed his hands together and said, "Well, John, how are you this day?"

John MacMahon closed his eyes wearily, then opened them again. "I'll be among you a while longer, I'm thinking."

"Is the pain so bad?"

John sighed. "I'll not say other than the truth. It was fit to tear me in pieces only this morning, but since the middle of the day it's been giving me a bit of peace. I'll be up again before long. For a while, at least." His eyes searched his old friend's face. "I'm bound and determined, Malcolm, to be with you for it on the night. You know that, I hope. I'll not be leaving you before then, God willing. You know that, do you not?"

Father Henning did not answer. Instead, he turned his head and glanced at the three men sitting against the wall. Without a word, avoiding his eyes, they pushed themselves to their feet and shuffled slowly out of the cottage.

When they were alone, Father Henning turned back to John MacMahon. "John," he said, "there's much we have to talk about."

MacMahon nodded. His head barely moved the pillow.

"Are you up to speaking of it now? We must be preparing for the time when you're gone, and when I'm gone myself as well."

Impulsively, he reached out and gripped John MacMahon's hand.

After a moment, without withdrawing his hand, Father Henning continued in a lower voice, "We'll need to pick others, see if they're right and they're willing."

MacMahon said, "We will. We will. But there'll be time yet for that."

They sat in silence for a long while, hands joined on the blanket that covered John MacMahon's thin body.

"Tell me of something else," MacMahon said at last. "The visitor, the one from America. Tell me about him." He turned his head and his eyes searched the face of the priest. "You know what I'm asking, Malcolm."

"He has it in the blood, I think," the priest said. "We've talked a bit and I know he's been . . . seeing certain things."

"Ah, it's so strange," MacMahon sighed. "A man comes such a ways and finds he's part of it all, and it so dark and deadly. I'd so hoped he'd be gone when the time comes. Is he seeing the lot, d'ye know?"

"He is, I think, from what he told me."

"But can you think why?"

"I cannot," the priest said, "only that he came here to look and learn."

"There was only the one before him that was touched, all those years ago. But never a one of all the others seen a thing."

"That's so."

"He'll be here at the time?"

"He will."

MacMahon closed his eyes.

"We'll have to speak of it, John," Father Henning said. "Whether to get him away from it or what."

"When I'm upright, we'll talk further on it, but not with me lying in my bed like a corpse that's almost cold."

"John, don't be talking so."

"There's no denying it."

They were silent again.

Outside the door of the cottage, there was the sound of voices talking, low and guttural. The wind whistled at the corner of the little house. The cracked wooden frame of the window rattled the cloudy glass each time the wind gusted.

"I suppose it's a fitting way to go off," MacMahon said after a while.

Father Henning clutched tighter at his old friend's bony hand. He leaned closer over the bed, his face near John MacMahon's. Tears welled suddenly from his eyes and ran through the channels of deepset creases in his face. "Oh, John, John," he whispered, "how I wish you weren't going and leaving me behind."

MacMahon's fingers tightened a bit on the priest's hand. "Ye've more to hold you up than I have," he said. "Ye've two things and I've only the one."

"Aye, that's so," said the priest. "Either that, or I've a double load to carry."

"All things is as ye see them," MacMahon said, his phlegmy voice turning soft and soothing. "Ye can but do as ye must, Malcolm. And then the day will come and we'll rest together, the three of us, you and Paddy and meself, and leave the doing of it to those that come after."

"It's that we must be speaking of, John," the priest said, his voice more urgent than when he'd mentioned it before.

MacMahon gently pulled his thin hand free from Henning's, then placed it over the priest's and patted his hand several times, regularly, as one might hold and pat the hand of a frightened child. "We'll talk of it, Malcolm. It's a long time I've been thinking on it already. And I've a few good days more in me still." Something occurred to him suddenly and he turned his eyes again up to Malcolm Henning's face. "How many days is it yet? When the pain comes on me, I lose the count."

"It'll be Sunday next," said the priest.

"Sunday next," said John MacMahon. "And then, God willing, I can go myself, peaceful-like." He was silent for a moment, then a sudden fierceness turned his voice harsh once more. "Malcolm," he said, "when my time comes, you must promise to do for me yourself so's it's done all proper. Will you promise me that, Malcolm?"

Father Henning closed his eyes. "I will, John," he whispered. "I will, John, my dear old friend. I'll do it with my own two hands."

CHAPTER 14

But of course it had not been Grainne, could not have been her.

He'd lain there on the floor in the open doorway, his legs hanging down on the hard concrete steps, for ... how long? It must have been three hours. When he awoke, he was stiff from lying on the floor and shivering with the damp cold wind that was blowing in from the Atlantic. The fresh salt scent of the air cleared his head almost at once but did nothing to ease his throbbing headache. He must have hit his head when he fell. He felt gingerly at his temples and around the side of his head. There was no sign of a bump or blow. The headache was—

With a rush that made him shiver violently, he recalled the touch of those cold clawing fingers at his arm, his throat, his face. And with that remembrance came the sight of the girl in the road, running in the road, knees pumping, her mouth and chin dripping blood as she ran.

"Oh, God!"

He managed to sit up without jarring his body too much, and settled his back against the wall. After a moment, when the pain in his head settled down from searing, shooting flames to a dull blaze that only crackled and roared, he stretched out one foot, gingerly hooked the edge of the door, and pulled it closed.

He sat there on the floor, in the dark, and tried very hard not to think.

He guessed later that he must have dozed off again because, when the telephone rang, he nearly leaped in the air.

The sound pierced his head like a needle, jangling and rattling at nerves already frayed. He caught his breath and looked around at the dark living room, Telephone. It was the telephone. Grainne.

Balancing himself with one hand against the wall, he stood up. His head was still throbbing, but now it was only a dull pounding ache rather than the fiercely blinding pain of before. The telephone went on ringing, the odd double burr he'd grown accustomed to. He groped his way across the room to where he knew the telephone was, and a lamp, only taking his fingertips from the wall at the last possible second. When he switched on the lamp, the sudden light hurt his eyes. His other hand groped for the phone.

"Hello?"

"Hello, Jack. It's Grainne."

"Oh, thank God," he sighed before he even knew he was saying it. With relief, he sank onto the couch. It felt wonderfully soft beneath him.

"Jack? It's Grainne. Are you all right?"

"Yes, I'm fine."

"No, you're not. What's wrong? Are you sick? You don't sound well."

"No, no, I'm not sick. I'm just . . . I'm not sick."

"What is it, then? Did you only come back from Galway today? You didn't have a crash on the road, did you?"

"No, no, nothing like that." He was struggling to make his voice sound normal, to make his breathing steady. He tried closing his eyes but that only seemed to upset his stomach. "Really, I'm all right. I . . . I was going to call you."

"Well, all right," she said, but she still sounded doubtful. "Was your trip good?"

"Yes. It was. We'll ... uh ... we'll have to go there again. Together."

"Jack, will you tell me what's wrong?" she said urgently.

"When are you coming?"

"Thursday or Friday, I think. Jack!"

"Okay, so I . . . I just don't feel very well. I'll be okay, I promise."

"Is it the same thing that's troubled you before?" she asked quietly, her voice coming gently even through the phone. "The thing that's worrying you?"

"What makes you say that?"

"Jack, do you take me for the fool of the world, not to know there's something troubling you? Will you tell me what it is or not?"

"All right," he said, relieved to give in at last to her insistence. But telling such madness into the cold receiver of the telephone was still more than he could manage. "I'll tell you, I promise, when you get here."

"Jack, are you sure—"

"When you get here."

She sighed, making sure he heard the sadness and concern in the sound. "All right, then," she said. "Are you tired out from your trip?"

"A little, yes."

"Then maybe you'd best just go on to bed. I only rang to see were you all right and to tell you I'm looking forward to coming."

"Grainne, I'm so glad you'll be here."

"I'll see you in a few days, then. Now get on to bed."

As soon as he hung up the phone, he felt his eyes growing heavy again. Before he could fall asleep on the couch, he made his way into the bedroom, pulled his clothes off and left them in a heap on the floor, and crawled into bed. His next-to-last thought was that Mrs. Mullen would not be horrified to find him sleeping on the floor in the morning. His last thought was of Grainne's voice and her sweetly smiling face. He longed to rest his cheek on her naked breast, and then he was asleep.

He was fine in the morning, absolutely fine. He awoke with his head completely free of pain and his thoughts crystal clear. He remembered the whole episode from the night before, recalled it in all its grim details from grisly start to frightening finish, but somehow it seemed now incapable of hurting him. Now, instead of fear, he felt a consuming curiosity.

When Mrs. Mullen arrived, he had already made a pot of tea and was drinking it in the kitchen. While she was hanging up her coat and tying on her apron, he put four slices of bread in the toaster and invited her to come sit with him.

Mrs. Mullen looked extremely uncomfortable and insisted that she had too much work before her to be sitting about now. She'd already had her tea and, if he was to have a meal set in front of him later in the day, she'd best be starting her work at once. Jack had to repeat the invitation twice, adding a note of firmness to his voice, before she finally yielded. Looking very unhappy and ill at ease, she sat at the table and poured herself a cup.

"Mrs. Mullen," he said pleasantly, "you know I'm writing a book that's set in Ireland. I was thinking you could help me out with part of it."

"Sure, what would the likes of me know about books?"

"You've lived all your life here in Doolin, haven't you?"

"I have." She sipped a little of her tea. Jack, watching her closely, thought she took it more for comfort than anything else.

"Well, then, you can help me. You see, I've reached a point in the book now where I need some background information. Local stories, that sort of thing, legends and tales related to this specific part of County Clare."

"I know nothing of such things," she said, and sipped her tea again.

"Now don't be so modest, Mrs. Mullen. You must know plenty of such things. You know, you might take the old tales for granted yourself and think nothing of them, but they'd mean a great deal to me. They really would."

"We don't take none of that for granted hereabouts," she said quietly and, for the first time, met his eyes.

"Well, then," he said, smiling, "what you've just told me is that there *are* plenty of local stories. I'd just like to hear some of them."

"The pub is the place for that," she said. "And not the kitchen table when there's work I must be doing."

She stood up and gathered her cup and the teapot and the plates the toast had been on.

She had her back to him as she stood at the sink and the counter. He watched her in silence for a while. Mrs. Mullen did not turn around.

"Tell me," he said at last, his voice carefully neutral, "do people around here often see visions of things that cannot be?"

She was silent a long time before she answered, but Jack saw that her hand had stopped moving on the plate she was wiping dry.

Her tone was flat but her voice trembled ever so slightly when she finally replied. "There's many a one sees things," she said, "coming home late of a night from the pub. You'd best be asking them."

It would have been both useless and cruel to press the woman further. But he had learned something definite.

He went into his office and closed the door. He turned on the computer so that, if she listened from the hallway, she would hear the familiar hum of its fans.

Then he sat for a quarter of an hour, saying over and over to himself, in a silent voice that, all things considered, he thought sounded quite reasonable: there is something actually going on and I am not losing my mind.

He spent three hours that morning writing it all down.

His fingers flying over the keyboard, he wrote quickly, sometimes using a telegraphed style, shorthand, strings of adjectives, bits of description, in whatever order his searching mind brought the details back.

When he thought he had it all down, he removed the disk from the computer and sat back in his chair. Only then did he realize how tensely he'd been sitting. His shoulders hurt and the small of his back was aching. He stretched to ease the pain.

Then he smiled a little, thinking of his agent. If he called her and told her about all of this, she'd be instantly worried and urge him to see a psychiatrist. Go to London and find a good one, she'd say, who ever heard of an Irish shrink? And if he could set her mind at ease, assure her that he really wasn't going loony, he knew just what she'd say to that. You can use this. Nothing is ever wasted for a writer. Everything is grist for the mill. Look at it that way. Etcetera.

His smile broadened when his eye fell on the computer disk he'd been using. Now there was something to think about, something to help put this business in perspective. Here he was, in the ancient Irish countryside, among hillsides so desolate that men had once, and perhaps still, thought them holy, surrounded by a way of life that hadn't altered essentially in hundreds and hundreds of years, and he was seeing grisly nighttime visions in the fog at the edge of the road. And thinking perhaps they were real. And recording the memory of what he'd seen on a computer.

And out there in the living room was a telephone. He could walk out there and pick it up and, in a matter of seconds, talk to Grainne in Dublin. Or his agent in New York. Or friends in London, or in Chicago or San Francisco. If he wanted, he could be in New York in—he thought for a second—say, ten hours or so. Door to door. With a pretty Aer Lingus stewardess serving him a meal and drinks while the plane rushed along at 35,000 feet of altitude and six hundred-and-something miles an hour.

How crazy could he be?

Not very.

How far from civilization was he?

Not far.

And if there *was* something weird going on, he could look into it and find out what the hell it was. Right?

Right.

He pushed his chair back from the desk, went into his bedroom and pulled on a heavy Aran sweater and a jacket, and told Mrs. Mullen he was going out.

The sky was overcast, heavy clouds rolling like gray smoke above the hills, threatening a fresh torrent of rain, as he drove into the village, slowed, then continued along the road as far as Nolan's.

There were about twenty people inside. Jack ordered a pint of lager and a cheese sandwich. The sandwich, thick and crusty on freshly-baked bread, arrived on a chipped and cracked plate. He ate his lunch at the bar, but there was no opportunity to talk with Liam Nolan as he'd planned. There were too many people here now, too many meals to be served. Jack flicked a hand in parting to Nolan as he got up from the bar. Nolan nodded briefly and went on tending to his other customers.

Later, Jack promised himself as he returned to the car and put the key in the ignition. He'd come back and talk to Nolan later.

He leaned forward and looked up through the windshield at the sky. It had grown darker, and the clouds even thicker and more ominous, while he was eating in the pub.

"Nothing daunted," he said out loud, trying to amuse himself as he started the car moving into the road, "our intrepid hero pressed on in the face of weather that could mean only one thing, rain up the wazoo! Like a mailman. Neither rain nor fog nor cold that freezes your ass can stop this certified madman from keeping his appointed rounds. Onward, Christian soldiers!"

He turned the car north, on the road that passed through Knockfin and on to connect with the L54, the same road on which he'd seen the girl the night before.

His smile had disappeared by the time the road topped the first rise and shadowy little Doolin had disappeared entirely from the rearview mirror.

He couldn't be certain but he thought he'd found the place. If this wasn't precisely it, the spot was somewhere right along here.

He stood in the road with the car's engine ticking quietly beside him as it cooled. He was wearing the brown tweed cap he kept in the car. His collar was turned up around his neck and his hands pushed deep in his pockets. The wind, rushing in unchecked from the sea, had grown steadier as he drove, buffeting the car and forcing him to slow down. Now it roared in his ears, flapped the tail of his jacket, and tugged at his cap. He reached up and pulled the cap lower on his head, then shoved his hands back in his pockets.

He looked up. It had to rain soon. Those clouds could not contain themselves much longer.

He hunched his shoulders and started walking.

Yes, it was somewhere right along here he'd seen her. He remembered the straight stretch of road. There were no landmarks, of course, only the sloping hills of gray-white rock, the Burren, stretching up to his right and down to his left to the sea. No way to tell for sure, but he thought this was the place.

And what exactly am I looking for? he asked himself. A little girl's footprints on the rock or on the asphalt of the road? An historical marker to point the spot?

He stood still, then slowly turned a full circle, looking all around him. The scene was worse than desolate and devoid of human life. Not even sheep grazed here, Irish sheep that could live and grow fat on moors and mountains. This place looked inimical to life itself, savage, fierce, unyielding, nothing but blackening sky, twisting gray clouds, screeching wind, cold air, bare rock, and the ceaseless crashing of the sea.

The rain came suddenly, heavily, the wind flinging icy, stinging pellets at his face.

He turned and walked back toward his car.

She was curled up on the road beside the door on the driver's side. Her bony knees were drawn up toward her chest and she appeared to be asleep.

He stood over her for what seemed even to him a horribly long time, not breathing, just stood there, looking down at her, wondering if she was real.

She had curled herself up tightly, arms wrapped around her legs, as if making a smaller target for the rain and the wind. The worn and shredded nightgown was already soaked through. Her pale white skin was soiled with dirt. The lashing rain struck it hard and, in places, made clean little rivulets where the lighter, fresher dirt washed away. Her stringy, greasy hair, thoroughly soaked now like her nightgown or shift, might once have been reddish blond. The skin of her face was almost translucent, almost revealed the bone structure beneath. Her lips had no color. Her eyes, closed now beneath lightly fluttering lids, were sunk deep beneath the ridge of her brow. Her arms and legs had no flesh at all, only knots for the elbows and knees. Her tiny hands were the claws of a bird.

"You're alive," he heard himself say, and the sound of his own voice startled him.

"My God," he muttered.

He knelt in the road beside her, ignoring the icy puddle that instantly soaked his pants, the chilling rain that ran down his neck beneath his collar. He reached out a hand toward the child.

And stopped it, poised, just above her shoulder.

"Are you? Are you real?"

He lowered his hand slowly onto her shoulder and touched wet skin as cold as ice, felt hard bones beneath. She shivered at his touch and drew herself into a tighter knot, as if she waited for a kick. Despite the rain crashing in wet silver geysers all around her, he clearly heard her whimper. He slid his hand along her upper arm, making certain she was real. His fingers felt her shudder.

"Oh, my God," he whispered, not knowing he spoke at all. "Here! Here! Out of the rain! I'll get you in the car!"

He slid a hand beneath her shoulders, a hand beneath her legs, and lifted her from the wet ground. She was still curled into a knot. Rain streamed into her face as he lifted her in his arms. She was no heavier than the thin cloth of her shift might have been without her.

Awkwardly, holding her feathery weight in the crook of his left arm, he got the rear door open and laid her gently on the blue vinyl of the seat. A chilling sheet of rain struck him hard in the side of the face. He slid onto the corner of the seat and got the door shut behind him.

Her eyes were still closed. The wet shift clung to her skin. Her ribs showed through it. Her breathing was shallow. She began to shiver violently, fingers clenching and unclenching on her arms.

He twisted into a better position on the seat, gently moved her frozen bare feet out of the way, and clumsily pulled off his jacket in the tight space. He spread it over her, pressing it in gently all around. Then he stretched forward through the break in the front seats, turned the key in the ignition, and switched on the heater. Warm air began blowing into the car.

There was a roll of paper towels on the floor in the back. Hands trembling, he pulled off three or four sheets and wiped her face to dry it. She twisted her head away at the first touch but then she lay still. He dried her face, wiped her hair and her neck, then dried her arms and legs and feet, keeping the rest of her terrible body covered with the jacket as he worked.

Her eyes were still closed. Her breathing seemed steadier. He thought she was sleeping.

A doctor. Get her to a doctor.

Taking care not to disturb her, he tried to climb into the front seat. The space was too cramped. He took a deep breath, threw open the door beside him, slid out and slammed it, grabbed the handle of the front door, and threw himself in. Already he could feel the cold rain soaking through to his skin. Not even an Irish sweater could keep off such wetness.

He started the engine and heard the heater die for a second. Then it began blowing again with renewed strength and warmer air. He switched on the windshield wipers at top speed. They did almost nothing to clear the glass. Rain washed across it in blinding sheets, as if the car were sinking beneath the sea.

He turned around to check on the child once more before moving the car.

His jacket lay on the floor in the back. The child was gone.

When he finally reached home, Mrs. Mullen and Deirdre Corcoran were still there, waiting for him.

He told them nothing, said as little as possible, only that he'd been caught on the road in the worst of the storm and that he'd gotten to a pub in Knockfin and spent several hours there, drinking a few pints and huddling by the fire. His damp clothes smelled still of the burning peat.

The two women got the wet clothes off him and put him into bed. Deirdre reappeared with a steaming cup and insisted that he drink it to warm himself. When that one was done, she brought another. He drank that too, and then dozed off to sleep.

When he awoke sometime in the night, coming groggily into wakefulness with an aching bladder Deirdre Corcoran was sleeping, snoring lightly, in the chair near the window. He climbed out of bed quietly, keeping his blurry, shadowy vision on her large dark form. When he returned from the bathroom, she was still asleep. He dozed off again to the sound of her gentle snoring and the patter of the rain at the window.

Tuesday and Wednesday of that week passed. He wrote a little, or tried to, but he did set down a record of his experience the day before, adding it to his previous notes, forcing himself to sit before the keyboard, just letting the words come in whatever way they would, until he'd put it all down. He did a lot of reading; reading was relatively easy, once he forced himself to concentrate on the pages.

In the afternoon he went out, driving the Escort all through the hills of the western part of County Clare. He drove to Ennis and Lahinch and Milltown Malbay and Lisdoonvarna and Ballyvaughan, some of it on roads he knew, some of it on roads that had no names or numbers. When he was hungry, not often, he stopped into a pub and ate whatever was offered. He only returned to the house when he knew that Deirdre Corcoran had collected Peggy Mullen and the two of them were gone.

On Wednesday evening, Grainne called to say that she couldn't come to Doolin until Friday.

On Thursday morning, he went to see Father Henning.

"You look terrible," the priest said as soon as they were together in the sitting room, and Jack saw that Father Henning instantly regretted his words.

"Well, that's an ungracious greeting if ever there was one," the priest said quickly. "What I mean to say is—"

"I look terrible," Jack said. "Yes, I don't doubt it. I don't doubt it at all."

"Have you been sick? If you'd like, I can have Deirdre get the car and we'll bring you to the doctor. My old friend, Dennis Nugent, is a fine doctor, a fine doctor. He's only over in Ennistymon and we could—"

"I'm not sick."

Father Henning studied him closely. After a moment he leaned forward and said, "But you're not well either, son."

"No," Jack said. "I'm not. And that's why I'm here. I want to talk to you, Father. I want to ask you some questions about what we talked about before, and I want some answers."

"Jack—"

"Father, listen to me. I'm telling you, as clearly as I can, that I think you have the answers to some questions, and I mean to get them."

"Jack—"

"Father, if you won't listen to me, and if you won't tell me what I want to know, I swear to you, I'll stand in the middle of the town and shout out what I've seen until somebody tells me what the hell is going on."

Their eyes bored into each other. Jack, determined now to win the day, prevailed at last. Father Henning dropped his gaze to his hands in his lap.

"The rain's let up a bit," he said quietly after a little silence. "Will you take me for a ride in that smart new car of yours? It'll be easier to talk."

Jack hesitated, then said, "All right."

The priest took his cap and scarf and coat but didn't bother to put them on.

Ignoring Deirdre Corcoran who had come to the kitchen doorway, they went outside to the car.

"This way," Father Henning said, and waved his hand to the right, toward the hills.

Willy Egan was sitting just inside the wide doorway of the barn when they arrived and came to a halt on the wet gravel outside. He was working on the spoke of a wooden cartwheel and did not look up until he'd finished what he was doing.

"Good morning to ye," he said as he put the wheel aside and stood up.

"Good morning, Willy," Father Henning said. "I've brought a friend along. This is Jack Quinlan."

Jack and Willy Egan nodded at each other. Jack felt, when their eyes met for a second, an odd union with the farmer, and guessed that the two of them were equally uneasy at the priest's bringing him here.

"Well, will ye come in from the damp?" Willy said to break the awkward silence.

"We will," Father Henning said, "but not before having a visit with that lovely lady of yours. Is she receiving visitors, do you suppose, Willy?"

"She is," the farmer said.

Jack couldn't make out what was going on, but he followed as the two men walked together into the barn.

The mare watched them approaching, eyeing Jack and the priest warily. When they were in front of her, she pushed her nose against Willy Egan's chest.

"Isn't she a beauty, Jack?" Father Henning said.

"She is, yes." Jack was amazed that such an animal would have a home in a place like this. She was no thoroughbred, he could see that in an instant, but she was tall and powerful and looked as if she'd been gotten up for a show. Willy must spend hours every day rubbing her down and combing her.

They stood with the mare for a few minutes, Willy and the

priest petting her, and then Willy said, "Well, then," and, as if by common understanding, they left the barn and walked across the yard to the cottage.

Jack had resigned himself to playing along with Father Henning's roundabout ways, at least to a degree. Whatever was going on here—and the priest's tacit acknowledgment confirmed that there was indeed a secret to be found out—would not yield to straightforward attack and investigation. It was something perhaps very convoluted, very subtle, and would reveal itself only in a convoluted and subtle way. Until his patience ran out entirely, Jack had promised himself on his way to Father Henning's house, he would follow along and let the priest answer his questions by his own methods.

He had to exercise that patience as they sat together in the dim interior of Willy Egan's cottage. Jack took no part in the conversation, only nodding occasionally, adopting the facial expression people use when they are party to an exchange about people and subjects of which they know nothing. The priest and the farmer spoke of people in the village, of the weather—colder and wetter this October than usual—and of the prices you had to pay for everything, even food, God help us all, these days. After twenty minutes or so, there was a natural lull in the talk.

"Will you take a drop of something, Father?" Willy Egan asked. "And you as well," he added, looking at Jack.

Jack caught the priest glancing at him furtively. Father Henning said they would, as a preventative of chills, and Willy Egan brought forth from a cupboard a stone jug. The priest drank first, right from the jug, exhaled sharply, and passed it over to Jack.

"Go easy, son," the priest warned quietly.

Jack drank cautiously from the jug. The poteen burned its way down to his stomach and ignited a roaring blaze when it arrived. His eyes watered and he wanted desperately to gasp for air, but he kept himself from coughing. The two others seemed pleased and an indefinable tension seemed to have gone out of the air as Willy Egan took a mouthful himself and put away the jug. It was clear that Jack had been put to some sort of test, or that he had, in fact, already passed some sort of inspection.

A few minutes later, back in the car, Jack said, "Did I pass your little test?"

"You did," the priest said solemnly.

"Because I kept that stuff down?"

"No. Because Willy Egan saw fit to offer it to you. Go back the road we came and then I'll show you where to turn."

Jack made himself keep quiet. He'd put the pieces together as the priest gradually revealed them. He steered the car back down the hill and followed Father Henning's directions along narrow country roads.

"Just ahead there on the right," the priest said after a while. "There's a little lane. Take care with it. It's rough and the ground'll be muddy."

It was a mess and Jack had all he could do to maneuver the car, but the lane was short. He sought a relatively solid-looking spot on which to stop in front of yet another stone cottage.

He looked enquiringly at his companion.

"This is it," the priest said, and opened his door and got out.

The cottage was dark inside. A single candle burned beside the bed, but the turf fire had died down to an orange glow.

Jack thought at first that it was a corpse in the bed with a blanket pulled up to its chin. Then he recognized the face of John MacMahon. One of his regular cronies rose from the single chair in the room as they entered.

The priest made formal introductions, as if they were all ambassadors meeting at a tea party and he were the local chief of protocol. The old man in the bed, who Jack clearly saw was dying, fixed dark, sunken eyes on him but only nodded his head in Jack's direction.

The priest took the chair vacated by Brian Flynn. For some while then, Jack thought he'd been brought on a priest's routine pastoral visit to a parishioner nearing his end, but at the same time he knew that could not be. Father Henning would not have subjected a dying man to the scrutiny of a stranger. This was part of the priest's explanation, if he could even call it that. It had to be. John MacMahon was the one Jack had seen at that gravesite, pouring something into the grave.

They spoke in quiet voices, Brian Flynn sometimes joining in, and Jack maintaining his impassive expression. Finally, John Mac-Mahon told the priest he thought he could be up and about the next day. The rest had done him good. Then, with his eyes fixed on Jack's face, he invited them, as Willy Egan had, to take a drop of something. Brian Flynn fetched the jug from a wooden chest in the darkness of a corner.

They drank again, the priest first, then John MacMahon, then Brian Flynn, and finally Jack. Jack noted that MacMahon barely wet his lips with the powerful liquor. Whatever the man was dying of, Jack thought, the raw poteen could serve either to kill his pain or to put him out of his misery once and for all. But the real value of the stuff, he saw, was at least as much in its ritual strength as any other. This time he was prepared for its burning. He drank it with hardly a shudder. When he was done, he saw that the jug was set on the floor near the foot of the bed, rather than being put away.

Father Henning turned to look at him over his shoulder.

"Jack, will you tell John MacMahon what you told me before."

The request startled him and it was a second before he replied. He looked from one face to the other.

"I've seen more since," he said.

"Tell all of it, then," John MacMahon said. His voice was low, weak, but there was a surprising softness in it.

Jack told what he'd seen, all of it, the words coming slowly at first, then more easily as the seeming absurdity of it all changed to certainty that these men were already familiar with it. They were hearing nothing new. When he got to the child he'd found in the road on Monday, it was as if he were speaking of a normal child in the village, a familiar child they all knew.

There was a long silence when he was finished. Then John MacMahon lifted an eyebrow toward Brian Flynn. Flynn reached for the jug of poteen and passed it around again. This time, Jack was grateful for the drink.

"We'll be seeing you again, son," MacMahon said to him.

Without even meaning to, Jack said, "All right."

Father Henning stood up and took his leave of MacMahon and Flynn.

"I'll be saying a prayer for you," he told MacMahon.

Then Jack and the priest were outside again and silently climbing into the car.

Somehow, they had tacitly agreed not to speak about it until they were well away from the cottage.

When they reached the bottom of the muddy lane, Father Henning said, "We'll drive to Doolin Point. Go this way."

It was a route that avoided the road through the village. They drove in silence all the way. Jack, close now to an explanation and feeling that he was going to learn something that would free his thoughts of the darkness he'd been seeing, concentrated only on the slick surface of the road.

The bare rock shelving of Doolin Point was taking the full brunt of the wind. Rain and spray lashed at the two men as the priest led the way out to the farthest point of rock. It was a wild and savage place. Beyond the edge of the shelving, they could see the curling white crests of breakers lashing at the shore, shooting spume high and higher against the walls of stone. Every fourth wave or so, more powerful or more angry than the others, shot spray higher than their heads. Near the end of the point there was a tumble of great squarish blocks of stone, the size of building blocks for a monster's castle. The priest stepped among them. The wind still roared past, but the bit of lee in the shelter of the stones would allow them to speak without having the wind steal away their words.

In spite of himself, in spite of the strange day and the strange meetings, in spite of the bonechilling damp and the screaming of the wind, Jack loved the spot. It was the most desolate place he'd ever seen, totally unprotected from the rage of wind and sea, yet standing steadfast against them.

"I love this place," Father Henning said.

Jack was surprised that, despite the noise of the wind all around them, the priest did not have to shout. The blocks of stone made a quiet place in the midst of chaos, and the priest had obviously been here many times before.

"So do I," Jack said.

They stood in silence, hunched over more to protect themselves from the rage of the wind than from the wind itself.

"Is your young lady coming?" the priest asked.

"Tomorrow."

"She's seen nothing herself?"

"No."

"Does she know that you have?"

"She knows something is wrong."

"How long will she stay?"

"I don't know," Jack said. "A few days. Maybe a week." His eyes met the priest's. "Maybe longer."

"And you want her with you?"

"Yes. Very much."

Part of Jack wanted to shout at the priest, take him by the shoulders and shake the life out of him, shake some explanation out of him. But he knew he wouldn't get it that way. This was like some crazy catechism the priest was putting him through, all these questions and answers.

"Do you love this girl?" Father Henning asked.

"I . . . I don't know. I might."

"Do you sleep with her?"

That was too much. "Listen, Father, this isn't a confessional!"

"Yes, it is," the priest said steadily, not taking his eyes from Jack's face. "Do you sleep with her?"

"No. Not yet."

"But you will?"

"Yes."

"If you were in trouble, or in pain, or in danger of death, could you count on her help and support?"

"Yes. I think so. Yes."

"And she could count on yours?"

"Yes. Of course."

The priest turned away and moved off a little distance. He stared out at the seething gray-green ocean for a minute, then moved back behind the shelter of the rock. He still did not look at Jack again.

"I will not, because I *cannot*, tell you what is going to happen here. Please hear me out. I cannot tell you, so don't be asking me again. When the proper time comes, I'll come for you. You'll know then, but you cannot know *before* then. Now I want to ask you another question. Then I'm going to give you my blessing, and then we are going to leave this place and carry on with our lives as if this had not happened. You have no choice now, you do see that, but to continue on this road. You'll learn nothing, and possibly be in great danger, if you do otherwise."

Jack clenched his teeth together but said, "Go on."

"If Grainne's life were in danger, in immediate danger, is there anything you would not do to save her?"

"No. Nothing."

"That horse we saw this morning at Willy Egan's farm, the mare. If it meant saving Grainne's life, could you drink that animal's blood?"

"Drink its . . . ?"

"Could you drink its blood?"

Jack whispered his answer. "Yes."

"Could you drink mine?"

"Yes."

"Or hers?"

"Yes."

A grave opened in the stone at his feet and a corpse with his own decaying face came toward him, blood dripping from its chin, and Grainne was beside it, holding one of its rotted hands.

"Or give your own for others to drink?"

"I—"

"Or give your own for others to drink?"

"Yes."

"Think. And then answer again."

He heard only the endless explosion of surf against the rocks, the crashing of seaspray, the blast of the wind, and the mad flapping of his collar near his ear.

"Yes."

"Oh, Lord," murmured the priest, "protect this thy servant in the hour of his direst need, which is almost upon him." He turned to face Jack and raised his right hand, thumb and first finger joined together, to make the sign of the cross. "In the name of the Father, and of the Son, and of the Holy Ghost."

CHAPTER 15

Grainne arrived, all smiles and cartons of books and parcels of food, just before three on Friday afternoon.

Jack had made up his mind that he was not going to let his own worry and gloom cast a pall over her visit. He had also made up his mind that he was not going to let her stay anywhere near Doolin for more than a day or two, not here, not where she might be in danger. He'd tell her he had to be away, in London, in New York, in Los Angeles, somewhere, to sign contracts or something equally urgent. She'd have to go back to Dublin but he'd be flying back as soon as he could and he'd see her there. He'd make it convincing; didn't he make his living by telling stories? At the same time, he didn't think for a minute that she'd believe him.

He'd been looking forward so much to seeing her, being with her, even though the strange things he'd experienced had been filling his thoughts. Through all of it, she was always there, a presence in his mind, a presence in his life, even though he could still add up the meager number of hours they'd spent together, the number of conversations on the phone. It was true, they hardly knew each other, and yet he felt this closeness and thought she felt it too. No, of course she felt it. If she didn't, she never would have come here in the first place and certainly would never have returned. He went back through the whole long list of factors he'd considered before—the fact that he was alone in a strange country, that there was no particular girlfriend at home in the States, all the rest of it—and wondered that he was no wiser at deciding if he was in love than he'd been at half this age.

But it was only when he came running out of the house into the bitingly cold air and saw her throwing open the car door and coming toward him—a flash of color: faded blue jeans, red windbreaker, white teeth in a happy smile—that he knew it all for sure. They'd spoken on the phone often since she'd left, usually every other night, and he'd treasured the sound of her voice, her inquiries about how his work was going, was he eating properly, was he dressing warmly, and he was always hungry to hear how she was herself and what she was doing, but no mechanically reproduced voice on a telephone could fill the place of her actual presence here, coming toward him, coming into his arms.

They came together as if they'd been separated for years. The joining took her breath away as well as his. Then everything was gone—wind, gray clouds, cold air, stony hillside, wet gravel underfoot—and there was only her body pressed tight against him, her breasts crushed hard against his chest, her lips full and warm against his own, her tongue seeking his. He wrapped her in his arms, would have wrapped himself around her, crushed her to him, feeling sudden alarm at the thinness of her body, the slightness of her, the fragility so easily damaged or broken. He held her with one arm around the small of her back and the other at her shoulders, his hand at the back of her head, fingers twined in her hair, pulling her close and hard against him.

Then they pulled apart at the same instant, hearts pounding, desperate for breath. She laid her cheek against his shoulder. He felt her hair against his face. Her arms were around his waist.

When at last they moved back and studied each other more calmly, neither one of them was smiling.

"Grainne," he said, and touched the silky skin of her face with the tips of his fingers.

"Jack," she said, and grasped his wrist with both her hands, held the palm of his hand against her cheek.

"It's so good to see you."

"I should have come sooner," she said. "I should have, I can see that. I'm so sorry, Jack. Whatever it is that's been troubling you, it's been bad, hasn't it? But it'll be all right now, I promise. I'll help you with whatever it is."

They stood for a moment, the wind pressing her hair against the back of his hand.

Then Jack said, "Let's get your things," and they moved apart and headed toward the car.

He couldn't tell her.

He certainly couldn't tell her, not this afternoon, not this evening, with the sight and the scent of her still so rich and fresh before him.

They moved about the house together, happily, easily, getting her settled in and her things put away. He'd emptied a drawer for her and made room in the closet. He'd even emptied a bookshelf for her to use. She kissed him again for that, but it only made him feel guilty, knowing he'd have to make her go away so soon, and that he'd have to tell her an elaborate lie instead of the truth.

He could not tell her the truth, as much as he wanted to. If he told her that, she'd either think he was crazy—he doubted she'd react like that, but she might, she might—or she'd insist on staying and seeing for herself what was going on. And Jack could only tell her the little he knew—if that was even the right word for it—and Father Henning's frightening ... what? Promise? Warning? No, he had to send her away, that was clear. And he also had to stay here himself.

He hated the gap of silence the secret set up between them. He did his best to act normal, casual—he did not have to act to show his joy at her really being here at last—but she knew something was wrong and, sooner or later, they would have to talk about it.

And there was another thing.

He wanted, with a hunger that almost frightened him with its intensity, to sleep with her, to hold her, touch her, taste her, be inside the comfort and warmth of her body.

But he could not. As terribly as he wanted that, he could not. Father Henning had asked if they slept together and implied very definitely that that link between them would establish a closeness, a union, that would irretrievably join their fates as one in *whatever the hell was going on.* He could not have that. If he could protect her in that way, even a bit, then he would not sleep with her. But what possible reason could he give her tonight? What could he say, short of telling her the whole ugly thing?

And yet, without all of this, they would have made love right there on the living room floor, before the car was unpacked, might not even have spent the time necessary to close the door of the house, might have let the heat of their bodies fend off the icy wind and the grayness of daylight.

He felt he was walking a tightrope, balancing between desire and selfishness on one side, and a need to protect her on the other. The battle made him restless, stolid rather than easy, polite rather than warm.

But his body ached for her. He was almost short of breath with the pain in his groin. Once, while she was unpacking her bag, he came and stood in the doorway, watching her. She was spreading out a blouse on the bed. He crossed the room, stood behind her, and put his arms around her waist. His hands felt the warmth of her stomach and she held them tight, pressed them tight against her. He slid his hands upward and made a sound deep in his throat when he felt the weight and warmth of her breasts against the palms of his hands. She covered his hands with her own and held him there, her head turned to the side, her face against his chest. Her nipples were erect, stiff against the pressure of his hands. She pressed her buttocks back hard against him. Neither of them said a word and, after a while, he eased away from her, kissed the back of her neck, and went out of the room. Afterward, neither of them referred to it.

The afternoon passed.

They made tea and sat talking in the living room. Jack spoke about his book, but he had to be careful of what he said because he'd actually been doing very little work. He let Grainne do most of the talking, about the shop and her girlfriend and a restaurant they'd enjoyed in Dundrum and the couple of films she'd seen recently.

It was Jack who grew sick of the pretending first.

A pause had developed in the conversation and, except for the unspoken tension that hung in the room, they would have been sitting in cozy silence, simply comfortable to be in each other's presence, without the need to talk. But it was not like that, this pretending, this waiting each other out. The things unsaid—Jack's secret knowledge and his plan to send her away, Grainne's obvious worry about him and her equally obvious intention to speak about it if he didn't do it first—were like a pall of sooty smoke hanging in the air, soon to cover everything beneath.

"Grainne, you can't stay here," he said. And instantly added, "Oh, shit, I don't mean it that way. I don't mean it as harshly as that sounded. Listen, I know you're worried about me and you think something's terribly wrong, but ... Well, look, I ... I just can't tell you the whole thing right now. Believe me, I wish I could, but I can't. It's ... It's just not the sort of thing I can tell you. Okay, okay! Yes, there's something wrong. If that's the right word, and I'm not even sure it is. But there's ... well ... something going on, something ... strange. And, no, it's not another girl and it has nothing, absolutely nothing, to do with you. But it worries me and just possibly there might be some danger. I simply can't let you be here now. I can't, and that's all there is to it. As soon as it's settled, just as soon as it's settled, I'll see you, we'll be together then, and I'll tell you the whole thing, the whole thing, I promise."

He'd stood up in the middle of that speech and was standing now halfway between the couch, where Grainne sat watching him, and the windows. The clouds above the ocean were turning from gray to threatening black.

"Grainne, please, just tell me you understand. I swear, it has nothing to do with you."

"Are you in danger?"

He studied her face, her dark eyes, her perfect white skin, her black hair, her fragile build combined with a full ripe body.

"Maybe," he said, "I'm not sure."

"When will you know ... what's going on?"

"I don't know."

"Is it the rest of your life you expect to spend in fear?"

He already knew that tone in her voice, velvet masking a razor's edge, and the definite Irish rhythms that were always more pronounced in her speech when she was angry or excited.

"Is it?" she said again, the two clear words pointing up the confusion of what he'd been saying.

"All right, listen," he said. He was still standing. "There is something wrong here, here in Doolin, this whole area around here. Something secret. The people here, or at least some of them, know what it is, or they're responsible for it, or they take part in it, or something of the sort. That priest, Father Henning, is in on it. And at least half a dozen others that I know of for sure. Maybe the whole village, for all I know. And somehow or other, it has something to do with me."

He stood watching her.

"Go on."

"And it has something to do with blood."

She said nothing.

"And with death."

She reacted to that, opening her lips in a gasp that she instantly stifled.

"I talked with Father Henning about it. He asked me if you were coming here again. He seemed . . . concerned that you'd be here. And there's something else, as long as you're dragging this much out of me. He wanted to know if we were lovers. From what he implied, I gathered that would make it worse. Whatever the hell it is."

They were silent for a minute, watching each other a little warily.

"Do you really not know what it is, what's going on or what it is that's going to happen?" Grainne asked at last.

"No," Jack said, then added, "Not really."

"Tell me," she said.

He turned away and leaned on the windowsill, looking out toward the darkening shore.

"The night we came back from the pub," he said slowly, "the night Father Henning came in and told that story. Do you remember?"

"I do."

"Do you remember the music the old fellow played on the pipes, one tune in particular that was very . . . excuse the expression, but it was very haunting. Do you remember that?"

"Yes," Grainne said softly.

When he heard the strange note in her voice, Jack turned away from the window to face her.

"You remember it."

"I do," she said. She was looking at her hands joined tightly together in her lap. "It followed us home across the hills and all the way to the door of this house."

He stared at her, seeing that everything was suddenly changed. "You heard it too. On the road just up the hill."

"I did." She nodded but did not look up.

He had to catch his breath before he could speak again. "There's no way, is there, it could have been real, no way the sound could have carried through the hills?"

"No," she said, "but I know it followed us home to our very door."

"Grainne . . ." He was almost whispering. "Grainne, Father Henning asked me about something else too. He asked me if you had . . . seen anything. Anything odd."

"The children at the house in the headlights of the car," she whispered: "The dead man in the road."

In an instant, he was kneeling on the floor in front of her, his arms wrapped tightly around her and hers wrapped around him. They clutched each other for warmth, and didn't speak, didn't move.

Jack's anger came a little later, anger at himself, and he stalked around the living room like a caged beast.

"I've been sitting here, waiting," he said loudly. "Just letting this stuff happen, all this crazy stuff. I thought at first I was going loony, you know, crackers, crazy!"

"You should have told me."

"*You* should have told *me*!"

"All right, we should have told each other. Jack, I'm sorry, but I was thinking a little the way you were."

He stopped his pacing. "A little?"

She turned her face away and looked confused.

"What do you mean?" he asked, making his voice more gentle this time. "What are you talking about?"

"There are such strange things that happen," she said. "Things no one really understands."

"Grainne, do you believe in"—he could not bring himself to use the word—"things like this, like the things we've been seeing?"

"No," she said. "And, yes, in a way. Oh, I don't know."

He closed his eyes for a second, sighed helplessly, and again looked out the windows at the still, dark wall of night.

"Jack," she said, "will you tell me why you stayed here? Why you just stayed and let it happen, without telling anyone, not me or a doctor or anyone? Why have you only stayed right here and waited to see what else would come?"

It was a long while before he answered.

"I stayed because ... because it's what I came here to do. I came here to see the country, learn about it, learn about the people, the way they live, the way they think. I've written down most of these things I've seen, described them as best I could. I don't know, a lot of reasons, I guess. Suicidal curiosity, maybe. A fascination with mysterious things. A determination to see it through. And, Grainne, the things were so real. I mean they were so goddamned *real*! Grainne, I touched that dead man in the road. I rolled him over, right out there in the road. And that little girl on Monday. I picked her up, for Christ's sake, I put her in the car, I covered her with my jacket. She was *real*! As real as you and me!"

"I wish I'd seen her too," Grainne said, almost whispering the words. "Then I'd know as much as you know."

Jack shuddered and gooseflesh ran up the back of his neck.

"Maybe we should go to see Father Henning," he said. "Despite everything he's said, and all the things that have happened, and the way he spoke about whatever is still going to happen, I can't really believe that he's involved in anything evil." He tried a thin smile but it didn't work. "Famous last words," he said quietly.

"Let's see him in the morning," Grainne said. "Maybe it makes a difference that I've seen ... I've seen the people too." She was watching him closely.

"The people?"

"What else?"

"All right. First thing in the morning."

There was a little silence, now that that was settled.

After a moment, Grainne asked, in a different tone, "If I fix you something to eat, will you eat it?"

Jack did a little better with the smile this time. "Keep up our strength," he said.

Grainne closed her eyes.

"They look like they starved to death," she said.

"Yes," he said. "They do."

They had eaten, doing their best to talk about other things, and when they were finished, Jack said quietly, "Let's take a walk."

They went outside, bundled up against the weather, and walked part way up the hill, then turned and went back part way down past the house toward the sea.

On the doorstep again, Grainne said, "They're from the Famine, from that time. They died in the Famine."

Jack turned away and stared at the dark that was drowning the hill. "I know," he said sadly. "I recognized the signs. I've thought so all along but I'm so sorry to be right."

Grainne put her hand on his arm. "You know I won't be leaving," she said. "You know that."

After a moment, Jack nodded.

"Will you not make love to me, Jack?"

"No," he said. "Not yet."

"Will you hold me very tight, then, Jack, as tight as you can?"

He opened the door and held it for her, then followed and took her in his arms.

"So you know them as well, do you?" Father Henning said, and then said nothing else for the longest time while brittle silence filled the room.

"I'll not be leaving this place," said Grainne, her words a whisper barely louder than the silence.

Father Henning did not move. After a long time, he looked up and his eyes, unfocused, swept slowly around the room as if he were seeking dire agreement from a primitive council. Then his gaze came to rest on Grainne's hand that was touching Jack's arm.

"Are you certain of it?" he asked her. There was not the slightest inflection in his voice, no hint, no warning, only the question.

"I am."

His gaze rose to her face and the lines around his eyes and his mouth shifted and softened.

"Have you the heart for it, girl?" he asked, and the sadness of his voice almost made her gasp.

She pressed her lips together and nodded.

The young woman and the old man looked long into each other's faces.

Jack watched the two of them, aware suddenly of some communication that eluded him, that was near, nearly within reach, almost within hearing, like the music among the hills, but that eluded him still. And at the same time, he knew that it would come, perhaps on a road or a flowing river of blood, but it would come, it would come, and soon.

"For God's sake, Father," he said heavily, "when is this going to be?"

Father Henning blinked. "Why, it's almost upon us," he said. He looked away. "Tomorrow. The Eve of All Saints."

"Halloween," Jack murmured.

Grainne squeezed his fingers.

"The Eve of All Saints," the priest insisted.

"What happens?"

He was still not looking at them. "The earth will open," he said. "The earth itself will open and the dead will issue forth. And when the night is done, some of them will have eternal rest. But only some." He shook his head. "Only some."

He was silent a moment, then asked them—it was not an invitation—to come to Nolan's pub that night and to Mass in the morning.

"Where does the blood fit in?" Jack asked.

"Blood is everywhere," the priest said, looking from Jack's eyes to Grainne's. "There is blood even in the sacrifice of the Mass. 'This is the cup of my blood,' Jesus said. 'Take and drink of it.' Blood is everywhere."

He would tell them nothing further.

Nolan's pub at nine o'clock was filled with a sullen crowd. Dark-clothed men still wearing their caps clutched pints of brown-gold stout and sipped solemnly from the glasses. A few women were scattered among the men, dressed just as darkly, sipping from glasses themselves and smoking like the men. Smoke hung in the air, a gray-blue cloud, as if the weather, warm only for the moment, had come inside. Mixed with the smell of cigarette smoke and the sweeter scent of pipe tobacco was the acrid aroma of burning turf, from the fire and from the clothes of the people, and the homey sour smell of rainsoaked wool. There was little talk.

Jack and Grainne had taken their pints from Liam with only a nod of thanks and, not speaking, carried them to the back of the pub. James Brennan was there before them, and Martin Gilhooley, but neither of the other two old men. Jack saw at once that space had been left on the bench in the corner, awaiting their arrival. He and Grainne found stools and pulled them near the table. As they sat, Martin Gilhooley nodded and grunted a greeting, and after a moment James Brennan did the same. Grainne lightly tapped Jack's leg with her knee, a secret signal: they were in deep now, as thick as thieves.

They sipped slowly at the pints and waited.

At a few minutes after nine, Father Henning appeared in the doorway, supporting John MacMahon at one elbow while Brian Flynn held up the other. A quiet wave of murmured greetings washed through the room as they made their way toward the back and installed MacMahon in his accustomed seat. Liam Nolan followed after with three brimming pints.

John MacMahon was a cadaver. His eyes stared from dark sockets deep within his head, yet burned with a glittering light that said only pain and pain again. His cheeks were sunken, the flesh all sucked inward and away, burned up inside him, leaving only bones that might at any moment tear through the parchment skin. Tiny flecks of white stood out from his dry, cracked lips. One hand, all bones and tendons like the foot of a bird, was knotted into the wool of his sweater against his stomach.

His other hand fluttered, moved, touched Brian Flynn's arm beside him on the bench. He cleared his throat, closing his eyes with the effort, and made a sound like the stirring of coal ashes.

"Is the piper come?" he croaked. His voice was the sound of a corpse that could speak.

"Aye, John," Martin Gilhooley said. He reached a hand across the little table and touched MacMahon's arm. "He's right here, nearby." He turned on his stool and looked past Jack and Grainne to where old Seamus Curtin in the other corner was smoothing the leather pad for the chanter on his knee. "You're ready to play, Seamus, are you?"

The farmer, settling the heavy pipes comfortably across his lap, only nodded his bald head and made a slight adjustment to the cloth bag strapped at his side.

"He's ready, John," Martin Gilhooley said.

"Let him play, then," said John MacMahon. The hand at his stomach flexed once and then was still.

Everyone in the pub was silent. The only sound was a wooden match being scraped into flame and the shuffle of heavy shoes on the time-roughened boards of the floor.

Not a soul had taken any special note of Jack and Grainne's presence in the pub.

Old Seamus, sitting straight on his chair, lightly flexed his fingers over the holes of the chanter. His closed eyelids showed the speckles of age. His right elbow moved, pumping the bag full of air. The bag wheezed for a moment, then the pipes filled the pub with music that was older than any person present.

The long slow notes of the tune sobbed from the pipes and curled throughout the room. They might have been the ancient lament of a widow for her freshly-dead warrior husband. They might have been the nighttime chant of long-robed figures in a hilltop circle of stones. They might have been the cry of a father as he watched the rooftree of his cabin pulled in by the bailiff, and his little ones whimpering at his knee. They might have been the sound of a priest murmuring the Latin of the Mass in a forbidden, roofless church. They might have been the whisper of water between Irish dock and foreign ship that carried away the land's sons. They might have been the slow, strong, weeping flow in the veins of all here present.

The tune rose and ebbed, rose and waned, like the blurring line of the tide, and then lengthened and softened and only crooned its sadness in lower notes as if played in a distant room.

When the music had sighed away nearly to silence, Father Henning stirred on his seat and coughed once, quietly, behind his hand.

"I've a tale to tell you," he said.

The music of the pipes dropped lower still but did not cease their lament.

"It's a terrible tale, in its way," said the priest, "filled with suffering and death and endless lamentation after. But it's a short tale and a true one, and the sort to be coming back in your mind for as long as you live."

There was no need for him to look around the room. All eyes were fixed on him, all ears filled with the sadness of the pipes and the voice of the seanachie.

"In the old days, although it wasn't so long ago as some might think, this very town, our own Doolin, was a place of green hillsides and the blazing light of the sun and the lapping waters of the sea. And the children grew fine here, as you may imagine, with bright eyes and strong limbs and laughing voices. But among them was one that was different from the others, always keeping to himself, private-like, never laughing, and his face always dark and grim.

"Sean, let's call him.

"As he grew older, it came to be told around Doolin that this Sean was different from all others in every respect. It was true that he had no parents to be raising him up and made his way in the world by lending a hand on the farms hereabouts, and his wages only a basket of potatoes, or only a handful of greens if nothing more could be spared. And when the evening darkened the hills, the boy went off to sleep in a place known only to himself, and it made no difference what was the weather, either fair and soft or wet and dirty.

"After a while, too, with the passing of years, there were none who could remember the date of his first coming to Doolin. He had not been here always, but it came to seem so to those who knew him. Or rather, to those who came in his path, for none could say that truly they knew the lad. Men said they could count on the fingers of one hand the times they'd heard his voice, for hardly a word ever crossed his lips.

"And when he came to be about eighteen years or so—for none could say what was his age exactly—a thing happened on the hills just above the town that none who saw it could ever forget.

"You'll know the shebeen on the hillside, I'm thinking, at the side of the road that leads to the cemetery. It stands there still today where it has stood these hundreds of years. In those days, the days when the lad walked the earth among men, the cemetery was off higher on the hill, growing higher too, so it seemed, with the burying of so many Christians in its soil.

"Well, one day here's a procession making its way up the road, slow and mournful, for the dead man was well loved in Doolin, and with yet a little ways to go up the hill, they stop at the shebeen for to take their ease for a minute. And while they're stopped and mopping at their brows, don't you know there comes from nigh the top of the hill, where the yawning grave lies open and ready, a terrible cry fit to tear your heart in two. It has the sound of every mother in Ireland crying for her dead sons, and every woman in the pangs of birth, and every skinny child with a belly aching from the hunger. It freezes their blood cold, it does, and they look up the hill to the graveyard yonder. But there's nothing, not a thing at all, to be seen.

"So after a bit, with their faces cooler and the sound of the cry from the hill carried far away on the breeze from the sea, they resume their way and pass on up the road and so on till they reach the cemetery and the side of the waiting grave.

"And then truly does their blood freeze up in their bodies for they hear the cry again. Only this time, it's rising up, you see, right from the ground at their feet. They can feel it right in the very soil they're treading, feel it right through the soles of their boots. There was one old woman among them, one of whom much was thought for her holiness and the likelihood of her attaining God's heaven when her time would come, who was without shoes and she declared after that her feet felt the burning heat of that scream. For scream it was, make no mistake about that.

"But that was only the beginning. Before a soul has even the time to catch his breath and slow the pounding of his heart, there comes the worst of it.

"All around them the earth itself is trembling and shifting, falling away in places and cracking open in others. A few old trees are wavering all around their heads and the few graves that are graced with stones and all the markers of the rest are shaking with a life of their own.

"And then a hand comes up rising from the earth, all black at the nails and in the joints, rising up from the grass-covered dirt of a grave near the one that's open. And no sooner do they clap eyes on that than another hand appears beside it, and hands, all clawing and black with filth, rising up from the graves all around. Then the heads appear, faces, the faces of the people's own dear departed, all of them covered with dirt and rising up from the soil, looking the way each of them did at the end. And in no time at all, there they are, each of them standing at his own grave, with the dirt all fresh-turned and tumbled this way and that, and they start walking toward the corpse.

"No one moves. No one speaks a word. They're all frozen to the spot in terror, you see.

"So the corpses or whatever they may be are standing all about, never speaking a word, just standing, with the dirt of their graves all falling to the ground at their feet. And then they start moving closer to the people. And then, don't you know, one of them steps forward like as if to show he's the leader. And it's the lad himself that we're calling Sean.

"There he stands, with the pallor of the grave in his face and the soil of the grave on his skin.

"They come forward, with himself at the head, and take hold of the fresh corpse with hands as gentle as the touch of a mother to a sickly infant. They take hold of it and carry it to the open grave, the one that's open proper, and carry it right down inside with their own hands, and before a minute has passed, the whole lot of them has been swallowed in the earth and the dirt of all the other graves is lying smooth and flat again so's you'd never know it was touched at all.

"Well, there's a priest with the mourners, you see, and he's a good man with his wits about him and before the others can run off in their fear, he starts up with the prayers for the dead and the deceased is laid away right and proper, the way any Christian soul has a right.

"Now the rest of the tale takes place a little after, as the mourners are making their way home and whispering among themselves.

"When they've nearly reached the town, they're passing along the road when they hear a woman crying over near a barn. They stop to see, and there's the woman kneeling over a body on the ground. It's the same fellow, the lad himself, lying there in his own blood and in something more besides.

"I'll tell you what happened, the way they pieced it out after. The lad was working at the farm and handling this fine old horse they had, a big one and strong but somewhat skittish of mood. The horse had let out with a great kick, as they could plainly see, for there was the mark showing clear on the lad's chest. But that wasn't the end of it. The lad, after receiving the kick, had some strength in him still, monstrous strength, for he'd grabbed ahold of the horse with his bare hands and dug into the animal's neck and, so the witnesses swore to their dying days, tore it open with his bare hands till the blood poured out red and hot. And there lay the lad and the horse, the two of them bled dry, their blood mingling together as it soaked deep into the soil. It was clear that the young fellow had been as dead as the horse before ever the mourners saw his figure rising up from the soil of the graveyard.

"All this was in the time of the Famine, which is why I told you at the first it was a while ago and yet not so very long either. And, what's more, the worst part of the tale is this: it has no ending. No ending at all."

They were all staring at the floor. No one moved until old Seamus in the corner let the dirge of the pipes die away to smoky silence.

Finally, after a long while, chairs scraped on the floor and people, murmuring, began to stand up. They filed out of the pub quietly as if this were the end, not of a seanachie's fireside tale, but of the holy Mass itself.

Jack and Grainne were far down the road after, wet now with freshening wind and rain, before either of them spoke.

"Are you determined to stay?"

"I am," she answered. "You've no need to ask. You know that."

"I could understand some of that story. I think. But not all of it."

"Tomorrow," Grainne said.

"Halloween."

She looked at him, the rain striking her face. "The Eve of All Saints."

They were coming down the hill toward the house. Just as they reached the gravel at the side, where the cars were parked, they saw the little girl.

She was standing in the middle of the road, just beyond the house. She was bone-thin as before, the flimsy nightshirt fluttering in the wind, clinging wetly to her fleshless body. Even in the dark they could see her shining eyes.

She raised one arm, slowly, slowly, as the fog crept up the hill and swirled around her legs, and beckoned to them. She took a step backwards down the hill toward the sea.

"Jack?" Grainne said and clutched at the sleeve of his coat.

"Let's take the car," he said.

The child was still there, gleaming in the white of the headlights, when he backed the car into the road and pointed it downhill. She beckoned once more, turned, and trotted away.

Neither of them spoke as they followed in the car. The child ran steadily before them, too light, too misty, for them to see if her feet even touched the ground.

She led them to Doolin Point.

The wind had grown now to an angry beast, whistling shrilly in their ears and flinging biting rain at their faces as they climbed from the car.

The child beckoned once and dashed off across the rocks toward the point.

Slowly, picking each spot to set down a foot, they inched across the rocks toward the high point above the crashing surf. The wind roared one moment and the ocean the next, contending for the greater power to frighten them off.

They followed the tiny figure as far as the tumble of boulders near the edge of the cliff, but she was gone by the time they reached it.

"This will either save us or drive us mad," Grainne breathed, and buried her face against his wet shoulder.

"Oh, Grainne, I've brought you into this," Jack said against her hair. "I never meant to."

"No, Jack. I was in this before ever you laid eyes on me. It's been waiting for me, lying in wait for me. And you, you've only just come home. Don't you see? You've come home. It was waiting here for you as well."

He took her shoulders and held her away from him, trying to search her face in the near blackness of the night. All he could see were her eyes, as bright as those of the child.

She was sobbing now, her eyes filling with tears that mixed with the rain to run down her face. "Oh, Jack," she cried, "won't you make love to me now? Won't you be one with me?"

He pulled her against him and buried his face in her hair for a moment. His hands fumbled madly at her, seeking her warmth to fend off the cold, seeking the comfort of her body, the joining of flesh at last.

Their hands flew at each other, pulling at awkward clothing, never minding the wind-driven rain that touched warm skin. Their mouths sought each other with the hunger of time and their sobs and sharp breathing were one voice in the pitch of the night.

She lay back against the rough stone and he stretched on top of her, his weight sinking with relief between her legs. She cried out when he touched her there.

Her hair caught on the gritty angles of the rock and tugged at her head as she moved. It felt as if misty hands, composed of wind and seaspray, rose from the rock itself to clutch at her body and hold her down while he took her. The rough surface scraped at the soft nakedness of her bottom, clawing at tender flesh each time he thrust his weight upon her, making delicious pain.

She opened her mouth to cry his name and rain and salty spray touched her tongue.

There would be blood on the stone after but the rain would wash it away and carry it back to the sea.

She moved her hands from the rock to his body, to the rock again and back to his body, feeling the sandpaper roughness of the stone and the smooth bunching muscles of his buttocks. Her ankles were held tight by her jeans but she inched her knees a little farther apart, making room to welcome him deeper. Their thick sweaters were knotted between them against their chests, but their stomachs pressed together—a place of warmth against the cold and wet of the air—and he filled the space between her thighs with his moving, thrusting weight. Her fingers caught at his skin and squeezed, let go, squeezed and let go.

He moved over her, within her, his legs, his body, his arms, his warmth, making a shelter from the rain and the wind, and at the same time pressing her into the rock so that the roaring waves that pounded below pounded at her as well.

The warmth rose within her, filling her legs, her chest, her face. Their knotted clothing rubbed hard against her swollen nipples. She opened her mouth and sobbed, and again, and tasted salt that might have been tears, might have been spray, and she moved with him, pressed herself up to receive him and . . .

. . . he moved as if only they existed in the world, only the two of them and the rock beneath and the water swirling and hammering below, foaming white and green and filling his ears with their sound and his heart with their urgent rhythm. Elbows on the hard, wet stone, rain soaking through to touch his legs and back and shoulders, streaming through his hair and down his face, he wrapped taut arms around her head and grappled her close and closer, the side of his face against the wet smooth skin of her forehead.

He felt himself grow bigger as she closed around him and drew him in, pulled him deeper and deeper, clutched him tighter as he slid within to the dark, warm depths of her body where ultimate shelter waited to hold him tight.

He groaned aloud, face turned to the side, and rain ran into his mouth.

The wind lashed his side and back and pushed him faster still. He was one with her body, one with the rock, and their moving warmth made a house of heat around them. Sweat ran acrid and hot beneath his clothes and slid between their bellies.

He felt the burning warmth rising and pulsing within him, clenched his teeth tight and groaned between them, thrust once more, yearning deeper still, then stiffened, breath held, toes braced against the rock, held and . . .

. . . they cried out together, fingers flexing, his in her hair, hers at his back, and cried again as he poured himself into her and she felt her body filled with the heat of his own. Held for the moment, all else gone but the joining, they did not move. Even after he was emptied, he shuddered and his pelvis thrust again, knees pressing hard against the rock. Her arms moved and wrapped his head against her face.

He groaned once more, a long shivering sigh. Their mouths came together, lips wet with rain and spray and saliva.

After a while, as they began to catch their breath, he slid softly out of her warm flesh. Their mingled wetness ran out of her and dripped from him to puddle in the crevices of the rock beneath, and the rain would wash that away too and mix it with the grit and the salt and the sea.

When at last they rose from the rock and pulled rain-soaked clothing into place, they spoke not a word. All was darkness. Hands clutched tightly together, they inched their way across the endless expanse of jagged, broken rock and relentless rain, back to the road that would carry them home and the night that would take them to morning.

PART FOUR

I believe that in every decisive moment of our lives the spur to action comes from that part of the memory where desire lies dozing, awaiting the call to arms.

—Sean O'Faolain,
"I Remember! I Remember"

CHAPTER 16

The night passed, long and dark and slow.

Even while they slept, their limbs touched, hips touched, fingers touched, sliding against smooth sheets, seeking human warmth. They slept fitfully. Jack coughed twice in the night, waking each time to turn over. Grainne clutched tight at the pillow, one arm crooked around it.

Outside, rain still clattered at the walls and wind pressed hard against the glass.

Jack woke first, a little before eight. Grainne shifted in the bed, trying to find a safer position. Her knees were drawn up near her chest, her neck bent, her face buried against the pillow. Jack watched her for several minutes, scarcely breathing. She was so lovely. She looked so fragile. The back of her neck was exposed and he thought of how easily she could be hurt. Killed. The thought chilled him and he shivered. He pulled the covers higher over his chest. The air in the room felt very cold, as if the night had come inside.

After a while, when Grainne still had not moved, he eased the covers down and climbed out of the bed. The floor was like ice. Shivering, he gathered up some clothing and carried it quietly from the room so as not to wake her. He dressed in the hall, then went to the kitchen and started water for tea. While he waited for it to boil, he stood at the window and stared out, trying not to think.

The day itself was gray, although the rain had stopped, leaving only dark wet earth on the hill, wet rocks, and silvery puddles reflecting the rippled gray of the sky. A cold-looking day.

When the tea was made, he fixed two cups and carried them into the bedroom. Grainne was still asleep, curled up in the big bed and looking very small. Jack's breath caught for a second, seeing her like that. He had brought her into all this. She had come willingly, true, but if it hadn't been for him, she would not be here now, would not be in danger. If indeed they were in danger.

Blood. Death. Sacrifice.

He put the cups on the nighttable. When he sat on the edge of the bed and put his arm around her shoulders, she opened her eyes in sudden fright, stared at him for a moment, then closed her eyes in relief and curled against him like a trusting child.

For a moment, he hated himself.

Without opening her eyes, Grainne curled her body closer to him. He felt the pressure of her breast against his leg. She raised one hand and touched warm fingers to his lips.

"It'll be all right," she whispered. "We'll make it all right."

By the lonely standards of Doolin, the road to the town was crowded this Sunday morning. Each lane that fed into the road had its family, its pairs of husband and wife, its old men, all making their way to the church. It was still not raining, but the air itself was filled with moisture and fog crept across the fields and sneaked up to the edge of the road, venturing in places onto the open surface and making forays at their feet. A few muddy and bedraggled sheep stood with heads hung low, watching as the people of Doolin passed in the road.

There were fewer greetings among the people than usual, nods alone and a muttered word serving for acknowledgment. There were no inquiries about health, no comments on the weather. After the mutter and the nod, they walked along in silence toward the town and the church. Behind their feet, the fog followed them as close as it dared.

Jack and Grainne had left the car at home. They joined the people in the road and walked in equal silence.

Grainne turned the collar of her coat up higher around her neck against the chilling dampness of the air. She had one hand hooked through Jack's arm, but after a while she withdrew it and stuffed it deep into a pocket for warmth. They walked close enough together so that their elbows brushed as they moved.

They saw the town and the church for the first time as they topped a rise in the road, then started down a long and winding incline. People were gathered already in front of the church. They stood in small dark knots, speaking quietly or not at all. A single cocker spaniel, its dirty blond hair looking wet and matted, wandered disconsolately among them.

As Jack and Grainne, with their fellow walkers in the road, drew close to the open space before the church, the heavy wooden doors were drawn back on creaking iron hinges and Father Malcolm Henning appeared on the step. The diffused gray daylight that lit the town was bright enough to make people squint, but the priest's face was marked by deep lines and wrinkles—deeper, it seemed, than they'd been the night before—and not even the daylight could erase the shadows. He pushed the door all the way back, latched it in place, and stood aside to welcome his people into church. Slowly, the crowd stirred and began moving toward the door and filing inside.

As if by previous agreement, Jack and Grainne took places at the side, near the rear, where they could see everything that went on. Slowly, the church filled around them. After a few minutes, the temperature rose a little inside, but not enough to dispel the dampness from the stone of the floor and walls.

There were so many familiar faces, those of shopkeepers in the town, farmers seen occasionally on walks or drives through the hills, faces of women from the street of Doolin, Liam Nolan, Peggy Mullen and her two silent sons at either side of her, the old farmer, Willy Egan, who kept the beautiful horse, all the faces dark and devoid of expression, eyes fixed on the altar, waiting for the priest. Jack thought he'd seen all this before.

When the church was filled and only the shuffling of boots on the stone floor could be heard and the occasional dry cough, the doors at the back were closed suddenly with a creak of iron and wood and a hard thud. Jack turned to look back. John MacMahon was being assisted by his cronies into a seat in the last row that had obviously been saved for him. Father Henning stood watching until MacMahon was settled, then left them and walked briskly up the side aisle on the left, past Jack and Grainne, and disappeared through a doorway into the sacristy.

He reappeared on the altar a few minutes later, followed by two little boys in crisp white surplices. He genuflected stiffly, made the sign of the cross, and began the Mass.

Jack was not surprised that there was nothing unusual about

the first part of the Mass. After all, there was only one way to say it; the great glory of the Church's central ceremony and principal sacrifice was that it was the same all over the world. When it came time for the reading of the gospel, Father Henning spoke out the words clearly and nothing in his voice suggested anything out of the ordinary. But when the gospel was done, the priest stood looking out over the church in silence for a long time. His eyes seemed to sweep around the church, touching each face for at least a moment. Then he cleared his throat and began to speak.

"We'll have no announcements this day," he said. "It is my wish instead to draw the attention of our hearts and minds to thoughts of our dearly departed. I'll ask you to stand now and join me in a special prayer for the repose of their souls."

The people shuffled to their feet.

Although Father Henning intoned the prayers in the business-like way of priests throughout the world, the congregation, Jack thought, gave the responses with unaccustomed fervor.

"May their souls," the priest concluded, "and the souls of all the faithful departed, through the mercy of God"—he lifted his eyes to the faces of the people watching him, and they all joined aloud in the final words—"rest in peace. Amen."

And the priest stepped down from the pulpit, the altar boys joining him immediately, to resume the rest of the Mass.

Jack looked sideways at Grainne. She met his gaze briefly, then looked back at the altar.

When it came time for the consecration, Jack listened carefully as Father Henning held aloft first the sacred host, then the chalice, and intoned the words of the prayers. "This is the cup of my blood. Take and drink of it." But he could find no special tone, no unusual inflection, in the priest's voice.

It took a long time for the priest to distribute Holy Communion because nearly everyone in the church rose from their seats and lined up in the aisles to stand before him at the altar to receive the sacrament.

Jack debated going up himself. It was easy to tell himself that it couldn't hurt; after all, he thought he could receive the sacrament properly even though he hadn't been to confession in years.

But a lifetime of training, ingrained from his youth, kept him in his seat. He was startled when Grainne suddenly leaned over and spoke to him.

"Can you make a good Act of Contrition?" she whispered.

Jack pressed his lips together and stared at his hands joined before him. It was really a theological debate with himself that he didn't want to get into, especially just at the moment. Had he committed what he felt were any mortal sins? Did he even believe, honestly believe, in all that Catholic business of venial sins and mortal sins? Was making love with Grainne a sin? He shook his head. No, his thinking was very different now from the things he'd believed as a child. And even more different from the way it had been at the time he'd first arrived in Ireland.

"Sure," he whispered back.

"Then let's receive," Grainne replied, barely moving her lips. "I think we should." She lowered her head and closed her eyes, leaving him to make his own prayer for forgiveness of any sins he'd committed.

He did not believe that most of the things the Church taught were sins really *were* sins, but he privately assured God that he was sorry for anything he'd done that was offensive. To his surprise, he found that his thoughts were quite sincere, free of the mild cynicism that had marked his thinking on the subject of religion in his adult years.

They rose from their seats and joined the line in the side aisle. When they stood at last before Father Henning and the priest placed the host first on Grainne's tongue, then on his own, Jack kept his eyes on the priest's face. Not a flicker of expression showed there.

They returned to their seats with everyone else. Father Henning finished giving out Holy Communion, then went back to the altar, put the chalice back in the tabernacle, and quickly finished up the final prayers of the Mass.

Then he turned to face the congregation, his arms spread wide, palms turned outward, as if embracing them all.

"The Mass is ended," he said, his head held high as his gaze swept over the people in the church.

He raised his right hand, thumb and first finger joined at the tips, the other fingers extended, and began the sign of the cross above their heads.

"In the name of the Father," he said, and lowered his hand before him, "and of the Son," and moved his hand first to his left, then his right, "and of the Holy Ghost," and joined his hands softly before him. "Go in peace. Amen."

As they did every Sunday after Mass, the people were lingering and gathering in small groups outside the church. Jack and Grainne stood with them and watched as John MacMahon was helped from the doorway by his cronies. The old fellow looked terrible, pale as death and his face drawn taut with pain. Several people moved close to him and quietly expressed their concern for his health. The old man nodded to each one but did not speak. It was hard to tell if he was even fully conscious of the people around him.

"Isn't that the old form of the prayer?" Jack said softly to Grainne. "Shouldn't it be 'Holy Spirit'?"

"Yes," she said.

Father Henning came to the door after a few minutes, wearing his dark raincoat. As he always did, he moved through the quiet crowd, speaking a word with this one, a few words with that one, touching a child gently on the head, gripping an elderly arm, passing slowly on to the next group, missing no one. When he came to where Jack and Grainne stood, they turned to meet him. He took their hands, first Grainne's, then Jack's, and pressed it tight between his own.

"You must fast today," he said quietly. "Eat nothing at all. Stay in the house and wait for me. I'll come for you when it's time."

And he moved away to take the hand of someone else.

They went home and waited, hardly speaking, just waiting.

Once, Grainne said, "I'll make tea if you'd like," then instantly added, "Oh, never mind then."

Jack went back to looking out the window.

The sky brightened a bit toward midday, then slowly began darkening as the afternoon crept on.

After several hours of endless and fruitless attempts to read or listen to the radio, Grainne finally went off by herself. When Jack realized she wasn't in the room, he went to look for her and found her asleep, stretched out across the bed.

He went back to the living room and looked once more out the window.

The little girl, pale and thin with daylight seeming to pass right through her body, was standing in the road, her deep dark eyes fixed steadfastly on his face.

He went back to the couch and, after a while, began to doze.

He only woke at the sound of the knocking on the door.

CHAPTER 17

It wasn't Father Henning at the door.

Jack stood looking in surprise at Brian Flynn, James Brennan, and Martin Gilhooley. Whichever one had knocked had retreated from the steps and now stood side by side with the others on the wet gravel.

It was late in the afternoon, with little daylight left, only gray that would turn rapidly now to dark. Behind the three men, fog crept up the hill toward the house.

"We've come for the both of ye," said Brian Flynn, and stood silently waiting.

No one spoke a word as Jack and Grainne walked with the three old men up the road and into the town, then through it and on up into the hills. All around them, night kept pace, following their footsteps, growing in strength and edging out the remnants of daylight. The fog followed them as well, sliding along at the edge of the road, creeping from rock to rock, gliding in wisps across the open spaces, hiding its face but staying with them all the way.

By the time they reached the shebeen on the hill that led to the graveyard, the dark was full upon them. The only light was the flickering yellow of a candle at the dirty window of the old stone cottage. The only sound, except for the wind that hummed just beside their shoulders, just behind their ears, was the hard crunch of gravel beneath their feet and the dry wheezing of the old fellows struggling up the hill.

There were no voices from inside. Whoever was there sat in silence. Brian Flynn rapped his knuckles twice at the door.

The door was pulled back by Father Henning. Brian Flynn nodded to Jack and Grainne, then stepped inside ahead of them.

"I've brung him," he said to no one in particular, "and her as well."

John MacMahon sat on the bench in the corner, held upright, to judge by his appearance, only by the angle of the two walls at his back. In the light of the guttering candle, his face looked to be more hollow than solid. His chest was sunk deep beneath his rounded shoulders. His hands, all knuckles and tendons, lay limp between his legs.

Besides the five new arrivals, the only other person present was Willy Egan. He was sitting awkwardly on the edge of the bench near John MacMahon. He glanced toward them and bobbed his head in brief greeting, but kept one thick hand on the old fellow's knee.

"Well, that's it, then," Father Henning said. He was still standing near the door, his hand still on the latch. He moved to where he could look outside and stood for a moment, as if taking the measure of the darkness. Still holding the latch, he turned toward them and said, "It's time now. We should be off."

Brian Flynn, James Brennan, and Martin Gilhooley moved toward John MacMahon and began helping him to his feet. Willy Egan rose stiffly from the bench and walked outside without saying a word. In a moment, the sound of his footsteps was swallowed by the night.

"Father . . ." Jack said.

The priest shook his head. "You're here now, lad, the both of you, and it's all set in motion. You've come of your own free will, and that's the main thing. It's time to be getting on with what must be done, and you'll not be backing out now."

He stood aside while Brennan and Gilhooley supported John MacMahon through the doorway. The old fellow's eyes were closed. His head lolled on his neck. The others followed them

out, Father Henning staying at the back, as if to prevent Jack and
Grainne from slipping away in the dark.

Outside, Willy Egan was waiting, holding the beautiful gray
mare by a rope bridle and softly stroking her nose.

They started up the hill, Brennan and Gilhooley supporting
John MacMahon between them, almost carrying him, with Brian
Flynn staying as close as possible behind the old fellow. Then
came Jack and Grainne, moving at the snail's pace of the others,
and behind them Willy Egan leading the mare and murmuring
to her in the lilting liquid tones of the Irish language, and Father
Henning following them all.

They moved with painful slowness up the hill. After a while,
Brian Flynn moved out in front. He pulled from his jacket pocket
a torch of dry twigs, lighted it with a match he scraped on his
thumbnail, and held the flaring torch high to light their way.

The silent procession turned left at the break in the stone
wall and moved even more slowly on the rough earth toward
the graveyard. A minute later, more torches were seen burning
brightly higher up the hill.

The mare snorted twice, loudly, and Willy Egan made his
voice deeper and more soothing and after a bit she was still. Her
hooves were almost silent now on the soft ground.

They passed the newest graves and moved higher up the hillside.

The entire town of Doolin, it seemed, everyone who had been
in church that morning and every other time, was assembled on
the hill, standing among the leaning stones. The light of torches
gave the area a flickering brightness, but long dark shadows
stretched away behind the circle of people and blended with the
night.

When they reached the circle, the four old men moved slowly
into the center. Jack felt a hand on his shoulder and turned his head
to see Father Henning holding him back and shaking his head.
Grainne pressed herself close, trembling cold fingers seeking his
own. He clasped her hand tight and she squeezed back. Father
Henning moved around them and stepped into the middle of the
circle. Jack glanced back again. Willy Egan was holding the mare
by her rope bridle, speaking softly to her, and patting her neck.

When Jack looked back at the circle, Father Henning was drawing a clear vial of what Jack thought must be holy water from an inside pocket of his coat. He removed the cap, wet his fingers, blessed himself with it, then carefully sprinkled it all around the circle, turning all the way as he did. Where the water landed on the ground, Jack saw, faint wisps of smoke rose up and drifted away. Either that, he thought, or the fog was just now reaching up the hill and that was what he was seeing.

He looked all around at the ring of silent faces and recognized every one, all the same faces he'd seen at Mass that morning, all the familiar faces he'd come to know in Doolin and some he'd only seen once or twice. Grainne's arm was pressed tight against his, her hand frozen in his own with a grip so tight it hurt, and he realized he must be hurting her too. He eased his hold on her hand but instantly felt her clutching at him. He looked back at the priest in the middle of the circle.

Father Henning was turning toward the other side of the crowd and holding out his hand for someone to come forward. After a moment, Peggy Mullen, her lips pressed grimly together, her eyes staring almost sightlessly with fright, moved slowly toward the priest.

When she reached him, he took both her hands in his and murmured something to her. She nodded but said nothing. Then he led her the few steps to where the four old men stood. She took each of their hands in turn and held it for a moment. She had to reach for John MacMahon's hand and lift it herself. Then the priest led her to where Jack and Grainne stood. Peggy Mullen raised her eyes to Grainne's face and murmured, "God bless you," and the priest led her back to the center.

From where she had stood on the other side of the circle, her elder son, Michael, came forward. He was carrying a stone bowl that appeared to be hugely heavy. He set it down at the priest's feet and backed away a short distance.

The only comfort Jack had as he searched the faces of the circle was that everyone looked as frightened and horrified as he knew he did himself. But the priest had indicated he would have a special role in this ceremony. What? He closed his eyes for a moment and realized he'd been holding his breath.

Michael Mullen was coming toward him. As everyone watched, Mullen gripped his hand for a moment, then returned to his place.

Willy Egan led the mare into the circle. She was nervous, nostrils flaring and muscles rippling beneath her coat. The man never once stopped murmuring to her, crooning as he might to a babe. She almost gleamed like silver in the light of the torches.

Father Henning had a knife in his hand.

Jack squinted and moved a little to the side to see it better. Grainne jumped and moved with him.

It was not a knife but more like a surgical scalpel. The priest was lifting John MacMahon's hand and gently placing the blade in it, holding it till the old fellow's fingers curled and grasped it securely.

With the scalpel in his hand, John MacMahon seemed to come alive. His chest moved as he drew in a deep breath. His head came up, his eyes opened, and new strength seemed to fill his frail body. This was what he'd stayed alive for, *willed* himself to stay alive for one more time. He balanced himself carefully for a moment against the arms that supported him, then took a tentative step away from them by himself. The others stayed close, ready to help him if he faltered. He moved slowly toward the trembling animal.

"Oh, God," Grainne breathed, but neither of them moved.

Father Henning sprinkled the last of the holy water on the mare, put the vial away in his pocket, then turned toward Jack and gestured for him to come forward.

His grip on Grainne's hand was crushing and hers crushed his in return. But then, even if reluctantly, she loosed her hold and withdrew her hand. For a moment, as he stood alone facing the circle, Jack was conscious only of the pounding of his heart, the flickering of the torchlight, and the damp air that prickled the back of his neck. He took a step forward and moved into the open space of the circle.

Father Henning gripped his hand tightly, held it for a long moment, then placed it in John MacMahon's free hand. Then he turned Jack gently, holding him by the elbow, and led him to greet in the same way the three other old men. When that was done, Jack found himself facing John MacMahon again.

The old fellow had to clear his throat painfully before he could speak. "God bless you," he managed to say, his voice like the creak of an ancient tree before a battering wind.

"And you," Jack murmured before he even realized he was speaking. The priest touched his shoulder gently as if in approbation.

John MacMahon fluttered a hand toward the bowl at his feet and Jack understood that he was to lift it. He swallowed, bent, touched the cold stone with his bare hands, gripped it. It was monstrously heavy but he lifted it, aware that every eye was watching and feeling, suddenly and surprisingly, that this was a terrible honor being bestowed on him. Brian Flynn was at his elbow, directing him where to stand. He was very near to Willy Egan and the mare.

Willy Egan held tight to the bridle, still whispering to the beast. John MacMahon came close to the animal and raised the blade near her neck.

Jack felt cold air chilling the sweat on his face. He swallowed again, hard, clamped his muscles in place to hold the bowl steady, and thought how none of this surprised him.

The other men, Brennan and Gilhooley, had moved to the far side of the mare. John MacMahon, his lips moving but making no sound, raised the blade and, with no obvious effort, slipped it into the animal's throat. When he withdrew it, a fountain of blood, looking black, arced out. Brian Flynn nudged Jack's elbow to get him in place but Jack needed no urging. The first blood spattered directly into the bowl, splashing up onto his hands and the front of his coat. Jack held his ground.

It took the mare a moment to realize she'd been cut, so easy was John MacMahon's movement. Then suddenly she snorted, her eyes went wide and white, and she screamed in terror, tossed her head violently, and tried to back off. Willy Egan, Brennan and Gilhooley held on tight, keeping her in place as best they could, but keeping their eyes on the bowl Jack held. Jack had to follow a few steps to keep the flow striking the bowl. Some of the blood spilled over the sides and felt hot on his fingers.

Then it was full and he knew he should set it down on the ground. The instant he began to lower it, Willy Egan was applying a clip and bandage to the tiny slit in the animal's neck and talking loudly to her, staying where she could see him with her left eye. The flow of blood stopped abruptly. The horse screamed once more, baring her yellowed teeth, but Egan and the others were already leading her away toward the trees through an opening people made in the circle. They heard her snorting and stamping and then the circle closed once more and all was silence.

Father Henning was holding a fresh scalpel. He gave it to John MacMahon and MacMahon turned toward Jack and held out his hand.

Jack thought he had never seen a face gentler, kinder, more loving, than that of John MacMahon. His fingers were sticky with blood, his clothing stained with it, but never in his life had he felt so firmly that he *belonged* exactly where he was, among these people whose blood flowed in his own veins and had flowed there all his life. He was no less frightened of the scene and the moment and the imminent letting of his own blood—John Mac-Mahon was coming close to him, reaching for his arm, torchlight gleaming on the blade—but he felt the deep satisfaction of having a place at last, of having, at long last, come home.

He extended his left hand, palm upward, and pushed the sleeve of his coat back as far as it would go.

The old fellow gripped his arm and held it in place. The incision felt searingly hot but, strangely, hardly hurt at all. Jack clenched his teeth but the pain was infinitely less than he'd expected.

He watched his blood flow into the bowl, mixing with that of the horse. Then strong hands were grasping his arm, his wrist, his hand, stanching the flow of blood, cutting it off to nothing, and binding his arm in tight wrappings. He felt dizzy for a moment, felt his clothing thoroughly soaked with sweat, thought for a moment that he might either faint or vomit, but then his vision cleared and he was all right.

Father Henning moved him back a few steps. The three old men—Brian Flynn, James Brennan, Martin Gilhooley—each gave their blood in turn. There was little from each, but it was enough for the bowl to overflow and soak the earth around it. That seemed, Jack thought as he watched the earth grow dark and wet, to be part of the purpose.

The priest embraced John MacMahon briefly before the old fellow added his own blood to the bowl. The instant it appeared, Henning reached for his arm and cut off the flow. When his arm was wrapped, MacMahon swayed for a moment against the priest but straightened himself at once, his eyes bright, satisfied, relieved that he'd lived long enough for this.

Then he bent forward, slowly and stiffly but with determination, toward the brimming bowl and dipped his fingers into it. He straightened up a little and put the fingers in his mouth. Then he lowered his hand from his lips and turned to look at Jack.

Jack, not permitting himself to yield to his revulsion, knowing that he must not and did not want to, stepped forward and did the same. The blood tasted warm and salty, like the water of a summer ocean.

He had to swallow hard to get it down. It helped to know that this would be the last.

Father Henning guided him back to the circle, back to where Grainne stood, wide-eyed and shivering. She snatched at his hand, the one that was still sticky and wet with the traces of blood.

Together they watched the priest.

He dipped his own fingers into the bowl, lifted a dripping handful, and, still bent over it, scattered it on the ground in a wide arc. He did the same again, and again, and again, slowly turning in a full circle around the bowl, spreading the blood evenly over the soil of the graveyard, until he'd completed the circle.

Then he stood, wiped his fingers on a linen towel that Peggy Mullen came forward and handed him, and lowered his head in silent prayer.

All around the circle, others did the same until all stood with heads bowed low.

The circle of people stood silent among the graves. Near Jack's feet, a stone, its inscription long ago blurred away by wind and rain, leaned over as if weary of its own weight. Jack opened his eyes and looked at the stone, trying not to see it, trying only to concentrate, but all he could think of was the sticky blood that joined his hand to Grainne's and the metallic taste of it in his mouth. He closed his eyes again.

Beside him, Grainne jumped and gasped. Her hand moved in

his. No, someone else was gripping his hand, pulling their fingers apart.

The pale little girl, as pale as mist itself or the spray of the sea, stood between them. He felt the weightless pressure of her thin body against his leg as she pushed gently between him and Grainne.

Grainne was watching her too. Their eyes met for a second and Jack knew that Grainne felt the same fear he felt, and the same calmness, the same sense of having come to the right place at last.

They opened their hands and the child edged easily between them. She reached up with both her hands and grasped theirs, joining them again through herself. Her fingers, little more than bone covered with skin, felt cold. Jack wrapped her hand in his large one to give it warmth. The child did not move, only looked up at his face and then at Grainne's. Jack remembered the time he had sheltered her on the road in the rain. Poor thing. Her tiny fingers moved and squeezed his hand in return. She stood silently between them, content to touch their hands.

When Jack looked up and around the circle of faces, he thought at first that there were twice as many people. He blinked, stirred from one foot to the other, caught his breath. Among the faces he knew and recognized, there were now at least as many again, all of them strange, pale, gaunt, some ghastly, many bearing what might once have been a family resemblance to those he knew, all of them silent, joined in the silent prayer.

He saw almost at once three haggard faces of men who might have been the man he'd found lying in the road near the house, the same one Grainne had seen. It did not matter which one he was; Jack knew he was there.

All the faces were there, standing still and mute among the people of Doolin, these earlier faces and lives of the town, come back now this one night of the year to be among their own.

Jack's heart was pounding in his chest. He squeezed the little girl's hand as hard as he dared without hurting her.

In the middle of the crowded circle, Father Henning raised his head and opened his eyes. Some of the torches had now flickered out and his face was partly in shadow. His lips still moved in prayer as he looked around the now crowded circle.

When he stretched his arms out as if to embrace them all, the gaunt and pale faces fixed their sunken eyes on him and, slowly, one by one, began moving forward, gliding between the people of Doolin toward the center of the circle and the still brimming bowl of blood.

The child loosed her grip on their hands. She was the first to reach the bowl and the other misty shapes inside the circle held back while she went ahead. Seeming almost to float toward the earth, she knelt beside the bowl and dipped her fingers into it, lifted her fingers to her lips and tasted the blood, and sucked her fingers clean. For an instant, no more than the momentary flare of a burning twig, her skin seemed to glow and fill out, as if the flesh itself were renewed. Then she shrank instantly back to pallor and returned to the circle. When she touched their hands again, her fingers were warm with life.

They took their turns and drank from the bowl, licking their fingers clean, and glided back to their places among the others.

When the last of them had drunk and the bowl was only stained and empty, Father Henning looked all around at the silent faces in the light of the last dying torch.

"May their souls," he said, and even the wind was stilled at the sound of his words, "and the souls of all the faithful departed, through the mercy of God, rest in peace."

"Amen," murmured the circle around him.

When Jack stirred, he felt Grainne's hand move in his. The child was gone, and gone were all the others who had come with her. Even so, he thought he could still feel the pressure of her hand, and the brief glowing warmth of it, between his own hand and that of Grainne.

The people in the circle blessed themselves, touching forehead and shoulders, and slowly began to disperse.

Grainne crossed the open space to walk with Peggy Mullen. Jack went to help Brian Flynn support old John MacMahon.

CHAPTER 18

By ten o'clock on Monday morning, everyone in Doolin knew that John MacMahon had passed away in the night. It came on him in his sleep, God rest his soul, and there was an end to his terrible pain at last.

By late afternoon he was laid out all clean and proper in the place of highest honor in the town of Doolin, the front sitting room of Father Henning's own house. It was only right, after all, said everyone, weren't the two of them boys together all those many years ago, and hadn't they been through the years like brothers, sharing each and all, the one with the other. God will rest his soul for sure, and a blessing on Father Henning for taking such care of old John even at the end.

They came alone and in couples and in families to pay their respects, to murmur a prayer while kneeling before the box, and have a drop of the poteen, and talk of other times.

The weather for the funeral Mass on Tuesday was the clearest, brightest day the town had seen in a month's time, bright sun shining on walls that seemed suddenly white and the ocean rolling blue in the distance. John MacMahon had lived for decades and decades in the town, all his life, and the shops were closed that morning and the Sunday suits and ties were donned and all were present in the church. They stood with silent, solemn faces as the coffin was carried out on the shoulders of Brian Flynn, James Brennan, Martin Gilhooley, and Willy Egan. And almost everyone followed the little procession up the hill to the old fellow's resting place.

Halfway up to the cemetery, Jack and Grainne silently turned off the road and made their way over the rough ground a short distance to the shebeen on the side of the hill. Its thatch, ragged and blown by the wind, looked dry and thick today in the bright sunlight. They went in and left the door open behind them to admit the clean fresh air. And sat on the polished wood of the bench along the wall, without speaking, and waited.

After a while, they heard the movement of feet making their way down the hill toward the town, and the soft murmur of elderly voices. And a little while after that, Father Malcolm Henning appeared in the doorway, ducking his head a bit beneath the low lintel. He stepped across the threshold and stood just inside the shebeen, and, behind him, the shape of Brian Flynn filled the doorway.

"God save all here," the priest said softly.

Grainne touched her hand to Jack's arm.

The two old fellows at the door looked at him hard for a long minute. Jack lifted his head and looked steadily back at them.

At last Brian Flynn said, "Have you the blood, Jack?"

"I have," Jack answered, and brushed a hand against the hard lump in his pocket.

Grainne's grip tightened on his arm. "*Mo ghrá thú*," she murmured close to his ear. "I love you, Jack."

"And I you," he whispered in return.

Then they rose together and went out into the light of the day, heading uphill toward the graves.

AUTHOR'S NOTE

There is a town named Doolin in County Clare, on the western coast of Ireland, but it and its residents share only a name with the Doolin I describe in *Cast a Cold Eye*.

The basic book on the period of the Irish Famine is, of course, *The Great Hunger: Ireland 1845-1849* by Cecil Woodham-Smith (E. P. Dutton, 1962). But I am more immediately indebted to *Paddy's Lament: Ireland 1846-1847* by Thomas Gallagher (Harcourt Brace Jovanovich, 1982) for an insight into what the experience of the Famine meant, not in political terms, but in human terms.

I am also indebted to the following friends:

Donald M. Grant, for suggesting a different book, which got me started on this one.

Jill Bauman, Tamzen Cannoy, Jim French, Craig Shaw Gardner, Charles L. Grant, Whitley Strieber, and Douglas E. Winter, for their constant support during the writing of the book.

Paul Mikol, Beverly Berg, and Scot Stadalsky, for wanting it in the second place.

Walter Berkov, Reid Beddow, and Michael Dirda for letting me stretch my mind along the way.

And my grandmother, Jenny Bjerre, who was born in Dublin in 1879, the daughter of Mary Mullen and Patrick Boshell, and who died in New York in 1969. She left Ireland in 1900, not once looking back, but having prepared for me a gift it took eighty years to find.

Alan Ryan
September 22, 1983

CPSIA information can be obtained
at www.ICGtesting.com
Printed in the USA
LVOW12s0055051117
555071LV00001B/21/P